TASTE OF THE PAST

THEO GALLOWAY JR.

© Copyright 2023
Published by P.S.S. Publishing LLC
P.S.S. Publishing, LLC.
P.O. Box 372425
Denver, CO 80237

All rights reserved. No part of this book may be reproduced in any form
or by an electronic or mechanical means, including storage and retrieval system
without the written permission of the publisher.

ISBN 13-979-8-9854145-4-7
Library of Congress
Cataloging–in–Publication Data
Cover Photo: ©2022 www.gettyimages.com

CHAPTER 1

It was an ordinary morning, no different from any other, where two minutes would change the life of Jerome Thomas forever. Jerome was walking to school with Richard Wilson, his best friend since third grade. Both were in the eleventh grade and known by everyone as JT and Rich. Jerome was the bigger and outspoken one, while Richard was quiet and laid back.

Jerome looked over at Richard. "Damn, I hate to go to Mrs. Wilkins' class. All she talks about is how we should be more than glad to learn about our forefathers. Nobody cares about that ancient crap."

Richard started laughing and in his mocking way gave his impression of Mrs. Wilkins. He cleared his throat then pretended he was looking over his glasses: "If you only knew what Black folk went through just trying to learn how to read and write, you would appreciate the opportunity you have to get a good education."

Richard paused, no longer Mrs. Wilkins. "Then she goes into those long stories her grandmother used to tell her that inspired her to become a teacher."

Jerome shook his head. "I'm in no mood to hear her stories today."

"We better get moving if we don't want to be late," Jerome said as he started running.

"Wait for me!" Richard said, trying his best to keep up.

The school they went to was a typical inner-city school with all its economic and educational challenges. It was greatly underfunded, which contributed to its condition as well as the quality of the teachers who taught there. It desperately needed repairs. Structurally, it boasted broken windows and light fixtures, which was only accented by graffiti on nearly every available surface. The few good teachers would leave when the first opportunity presented itself, giving the students the impression that their teachers did not care for their school or for them.

As a result, most of the students did not feel they had any reason to learn, which contributed to the school's test scores being far below the state standards.

When they made it to the school, a look of disappointment flashed across Jerome's face. "Damn, you mean to tell me we ran all that way to get to this dump?" he asked, as though he was seeing the school for the first time.

Richard bent over with his hands on his knees, trying to catch his breath. "Looks that way, and what makes matters worse, we're late and you know old lady Wilkins."

Mrs. Wilkins, born Ruth Marie Baker, was a formidable woman in her early eighties. She could have retired many years ago but loved teaching and devoted all of her time to the Black history program at the high school. She had grown up in a small town in northern Louisiana. Her mother died when she was born, and her father was never around, so her grandmother raised her. Her grandmother called her Bitty because she was so small when she was born. When her grandmother saw her for the first time, she said, "She is such a little bitty thing." From that point on, her grandmother would call her Bitty.

Bitty's grandmother would take her to the house where she worked. She noticed the schools on the side of town where the White folks lived looked much better, yet she did not understand why she could not go to them. There was a little White girl who lived in the house where her grandmother worked who was just her age. They would play while her grandmother would work. The little girl's bedroom looked like a room fit for a princess, which made Bitty more than a little envious. Being the bright, observant child that she was, she took advantage of everything she could while she was there. She saw the schoolbooks the little girl had, which were much better and more advanced than the ones at the school she went to. She would read them every chance she could get. She would even help her little White friend with her homework, which gave her even more opportunities to read her books.

One day on the way home, she asked her grandmother why she could not go to the schools on that side of town. She declared that she was smart enough and explained how she would help the little White girl with her homework. Her grandmother took her into her arms that day and explained why Black and White children did not go to school together. Her grandmother said, "Bitty, White folks do not care about Black folks' education, and you should learn all you can so that when you grow up, you can help Black children get a good education."

She would never forget how her grandmother looked at her and said that there was a time when White folk did not allow Black folk to read or even write. Then she would tell her about the struggles Black folks went through to obtain their right to equal education, and how even then, it was not quite equal, but how it would all work out if they put their faith in God and stuck together. She would sit there, content to listen for hours to her grandmother's message of hope for the future.

The classroom door slowly opened, and Jerome and Richard entered. Mrs. Wilkins glanced up as they tiptoed in. "And what do you two have to say for being late again?" she said, with a disappointed look.

Jerome looked at Mrs. Wilkins defiantly. "It's just Black history. Nobody cares about it anyway." Richard just headed for his seat, not daring to say anything.

Mrs. Wilkins stiffened, and addressed the class. "Do the rest of you feel that way?" she asked disappointedly.

Several remarks came from the class:

"I don't see what good it does to know this stuff."

"This stuff ain't going to make me any money."

"It ain't nothin' but slavery and killing Blacks. That don't do nothin' but make me mad."

"Well, I'm sorry you all feel that way, because there is a lot of good that can come from learning about our past. But before you can get anything out of this class, you need to know the value it can bring. So for your homework assignment, I want everyone to write a paper on how learning about our past can help you in the present. You should be prepared to read it aloud and discuss it with the class." A number of disgruntled remarks sounded from the class about doing the paper, but the noise ceased as soon as Mrs. Wilkins threatened to have them do even more homework.

As it was getting close to the end of class, Jerome kept his eyes on the clock, waiting impatiently to leave what he considered the worst hour of the day. When the bell rang, Jerome headed for the door.

"Hold it!" Mrs. Wilkins called before Jerome and several others could make it to the door. "I did not dismiss this class, so where do you think you are going?"

Jerome looked at Mrs. Wilkins. "Don't want to be late to my next class."

"It's too bad you don't try that hard to get to *my* class on time. Everyone, go sit down," she said in a demanding voice.

There were several murmured remarks as they went back to their seats. "Now don't forget the homework assignment. I want a report from everyone, and be prepared to read and discuss it in class tomorrow. Everyone may leave except Jerome and Richard."

Jerome and Richard sat in their seats with their chins resting in the palms of their hands. Mrs. Wilkins walked to the front of her desk and leaned back on it. "What am I going to do with you two?" she said, shaking her head in disappointment. "You are late every day; you don't do your work. Richard, I want to hear something out of you this time," she said sharply.

Richard turned his head and looked out the window.

"Well, say something," she said in an exasperated voice.

Richard turned toward Mrs. Wilkins before replying, "We were just late to class. We're sorry. Can't you just leave it at that?"

"No, I can't. If I do, that will mean I have given up on you two, and you both have too much potential for me to do that. You know you are very bright young men, and I am very surprised at you, Richard. I've had you in classes before, and you have done very well. You need to stop letting Jerome influence you and start doing the things I know you are capable of doing."

"Jerome, you need to start making better choices when it comes to school. You both must start taking responsibility for your actions like young men your age should. You will need a good education to make it in this world as Black men today. It's not like it was when Blacks were beaten and killed for trying to learn to read and write."

"Here we go again," Jerome said under his breath.

Mrs. Wilkins looked at Jerome. "You will continue to hear it until I get you to understand the importance of learning from the past. You two may not want to hear this, but a good education will open many doors that will be closed without it. Education is there for the taking, and if you take it into consideration, you can become anything you want. If you took education as seriously as you take basketball, I wouldn't have any problems out of you two. Now you may go and please, for the love of God, be on time tomorrow."

As they left the room, Jerome said, "Man, that woman crazy; basketball can make me some money. That ancient history junk she teach can't make me no money."

Richard shook his head. "You may be right, but if we don't get our grades up in her class, we won't be playing basketball at this school or anywhere else. Since we have a free period now, do you want to go and work on the paper?"

"Man, it sounds like you scared."

"I ain't scared…just want that woman off my back."

"You are scared."

"I said I ain't scared."

"Well, let's get to the gym, because it's basketball time."

Jerome started jogging down to the gym, and Richard shook his head and followed behind.

There was a slim built six-foot two guy working on his dribbling skills waiting for the game to get started when they came into the gym. "Say JT, Rich, where you been? We're about to start."

"Old Lady Wilkins held me and Rich up again. I think she's out to get us."

"You ain't by yourself."

Jerome held his hands out and called, "Pass me the ball."

Jerome shot a ten-foot jump shot. "All day!" he exclaimed as the ball hit nothing but net.

The pickup game started in its usual way, with trash talking, fussing, and cursing. Jerome and Richard were always on the same team. Richard would handle bringing the ball down, Jerome would make most of the points, and the other guys would be the supporting cast. The score of the game stayed very close, which made the trash talking, fussing, and cursing level even higher. The score was tied fourteen to fourteen, bringing upon a sudden death situation, and the next score won.

Richard brought the ball down, giving Jerome the look which he knew was the signal for him to get ready for the alley-oop. The pressure was tight, but Richard could handle the ball better than most. Jerome was running through screens trying to get open for Richard's lob. Richard knew the timing had to be right for the play to work.

There was the opening; Richard lobbed the ball in the air; there was Jerome, high above the rim.

"Ahhhhhh," he hollered as he slam-dunked the ball into the basket. When he made the winning point, the rim broke away from the backboard. Jerome came down hard, and shattered glass rained down upon him. His head hit the floor with a loud crack.

Richard ran over to where his friend lay on the floor. "Man, are you all right?"

All the other guys were looking on with concern, uncertain about how to help their friend. Lying on his back, Jerome looked up at Richard. Everything seemed to be spinning around and going in and out of focus. He blinked his eyes and shook his head, trying to get the fogginess, confusion, and dizziness to stop. He could see the concern on everyone's faces as they watched.

Richard said frantically. "Get some help, hurry up!"

Jerome could hear the remarks from everyone as he lay there, fading in and out, but everyone became more and more out of focus, and the voices seemed to sound like a distant echo. Just then, Jerome became confused and began attempting to articulate rambling words that weren't making any sense. He continued to shake his head, trying to understand what was happening, but not having any idea where he was or what was going on. His head finally fell to the left, and all movement stopped.

CHAPTER 2

Jerome found himself sitting by a big tree next to Richard. Confused, they both sat speechless and stunned at what they were seeing. Neither one of them looked at the other as they stared straight ahead. There was nothing but open fields as far as they could see. There was no school, no buildings, and no familiar sounds. They recognized nothing.

After taking in their surroundings, Jerome and Richard slowly turned toward each other. "Where the hell are we?" Jerome asked.

"I don't have a clue. We were in the gym playing ball, you hit your head on the floor and passed out, and then all of a sudden we are out in this field next to this big tree."

Just then a voice of a girl came from behind them. "What y'all doing on Massa land?" she asked them. "Is you runaway slaves?"

Jerome and Richard looked at each other and then slowly turned to see where the voice had come from. There was a young girl about their age, wearing a worn dress and carrying a worn-out book in her hand.

"Massa find y'all out here, you gon' be in a heap of trouble," she warned.

Jerome stared at the girl. "What you mean runaway slaves?" he asked.

Richard chimed in, "Yeah, what's this runaway slave crap? Is this some kind of joke?"

"Won't be a joke if Massa fines y'all here," she said, glancing around nervously, but when she didn't see anyone, she looked back at them.

"Where is here?" Jerome asked, confused.

"Why, this is the Williams' plantation, of course," she said, gesturing to the land around the tree where they sat. "And Massa John won't take kindly to colored folk he don't know on his land. Y'all best be on yo' way."

As Jerome stood up, she took a cautious step back. "I'm JT and this is Rich. We don't know how we got here or where we're at."

"That's yo' names? I never heard names like that before."

"My name is Jerome but everyone calls me JT, and his name is Richard but everyone calls him Rich."

"Well, I is June and everyone just calls me June."

"Okay, June, nice to meet you. Now can you take us to this John fellow? Maybe he can tell us where we are," suggested Jerome.

"Yeah," Richard said, "because this is starting to seriously freak me out."

"I can see y'all ain't from around here. Y'all dress funny, talk funny, and if'n you think you just gon' walk up to Massa John, you must be crazy too." She seemed certain.

Richard stood up and brushed the dirt from his pants. "What's crazy is we were in school, and the next thing you know we end up here. Now, if anything is crazy, it's that."

"Y'all go to school?" she asked excitedly. "I ain't never known any colored folk that go to school. Can y'all read and write?"

"Of course we can," Jerome said, as though that was a ridiculous question. "Can't you?"

June tilted her head down to stare at her feet. "No, colored folks around here can't read or write. If coloreds get caught trying to read and write, they would be beat plenty bad."

"Then what's with the book?" Richard asked, pointing at the worn book in her hand.

"Oh, this? I just make believe I can read. If Massa knew I had this book, I'd be beat fo' sure."

Richard was genuinely more confused than before. "Why are you walking around with a book if you can't read?"

"I just be looking at the books, pretending I can read. I wish I could read like Massa John and the White folk."

Richard looked at Jerome, who shrugged his shoulders as if to say, "It don't make any sense to me either."

"I work in the big house with my mama," she added, rocking back and forth onto her toes. "When I can get away, I sneak books out. You won't tell, will you?" She seemed genuinely concerned that they might, but then it appeared that her curiosity got the better of her and she continued. "Can you read a book like this?"

"Of course," Richard said.

"Can you read something for me?" June asked, all excited now, and she thrust the book toward Richard.

Richard took the book and started reading. June's jaw dropped in disbelief, and her eyes bucked wide open. "I is never seen a colored read. You read better than Miss Ann," she stated, awestruck.

"Who's that?" Richard asked.

"That's Massa daughter. She reads to the little children. I listen in sometimes when I'm cleaning, but I don't let her know. No sir, 'cause she gets real mad. One time, she caught me looking at the book when she was reading. She said, 'Is you trying to read?'" Her eyes widened. "I said, 'No, Miss Ann, I ain't trying to read.' She looks at me real mean. Oh, that look made me shiver and it sent cold chills up my spine. Then she say I better not be trying to read. Niggers don't have any reason to read."

"This is crazy. What the hell is going on?" Jerome asked, stunned by what he was seeing and hearing.

"It don't make sense," Richard said as he looked over at Jerome.

"Y'all must not be slaves, being able to read and all. Is y'all from up north? I hear coloreds are treated much better up there. They say some coloreds even go to school." She paused, looking wistfully at the book in her hand. "I'll do anything to go to school. One day, I is going up north where I can get me some proper learning." She seemed determined now. "Yes, I is. I'm gon' leave this place and never gon' come back."

Jerome interjected. "You may be thinking about going north, but me and Rich need to figure out how to get back home, because we sure don't belong here." Richard glanced around nervously, then at Jerome. "JT, we can't stand out here in the open; we need to find a place where we can think and figure this out. Someone might see us and have more questions, and that we don't need."

"There is an old barn not too far from here that y'all can stay in." She gestured toward the horizon. "Nobody goes down there," she continued. "You can stay there until you figure out what you gon' do. I can show you where it is."

They didn't have much of a choice, and this seemed as good a bet as any. As strange as the situation was, it was beginning to dawn on them that they were somewhere they weren't supposed to be, and that it might not be safe for them to stay. Echoes of the teachings of slavery rang in their ears, and suddenly, those lessons felt very real.

CHAPTER 3

The three headed for the barn. Jerome and Richard were following June, making sure that they were not seen. The old barn was no longer used and was beginning to fall apart from the years of neglect and disrepair. They walked about a quarter of a mile away from where the slaves lived before they reached the barn.

"Here we is. Y'all can wait in here until you can think of what you gon' do. Nobody comes down here anymore. That's why I sometimes come down here to look at the books."

The barn was a large wooden structure, spacious inside. There was a dirt floor, and small dust motes floated in the sunshine coming through the windows and slats in the wood.

June gave them the quick tour of the barn, clearly proud of the space. "I call this my school. I can sit in here and not worry about anyone finding me. This is where I was going when I saw y'all."

She paused, and then continued, "I better get back before someone misses me, but I'll come back later." She began running down the trail as Jerome and Richard watched.

They closed the barn door and started looking around.

"Look at this dump," Jerome said as he picked up an old crate and dusted it off to sit on. He scoffed, "And she calls this her school? Say, Rich, you know what I think?"

"What's that?"

"I think we were sent back into time as some kind of punishment."

"Punishment for what? We haven't done anything. Besides, it don't make any sense. People just don't go back in time. This isn't some science fiction movie."

"Do you have a better explanation for what's going on?" Jerome asked.

"No, not really, but whatever it is, we need to figure it out and quick."

"You're right about that," responded Jerome. The two just sat quietly, both in deep thought, not knowing what to do. They'd dealt with various situations over the years that had required quick thinking, but this was outside of their wheelhouse and they knew it.

After a while, Richard spoke. "Say, JT, you know who I was thinking about?"

"Who's that?"

"I was thinking about Mrs. Wilkins."

"Mrs. Wilkins? What made you think about her?"

"June." Even though the two of them often got each other in trouble, Richard was far more introspective than Jerome, who was prone to acting first and thinking later.

"June?" Jerome said with a confused look. "What about June would make you think about Mrs. Wilkins?"

"You know how Mrs. Wilkins is always getting on us about taking advantage of the opportunities we have?"

"Yeah, so?"

"Well, look at June. She is around our age and she can't even read or write. If she is even caught with a book, trying to learn it could mean big trouble, but that don't even stop her from trying. She would risk taking a beating for the opportunities that we have."

Richard stopped. "It's amazing how June would take that kind of risk for the opportunities that we take for granted. I can't wait to get home and throw down my backpack so I can play ball."

"I see what you mean. She did get excited when she heard you read, and just think, you can't even read that good," Jerome said as he held his hand out for Richard to slap.

"Real funny," Richard said, high-fiving him, and the two started laughing.

"Quiet, Rich, did you hear that?" Jerome whispered quickly.

"Hear what? I didn't hear anything," Richard responded, also in a sharp whisper.

"I think someone's coming. Let's get behind those old crates."

Jerome and Richard ducked behind the crates moments before the barn doors opened. "Y'all in here?" June asked hesitantly as she closed the barn door behind her.

Jerome and Richard both let out a sigh of relief when they heard June's voice. Just as they were about to come from behind the crates, the barn door opened again, and they ducked back down. There was a slender White man in dirty overalls with a wad of chewing tobacco in his mouth standing in the barn, spitting juice on the floor next to him.

"What you doin' sneaking up here?" he drawled. "I been watching you, and I thought you were up to something. Is there a nigger boy in here?" he asked June, spitting again.

"No, Massa, ain't no nigger boy in here. I just come up here to be by myself and think," she said quietly. She looked nervous.

"What a nigger gal got to think about? You up to something?" he asked.

"Naw, suh, I ain't up to nothin'," June said as she started to back up.

The slender White man's name was Billy. He was poor White trash, not much better off than the slaves who worked on the plantation, so when he got a chance to show them that he was above them, he took it. He was hired on by the plantation owner to do odd jobs and sometimes to oversee the slaves as they did their work. He was the worst of the overseers to work for, because he always had to show that he was superior by being unnecessarily tough on the slaves. He made their lives even more miserable with his cruelty, and as much as they resented him for it, they feared him as well.

"Well, well," Billy said as he closed the barn door. He spit the wad of tobacco on the ground and wiped the drool that was running down from his lips onto his chin. A big grin came over his face, showing his brown teeth caused by the constant chewing of tobacco.

He had a menacing look in his eye as he moved toward a frozen June. "I've had my eye on you ever since you were little. You about ripe now." Billy started taking the straps from his overalls off his shoulders.

June started backing up, knowing what was about to happen. "No massa, no massa," she pleaded as tears ran down her cheeks.

"What are we going to do?" Richard said in a low voice.

"I don't know. Let me think," Jerome said as he rubbed his head.

Billy grabbed June's dress in the front, ripping it to expose her breast. She could see the lust in his eyes, just as he could see the fright in hers. June closed her eyes and stood there, frightened, not knowing what to do as Billy felt all over her breast. Her mother had warned her about these men, but fighting might make the situation even worse. June was terrified.

"I got it!" Jerome said quietly. "You stand up to get his attention and lure him over here, and I'll knock his butt out with this board." As scared as Jerome was, he wasn't about to let anything happen to his newfound friend.

"Are you sure about that?" Rich whispered back.

"Do you have a better idea?"

"Okay, here I go." He jumped up. "Hey, what the hell you think you're doing?" he yelled at Billy, taking him by surprise.

Billy took his attention away from June, startled to have been interrupted. "Well, well, what do we have here? You do have a nigger boy in here," he accused.

"Who you calling a nigger, you White piece of trash?" shouted Richard, angry now.

"Oh we have a nigger boy who don't seem to know his place," said Billy, pushing June down. "You better not move. I'm not finished with you," he said to June as he left her and started toward Richard.

Richard, having lost the element of surprise, stood still, hoping that Jerome would jump in any time now.

"Here he comes," Richard said in a low voice, trying not to move his lips. "When I duck, you let him have it," he hissed.

Billy got closer and closer, putting the straps of his overalls back on his shoulders as he moved, clearly unthreatened by Richard.

"Now!" Richard ducked down. Jerome jumped up from behind the crates, swung the board as hard as he could, and hit Billy across the forehead with a loud thwack. Billy hit the ground and was out cold.

There was a moment of stunned silence in the barn.

"Ah, man, you laid his butt out!" Richard said as he looked down at Billy.

"He won't ever put his hands on no one else!" Jerome threw the board to the ground.

June scrambled to her feet, holding her torn dress over her chest so her breast would not be exposed. "Is he dead?"

Jerome nudged him with his foot. "I don't think so, but he's going to have a serious headache when he wakes up. Rich, let's see if we can find something to tie him up with before he wakes up." Jerome and Richard started looking around. June stood holding her dress, still frightened, not knowing what to think or do.

"Say, JT, I found some rope that we can use," Richard called from one end of the barn.

"Good, let's tie him up so we don't have any more trouble with him when he wakes up." Jerome pulled Billy's unconscious body over to one of the beams that held the loft up, sat him up against it, and pulled his hands back and tied him to the beam. Richard held his feet together, and Jerome tied them up too.

Not a moment after they had finished tying, Billy began to stir. "Oh, my head," he mumbled.

"He's waking up," June said urgently. "What we gon' do?"

Jerome walked over to her protectively. "Don't worry we have him tied up real good, he can't get loose."

"What the hell?!" Billy cried as he became fully conscious and realized that he was tied up. He tested the bonds, wiggling his arms furiously against the ropes, but they had tied him securely.

Billy looked up, and there standing above him were Jerome, Richard, and June looking down at him. "You niggers gon' be in a heap of trouble. Y'all better let me go," he threatened as he struggled to get the ropes loose. Not getting anywhere with his threats, Billy directed all his attention to June. "Girl, you better tell them to untie me right now." He gave her the kind of look that pierces right to the soul.

June stood there, trembling, knowing the type of man he was. She had seen and heard the stories of slaves being disciplined for getting out of line. She stood there with many thoughts running through her mind. *What should I do? How can I make this right?* But she knew he would not let a thing like this go, even if they untied him now.

CHAPTER 4

Jerome put his hand on Richard's shoulder. "Let's move so we can talk. We got to figure some things out."

The three walked over to the other side of the barn so Billy could not hear what they were saying.

"What's up?" Richard said.

Jerome looked at June. "Looks like we got you into a big mess," he said apologetically. "We can't stay here, and it looks like if you stay, it's going to be big trouble for you."

"Where am I gon' go? This is the only place I know," she said mournfully.

Richard snapped his fingers. "I got it! You said that you wanted to go north. We can take you there, and on the way, maybe we can figure out what we need to do to get back home, wherever or whenever that is."

Even though they hadn't discussed it, Jerome knew Rich was right. They couldn't very well leave June here to fend for herself, and right now, it seemed like they were the only people in the world who could protect her.

"Well, what do you say?" Jerome asked, looking at June.

A look of excitement washed over her face. For the first time in her young life, she felt as though she might have an opportunity to do some of the things that she dreamed about.

"I can't stay here. He gon' kill me," she said sadly but with certainty.

"Good," Jerome said. "You go change and meet us back here. Don't let anyone know what you're doing, not even your mother. "We can't take a chance of someone finding out what took place here."

Richard told June, "You need to make sure this is something you want to do, because once we leave there's no turning back." He was cautious but his tone was serious.

June stood there for a minute, knowing that she might never see her mother and friends again. She also knew that she could not stay because of what had happened with Billy, even though he had been the aggressor.

Her mind was made up. "I'll be back," she said.

As she opened the barn door, Billy looked up, conscious and certain to have one serious headache.

"Where do you think you're going? You better tell them to let me go," he said as he struggled to get loose. Even as Billy found himself completely helpless, he still imagined that his authority would override the free will of his captors.

"Don't worry, June, we'll take care of him," Jerome said as he closed the barn door behind her. Jerome and Richard found some old rags and stuffed them in Billy's mouth to keep him quiet.

About fifteen minutes later, June came through the barn door. Jerome and Richard were behind the door just in case it was someone else.

"We thought you would never get back," Jerome said as he closed the barn door behind her.

June looked at Jerome and Richard with a sad expression on her face. "I'm gon' really miss my ma," she said tearfully.

Jerome put his hand on her shoulder. "It's not too late to change your mind, and we will understand, but me and Rich can't stay. You know that."

"We have to leave and figure out how to get back home," Jerome added.

"I'll be okay," June said as she wiped tears from her face. "I told my ma that I had to help a friend who is sick, and I'll be there all night, so she won't miss me."

"Now that we got that worked out, do we know where we're going and how we're going to get there?" Richard asked.

"We'll have to work that out on the way," Jerome said as he opened the barn door. The three left the barn, leaving Billy behind still struggling in vain to get loose.

Jerome, Richard, and June could see and smell the smoke from the food that was cooking from slave row, which they had passed on their way to the barn. June turned around to take a last look at the place she called home all her life. She had mixed emotions about leaving her mother and the only life she knew. She knew she could not stay after what had happened, but worried how Master John would treat her mother when he found out she was gone. Would he think her mother had helped her get away? Would he beat her?

Richard looked at Jerome and said, "We got to go."

Jerome walked over to June. "It's time to go now," he said softly.

She turned around with tears running down her face and said, "I know," in a low, soft voice.

The three started jogging down the trail and never looked back. As soon as they could, they got off the main trail. The brush was thick around them, and they could not move as fast as they could have if they'd been on the main trail, but there would be less chance of being seen if someone came down the trail. It had become completely dark as night had fallen, but there was plenty of light from the full moon.

They did not know where they were going. All they knew was that they had to get as far away from the plantation as they could before June was missed or someone discovered Billy tied up in the old barn. They had been moving at a good pace for several hours.

"Wait," June said in a soft voice as she stopped and bent over, leaning against a tree, trying to catch her breath. "I needs to rest. I can't go no more."

The three fell to the ground, not saying a word, all breathing heavily. On their backs, looking up at the sky in the darkness, they lay there quietly as they felt their heart rates return to normal. All three were at peace in that moment, but they knew they could not enjoy it for long.

CHAPTER 5

Jerome finally sat up. "We don't have a clue where we are."

Richard turned on his side toward where Jerome and June lay, resting his head in his hand with his elbow on the ground. "We been on the move for quite a while," he said.

"We don't know where we're going or how we're going to get there. This can't be real," he said, the disbelief catching up with him. "I hope we didn't make a mistake by leaving."

"What do you mean?" Jerome said.

Richard sat up. "I'm just saying, maybe the key to getting home is where we started, near that big tree."

"You know, you could be right. Maybe we should go back and try and figure this out where it started," Jerome responded. He'd seen enough superhero movies to know about things like portals, magic, and time travel.

"We can't go back!" June said in a panic. "No, no, no. Massa kill us as sho as we standing here."

"Maybe if we explain to him what happened, he will understand," Jerome said, still trying to make sense of what was happening.

"You don't understand. People have died fo' less than what we did," she said with panic in her voice. "If we want to live, we can never go back."

"That's ridiculous," Richard said. "No one will kill you for hitting someone. That just don't make sense."

"I can't go back. Don't make me, please don't make me," June said, crying now and pulling on Jerome's shirt.

"Quiet, do you hear that?" Jerome said suddenly, looking at Richard and June.

"Hear what? I don't hear anything," Richard said.

"I hear it," June said, sniffling a little as she composed herself. "Those is dogs; we got to get out of here."

They started running back the way they came, since the sound of the dogs was coming from the way they were going. As they continued to run, they could hear the sound of the dogs getting closer and closer.

"Let's head for that ditch. We can hide there," Jerome said, thinking quickly. The three jumped in the ditch and ducked down. There was a broken tree branch lying across the ditch that gave them extra cover. They could hear the dogs getting closer and closer. They also could hear the voices of men.

"We got him now."

"We got that nigger now."

"We gon' teach him he can't run from us." The voices of the men echoed all around them, seeming to come from everywhere.

Suddenly, they heard a man's voice screaming in the dark night.

"Haaaaaa, call 'em off, Massa, call 'em off, please call 'em off!"

Jerome and Richard peeped over the tree branch to see what was going on. June stayed down nervously, shaking her leg and covering her ears, trying not to hear the frightful sounds. They were several feet away and could see the dogs biting at the man's bare feet as he kicked and fought, trying to keep them off.

"Look at that nigger kick," one of the White men jeered as the other two men watched and laughed. Jerome and Richard looked at each other, dumbfounded at what they were seeing.

"All right, all right, you've had your fun. Call 'em off," one of the men said as he gestured to the other men. "We have to bring this nigger back in one piece. He does Mr. Jackson no good if'n he can't work." The two men grabbed the dogs and put their chains around their necks as they continued barking and trying to get to the man on the ground. The man who'd been screaming sat up, breathing hard, as the blood from his wounds covered his bare feet. With his head down, the broken man sat there breathing heavily as perspiration dripped from his forehead.

The White man who appeared to be the one in charge slowly walked over to where the man was sitting on the ground. He leaned over the man with his hands behind his back, shaking his head.

"Now why you go do a dumb thing and run? Don't Mr. Jackson treat you niggers good?"

"Yassuh," the man said, as he sat there with his head down, cringing from the pain of the dog bites.

"So, you think you can do just as you damn please?" the White man asked.

The man on the ground looked up at the White man and cried out, "He took my little girl! Why he had to take her? He had no right to do that!" The pain in his voice was beyond the physical pain that he felt.

"You better watch your mouth, boy. Mr. Jackson can do what he damn well pleases with you niggers. He owns all of you and your nigger offspring."

The man sat there and mumbled in a softer voice, shaking his head as he looked down at the ground. "Why my little girl? Why he had to take my little girl?" he asked again, sadly.

"Ya see, that's the problem with you dumb niggers. Ya don't know how good ya got it. Mr. Jackson gives ya everything ya need and you treat him like this, running. You'll wish you never ran when I finish with you." The White man's voice was low and threatening.

From his belt, he pulled out a whip and snapped it. The sound was like a crack of thunder, which made the dogs bark and pull at the chains even more.

"Man what we gon' do?" Richard whispered to Jerome.

"We can't do nothing but stay right here and hope they don't find us." Jerome had never felt fear like this in his entire life, but he knew that trying to stand up for the man would only lead to more trouble, and this time, trouble they couldn't talk their way out of. Jerome and Richard looked on helplessly as June stayed down with her hands over her ears, not wanting to see or hear anything.

"Stand up, boy," the man with the whip said callously.

"This gon' be fun," remarked one of the men holding the dogs' chains, as the dogs barked, clamoring to be let loose.

The man on the ground slowly stood up. The look on his face said he was in a great deal of pain.

"Turn around," the man with the whip said as he cracked it for the second time. The dogs again started barking and pulling at the chains. The man, now standing, turned around, holding his head down, anticipating the pain from the whip.

"I'll teach you not to run!" the White man said angrily, and he pulled back the whip and swung it forward. The whip hit the man's back, tearing through the shirt and ripping the skin on his back.

"Haaaaaa!" the scream echoed through the darkness as he felt the pain from the whip. The scream excited the dogs even further, which started them barking and pulling at their chains again.

"Look at that nigger scream like a pig," one of the men said as they looked on and laughed. With another hit from the whip, screaming from the pain, the man fell to his knees.

The White man continued to hit him until the Black man fell facedown on the ground. He lay there, unmoving, lifeless in the dust as the blood saturated his shredded shirt.

The White man with the whip kicked him. "Get up get up we ain't got all night."

The man groaned. Moving slowly, he made his way to his knees. The pain with every move was unbearable as he stood up. The man with the whip put shackles around his ankles as he stood there, with a clearly broken spirit.

"I bet yo running days are over," the White man said as he clamped the pin in the shackles. "Let's move it. We ain't got all night, and we got a long way to go."

He then pushed the shackled man in the back with the butt of the whip, causing the man to flinch in pain because of the welts on his back. The group started walking, the two men with the dogs following behind, talking and laughing.

Jerome and Richard watched as they walked off, speechless. When they were no longer in sight, they sat down next to June, in shock after witnessing something that they only heard about in Mrs. Wilkins' Black History class.

"Rich."

"Yeah, man," replied Richard.

"When Mrs. Wilkins talked about the beating that Blacks took, I didn't think much about it, but after seeing that, I know one thing. I'll never forget it as long as I live."

"I know what you mean," Richard said, shaking his head.

"Now you see why we can't go back," June said as she looked up for the first time since they had been in the ditch. "They kill us and think nothin' of it fo' what we did."

"She's right. Ain't no way we can go back there," Richard said.

"And we can't stick around here," Jerome said, rubbing his head.

The three got out of the ditch and headed in a different direction from the way they came or the way the men went. They knew it would only be a matter of time before they would be hunted like the man they had just seen. Not sure of where they were going, they worked their way through the tall brush. The mosquitoes seemed to bite and aggravate them every step of the way. They began to get tired, but they knew they had to keep moving. Hour after hour, they moved on, not saying a word, just hearing the heavy breathing from each other, and fearing that they, too, would be hunted down like an animal and treated like the man they had seen.

CHAPTER 6

June, unable to keep up the pace, started to fall behind. "We is got to stop and get some sleep or we ain't gon' be able to continue," she panted.

Richard looked around, not seeing anywhere remotely hospitable for rest. "Sleep where? There ain't nowhere to sleep around here," he said.

"We just gon' have to sleep on the ground," she replied.

"The mosquitoes are tearing us up as it is and you want to lie on the ground?" he asked, exasperated at the thought. "You got to be kidding me."

"I'm gon' lay down here and get me some sleep. I is too tired to go any mo' without no sleep."

Jerome and Richard could see the fatigue on each other's faces. They'd never been in a survival situation like this before, and even though neither was comfortable with their surroundings, they were resigned to the fact that there wasn't a whole lot they could do to change it.

"I am tired," Jerome said. Richard shrugged his shoulders in reluctant agreement, and the boys started looking for the safest place to rest. They spotted a relatively flat spot that would partially obscure them from view of anyone passing by. Deciding that was the best option, they all settled in to try to get some rest. Jerome and Richard lay down on either side of June to protect her as they slept. Despite the discomfort, all three fell fast asleep nearly immediately, unaware of their surroundings. Maybe it was because of the late hour when they'd stopped, or because of their exhaustion, but the three slept straight through the sunrise.

"Well, well, well. What do we have here?"

Jerome, Richard, and June all looked up, startled, squinting from the morning sun that was shining in their faces. Surprised that they had slept through the night with no interruptions, they saw a big burly man looking down at them holding a shotgun in his hand.

Big Jake was his name. Big Jake was a three-hundred-pound man who traveled from town to town in his wagon doing odd jobs and selling things to make a living. Looking down at the three of them, he saw a big payday. Believing that they were runaways, he felt there would be a reward if he returned them.

The shotgun clicked as Big Jake pulled the trigger back, capitalizing on the element of surprise. "Get up, get up from there and don't try nothin' or I'll drop you right there," he ordered.

Keeping his eyes on them, he spit the brown juice from the tobacco he was chewing as he leaned over them. The three of them got up, still groggy and sore from the hard night they had.

Jerome raised his hands defensively. "What's up with the gun, man? We ain't done nothing. If this is your land we'll leave."

"Ain't no niggers out here unless they running. Where yo' papers?"

"Papers for what?" Richard asked, looking at June questioningly.

"Papers that sho' us free or giving us permission to leave the plantation," she replied, her brain still groggy from sleep, but her body humming with concern.

"Something ain't right," Big Jake said, with a puzzled look on his face. "I ain't never seen niggers around these parts that look like you two." He paused, clearly trying to work something out in his mind. "Now, she looks like the niggers round here."

June just stared at the ground, not saying anything. Jerome and Richard, knowing they were out of their element, didn't know quite what to say.

"Y'all better speak up and tell me what the hell's going on," said Big Jake, spitting tobacco juice forcefully on the ground near them.

"You right, we ain't from around here and we ain't no niggers," Jerome said defiantly, looking him straight in the eye. "We're African Americans, so why don't you put that gun down?"

"African Americans, what the hell is that?" asked Big Jake, confused at the term. "I ain't ever heard of no African American. You is either an African or you is an American and if you ain't got no papers, you is in deep trouble."

The three of them were concerned. This situation was not good, and it was only getting worse by the minute.

"Now y'all walk over to that there wagon and don't try nothin' or you gon' be dead, whatever the hell you is."

The three stood up, reluctantly, and started walking over to the wagon with Big Jake following with his shotgun pointed at them. Their eyes scanned the surroundings, looking for a way out but there wasn't one that they could see.

"Stop," he said harshly, keeping his eyes on them as he walked to the back of the wagon. He reached into the wagon and pulled out three sets of chains and then casually tossed them over to them. "Clamp these around y'all ankles and don't try nothin'," he directed.

They put the clamps that were connected to the chains around their ankles. "Now get to walkin' that a way," Big Jake said as he pointed with his shotgun in the direction he wanted to go. As they started trudging forward, Big Jake struggled to climb into the wagon, as his weight made it tough for him to climb in or out. Breathing hard as he clambered up into the seat, he yelled, "Get to walking; we have a long way to go."

The three started walking more quickly as Jake followed close behind in his wagon.

"Now what?" Richard whispered.

"I don't know, but we need to think of something fast because we can't end up going back to some place we don't belong," Jerome said, thinking about the man they saw get beaten and attacked by dogs the night before.

They continued to walk as the sun beamed down and drained them of the little energy they had. They were thirsty and hungry, not having eaten since they'd arrived, but they continued to trudge along, hearing the steady clanking of the wagon not far behind.

After several hours, Richard, who was in the back of the three, hollered, "It's hot, we need some water!" He didn't look back, waiting for a response. He continued walking for a minute or so but didn't hear anything except the clanking of the wagon. Richard turned his head slightly and looked back. He saw Big Jake with his head down, slouched over, the reins dangling limply from his unmoving hands.

"He's asleep! His fat sloppy butt done fell asleep!" he whispered urgently and excitedly. Now was their chance, maybe the only opportunity that they'd have to get away.

The three stopped walking. The wagon kept going, guided by the horse. Jerome grabbed the reins to stop the horse, halting the wagon. Still chained, they looked at Big Jake cautiously.

"I think he's dead. He should have woken up by now," Jerome said. Big Jake had not so much as stirred or shifted in his seat since Richard had turned around.

"Good," Richard said. "Let's get these chains off and push his big sloppy butt out the wagon and we can ride."

"Are you crazy?" Jerome said. "If someone finds him and then sees us in this wagon, we will get blamed for killing him. That's all we need is to have that hanging over our heads. We need to get these chains off and get as far away from this wagon as we can."

After they removed the chains, Jerome climbed in the back of the wagon to see if there was any food or water they could take. He found a bag with some jerky, a couple of biscuits, and a canteen half full of water. He handed the bag and canteen to June, who was waiting by the back of the wagon to help, then climbed out the wagon.

Jerome was thinking quickly about their situation, wondering what the best course of action might be. Finally, he had a thought. "Rich, let's turn this wagon around and send it the way we came from."

They all agreed that was a good idea, as the farther the wagon got away from them, the more difficult it would be to track them, giving them distance from the dead man. They turned the wagon around, smacked the horse's backside, and watch it slowly move down the trail.

They then took a drink from the canteen and went into the brush to keep from being seen as they continued in the direction they were going, now free from the chains they'd worn all morning. All three were quiet. None of them had experienced anything like this, and June had never imagined she'd get so far from the only home she'd ever known, especially not like this. For all of their brave talk and attitude back home, Jerome and Richard were living a reality they'd previously refused to understand. Either of them would have given anything to be writing that paper back in Ms. Wilkins class rather than being here, lost, confused, and more scared than they'd ever admit.

Picking carefully through the brush, they continued moving forward, knowing that time was their enemy. They knew it was only a matter of time before Billy or someone from the plantation would be hot on their trail, so they had to put as much distance between themselves and the ones who would be tracking them like a hunter after its prey. After several hours of slow progress, they finally saw a house in the near distance.

"Finally," Richard said. "I didn't think we were ever going to run across anything except more weeds and bugs."

"We have to be careful," Jerome cautioned. "We don't know how they will react when they see three Blacks walking up to their house. We need to think this through."

"I am hot, tired, and hungry. I don't care about thinking anything through," Richard said, frustrated by Jerome's hesitation. "I just want to sit down somewhere other than the ground and eat some real food. Let's just walk up to the house like there is nothing wrong."

"All right, let's go," Jerome said in a hesitant voice.

The three started walking up to the house, very cautiously, not in a hurry to find out who was on the other side of that door, but hopeful at the thought of finding relief from the elements and the threat of White men.

CHAPTER 7

June, starting to panic, stopped suddenly. "Maybe we should keep going and not stop here."

Jerome said, "We done came this far; we might as well see it through."

All of a sudden, the front door opened and a middle-aged White man came out to stand on the porch. "Hurry, hurry, we don't want you to be seen!"

The three looked at each other, momentarily baffled, not knowing what to make of what the man was saying.

"Come on, come on," he urged, gesturing rapidly with his hand. The three ran up to the house. The man ushered them in and glanced around to see if anyone was watching, then closed the door. He didn't address them, but instead, looked out the window.

"Where are the rest? Did something happen to them?" he asked, concerned.

They did not say anything, just shared a confused look between them.

"This does not look good," he said, shaking his head.

Bill Cummings and his wife Rachel had moved from Boston to Louisiana several months before as part of an organization that worked to help slaves escape to the safety of the North. Hearing all the stories of the inhumane ways Blacks were treated in the South, when the opportunity came, Bill and his wife wanted to help.

They had uprooted their lives in Boston and trekked down to Louisiana in order to accomplish their goal. This was their first experience at helping with an escape, and they wanted everything to go right, knowing that any mistakes could cost them and others their lives.

All of Bill's friends in Boston told him that they thought he was making a big mistake by making this move to the South. They said he should think about his wife. Bill, being a very timid person, felt he had something to prove. He wanted to show everyone that he could make a difference. Many of their friends had talked to Rachel, hoping she could talk some sense into him because they knew that she did not want to leave her family and home, but she stood by her husband and the decision he made, understanding and appreciating that his compulsion to assist was larger than himself.

"What's wrong?" Rachel asked as she came in the room and saw Bill pacing back and forth.

"Everyone is not here like they're supposed to be, and you know a mistake could cost us and the organization," Bill said testily.

"Calm down, calm down," she said as she put her hand on his shoulder, trying to reassure him.

Jerome raised his hands. "We're just passing through, trying to find our way to the next town."

Richard hit Jerome on the arm excitedly. "Dude, this is part of the Underground Railroad!"

"What?" Jerome asked, looking at Richard.

"If you were paying attention in Ms. Wilkins' class, you would know what's going on," he said. "This is the Underground Railroad. We are actually experiencing the Underground Railroad. Wow, I can't believe this."

Jerome just looked at Richard and shook his head.

"You mean you were not sent here by the organization?" asked Bill.

"I'm afraid not," Jerome said.

"Oh, this is not good," Bill said as he nervously fumbled with his fingers.

"If you just point us in the direction of the next town, we'll be on our way," said Jerome apologetically.

"On your way? You can't leave now. What if you get caught?" Bill asked. "People have a way of getting information out of you, and before you know it, people will be showing up here asking questions."

"Come on, let's go, we'll find our own way," Jerome urged as he started walking toward the door of the house.

"Wait, everyone calm down," Rachel said, trying to be a voice of reason. This may not have been something that she had wanted to do, but now that she was here, she was going to make sure that she took care of everyone. "I know it's been a long night and you must be tired and hungry. Why don't you let me fix you something to eat?" she asked calmly. "After you eat, you can get some rest and then we can talk about what you should do."

Richard rubbed his hands together. Hearing her motherly voice calmed him, and his teenage body was now feeling a strong sense of hunger. "Now that's the best thing that has been said so far," he said, feeling relief run through him.

"Eat and rest sounds good to me," Jerome agreed, taking a deep breath, then pausing for a moment. "We are tired and hungry."

Rachel started cooking while Jerome, Richard, and June sat at the wooden table watching. The smell of the bacon, eggs, and biscuits cooking took their minds off of leaving, the running, and their near brush with the slave trade.

June was very surprised as she sat at the table of a White lady for the very first time, watching her doing the cooking for her. If she had not seen it with her own eyes, she would have never believed it. This was a surreal experience for her, the exact opposite of everything she'd ever known, and she wasn't sure how to feel or respond. She was apprehensive, of course, but she was also hungry and feeling safe for the first time since she'd met Jerome and Richard.

Rachael put the food she had prepared on the table, and Richard started rubbing his hands together in anticipation. "That's what I'm talking about," he said.

"This smells good…thanks," Jerome said as he pulled the plate close to him.

"Thanks, ma'am," June said with her head down, not wanting to look Rachel in the eye.

"Bill, come on, breakfast is ready," Rachel called out as she put his plate on the table. Bill came in and sat down next to June. June stopped eating reflexively and put her head down.

"You'd better eat before it gets cold," Bill said to June as he took a bite of his warm biscuit. June started eating again at his direction, feeling uncomfortable, since she had never before eaten at the same table with a White person.

Bill looked up after taking a sip of his coffee. "Where are my manners?" he asked, having recovered from the shock of their introduction. "What are your names?"

"My name is Jerome, and this is Richard and June," said Jerome, pointing at his companions.

"Now, I have never seen any coloreds that look like you two down here," Bill said, pointing at Jerome and Richard. "In fact, not even back east. You two dress different and talk different. There is something about you that is very different," he said, appraising them with his eyes, waving his biscuit around as he talked. "Where are you two from? Because you are not from around here, that much I am sure of." Bill may have been anxious, but he was also certain that the two of them did not belong.

"No, we're not from around here," Jerome said. "We met June and we're just trying to get her to a safe place."

"Let them eat, dear," Rachel said, pausing her work washing the dishes, since she had eaten her breakfast earlier. "There will be time to talk later."

June finished eating and was just sitting still in her chair, astonished that she had been able to sit next to a White man and have breakfast that was cooked by a White woman. Now she was sitting down and the White lady was doing the cleaning. This seemed so impossible to her.

Rachel cleared the table to finish washing the dishes. Bill was drinking his second cup of coffee, and Jerome, Richard, and June were at the table feeling relaxed, full, and about to fall asleep.

Bill took the last sip of coffee. "Looks like you three could use some rest. You can go down in the cellar, where you can rest and be out of sight just in case someone comes by."

Richard rubbed his eyes, exhausted now that he'd eaten. "We could use some rest before moving on, thank you." He turned to Rachel, who was finishing drying the dishes with a towel. "Thank you for your kindness, ma'am."

Bill walked into the other room with the three of them following. He moved a wooden rocking chair and the rug that was under it, lifting up the door to the cellar. He walked down the stairs and lit a lantern that was hanging from the low ceiling. "Come on," he said as he gestured to the three to join him in the cellar.

Jerome and Richard looked at each other in hesitation, but knowing they didn't have any other options, they went down to the cellar with June following them.

"You can rest down here and after you rest, we can discuss your next move," Bill said as he started heading up the stairs.

"Hey, you're not leaving us down here?" Jerome asked.

"You'll be safe down here, just in case someone shows up looking for you." Bill could see their hesitation, but wasn't sure how to reassure them. "You'll be fine," he said as he walked up the stairs and closed the door above them. He then put the rug and chair back in place to hide the door to the cellar from prying eyes.

June found a spot and settled down. "Is y'all gon' get some rest?" she asked, relieved to be out of the elements.

"In a second," Jerome said. He then pulled Richard out of June's hearing range to discuss their situation. "Man, I really don't like this."

"Being locked down here is making me nervous," Richard agreed.

"I hope we didn't make a mistake," Jerome said.

"I was thinking the same thing," replied Richard. "But they did seem like they wanted to help, and it seems that they have a lot at stake if someone finds out we are here, so I say let's take advantage of this and get some rest. I mean, how much worse could things get?"

Meanwhile, Bill and Rachel were upstairs. "We have to convince them that they need our help," Bill said with a worried look on his face. "I should have found out who they were before I assumed they were the ones we were waiting for, and now they know too much."

"Well, there is nothing we can do about it now," Rachel replied.

"We just have to make sure they get to the next station safely, because if they get caught, they put our lives and the organization in danger," said Bill.

Rachel nodded in agreement.

"I got it!" Bill said as he hit the table with his hand. "We can have them go with the others that are coming later. They will have a better chance of making it if they're traveling with the conductor."

"That might work. We just need to convince them it is in their best interests to join the others. I worry about them, being so young and on their own."

"That might be a challenge, but it's worth a try," Bill replied, before he got up and went outside.

Bill was out back doing chores and Rachel was in the house, both going about their daily routine, anticipating the arrival of the others.

Rachel looked out the window and saw two men on horses riding toward their house. She ran to the back door.

"Bill, come quick, there are two men riding up!" she called urgently.

Bill stopped what he was doing and ran into the house trying not to appear agitated. "Okay, let's not say much until we find out what they want. I don't want to make that mistake again."

Two men rode up to the front of the house, dusty from a long ride. They got off their horses and brushed the dust off with their hats. Bill opened the door and walked out to greet them.

"Why, hello, strangers. What can I do for you?" he asked, trying to appear hospitable and desperate to conceal his apprehension.

"We have been riding for a good while. We'd like to water our horses, if you'd be so kind as to accommodate two weary travelers," said the first man.

"Sure, you can take the horses out back," said Bill.

"Thank you kindly, sir," replied the second man. Bill looked at Rachel, who was standing in the door.

"All right, when they come back let's find out what they want and get them on their way," she said. "We can't have them hanging around too long when we got those others coming in soon."

Rachel turned to Bill for direction, and he responded, "Maybe they just want some information or directions," he said hopefully.

"Let's hope so," Rachel responded. "We got to get them away from here."

The two men stomped their feet on the porch, getting the dust off their boots before walking into the house. The stomping echoed down to the cellar, which woke the reluctant travelers from their rest.

"Quiet, I think someone is coming into the house," Jerome whispered as the three sat up.

"Come on in, how 'bout a cup of coffee?" Bill said as he met the two strange men at the door.

"After a long ride, coffee sounds good," one of the men said.

"By the way, my name is Bill, and this is my wife, Rachel." Bill hadn't forgotten to be hospitable and thought that familiarity might help ease the anxiety that was coursing through him.

"Good day," Rachel said with a smile, trying not to look nervous.

"Nice to make your acquaintance, ma'am," said the first man, tipping his cap in Rachel's direction. "I'm Billy, and this is Matt."

"We got something in common," Bill said with a little chuckle, trying to ease his nervousness.

They all sat down at the wooden table, and Rachel started the stove and put the pot of coffee on, busying herself with her womanly duties. It eased her anxiety to be able to move around and fuss with coffee.

"So, what brings you all out this way? We don't get much company," Bill said, hoping to hear that they were just passing through.

"Looking for some runaways, and when we catch them, there will be hell to pay," Billy said as he hit the table with his fist, startling Rachel, who nearly dropped the cup she was holding.

"Calm down," Matt said as he gave Billy a pat on the back.

"Ain't no niggers gon' be getting away with what they done did to me," said Billy, a determined look in his eye. His rage was palpable.

Bill looked over at Rachel, and at that moment they both knew that the three runaways in the cellar were the ones the two men were looking for.

"What they look like?" Bill asked, trying to keep them talking.

"Two nigger boys and a nigger gal. Them nigger boys look real different; ain't never seen no nigger look like them two," said Billy.

"Looks like they may have headed this way," added Matt.

"Seen any niggers like that around here today?" Billy asked.

"No, haven't seen anyone like that," Bill said, acting like he was really thinking.

"How 'bout you, ma'am?" Billy asked, looking over at Rachel.

She turned from where she was tending to the heating kettle. "No, can't say that I have," she said nonchalantly, channeling the carefree wife she hoped to portray. "Wait a minute," she said, looking up after a long pause.

Billy stood up, clearly excited by this potential revelation. "Do you remember something?" he asked.

"I do recall hearing some noise out back early this morning. The chickens were frightened by something, but when I went out there, I did not see anything," she said.

"That could have been them. We got to go," Billy said, looking over at Matt. They thanked Bill and Rachel for their hospitality and headed for the door.

"Come on, Matt, that had to be them; we may be getting close," Billy exclaimed excitedly, nearly running toward his horse.

The two got on their horses and rode off. Rachel busied herself with the dishes as Bill peered out the window. It wasn't until they were out of sight that Bill and Rachel breathed a sigh of relief.

He looked over at Rachel, relieved but now determined. "We've got to get them out of here and send them on their way before the others come," he said. "Sending them with the others is only going to complicate things."

Bill headed to the cellar door, pushed back the chair and the rug, then opened it up and hollered down at the travelers.

"Y'all up?" There was an urgency in his voice.

"Yeah," Jerome said. "Sounds like you had some unwelcome company."

"Yes, we did, two mean, unhappy fellows, and they are looking for you three," Bill said. "We got to get you out of here. I think it's best that you head out on your own. Rachel is putting together some food and water for you to take with you."

It was clear to the three that they were no longer welcome here, but despite the brevity of their rest, they felt refreshed, but now newly aware of the dangers that lay ahead. They hurried up from their hiding place in the cellar and stood nervously in the main room.

Rachel handed them the bag of food that she had prepared, as well as a large canteen of water. "You will need to make this food and water last until you can come across some more," she warned. "Good luck and God bless," she said as they headed out the door.

Bill pointed them in the direction they should go. They thanked them for everything, and reluctantly, the three ran off. They knew Billy was furious and determined to do whatever it might take to find them and get the justice he felt he deserved. They knew they had to outsmart him and move faster to evade his rage.

CHAPTER 8

The hot sun showed no mercy, draining their energy with every step they took. Trudging through the unfamiliar landscape had proven difficult and slow-going.

"Let's take a break." Richard stopped and propped his worn body against a tree, which cast a bit of shade that was well appreciated. The three travelers sat down under the tree. They all took sips of water and ate something, being careful not to eat or drink too much, since they did not know when they would come across any more food or water. They knew Billy would not stop at anything to find them, so they could not rest for long.

June asked Jerome and Richard, "You think Massa Billy gon' catch us?"

Richard looked up from where he was leaning under the tree. "After what we did to him, I don't see him giving up any time soon."

"That's for sure," Jerome said. "So we have to make sure we stay one step ahead of him. There is no telling what he's going to do if he catches us."

"He gon' kill us as sure as we sittin' here," June said with a worried look on her face.

"We just have to come up with a plan," Jerome said as he sat there tapping his finger on his knee.

"What you got?" Richard asked.

"Well, when they find out we didn't go in the same direction they went, I have a feeling they will be coming back this way looking for us. Since they are on horses and we are on foot, it won't be long before they catch up with us, so we have to outsmart their country butts."

Richard listened to Jerome and shook his head. "After seeing that dude get beat and run down by those dogs, there is no way we can let those guys catch us."

The three sat there for several minutes before Jerome exclaimed, "I think I got it!"

"What is it?" Richard asked as he and June turned their attention to him.

"They most likely will be heading this way, so if we cross over and head back in the direction they went, we should miss them."

"I see," Richard said, considering Jerome's proposal. "Since they already went that way, they most likely would go in a different direction looking for us, not thinking that we'd double back."

"That's what I'm talking about!" Jerome held his hand out for Richard to slap it. June was puzzled, not understanding what they were doing. She figured that gesture was just one more thing about the two that was strange to her.

They stood up and gathered their things, energized by the hope of escaping from the chase. Richard looked around. "Now what? We don't have a clue how far this town is. We don't even know the name of the town where we're headed, so it's not like we can ask for directions."

"There can't be many towns around here, and besides, it doesn't matter," Jerome said. "As long as we head in a different direction from where we think they will be heading, or they think we'll be heading, we should be able to put space between us. Maybe enough space that they'll give up."

"We have to think like they think. We can't just go running thinking they won't catch us, because if we do, you know they will." Richard was cautious, trying to remember that word that they'd learned in school that meant too much confidence. He couldn't put his finger on it.

After several hours of heading in a direction they believed would be safe, they came across an old, abandoned house. "This looks like a good place to rest," Jerome said.

"It does? It could have fooled me," Richard said with a displeased look on his face. The house was in clear disrepair, an old clapboard house with weathered wood around the outside and a dilapidated brick chimney stretching up into the sky.

They walked to the front of the house after they'd spent a while sitting in the trees that surrounded it, to make sure no one was home, and then went inside.

June looked around. "With a little cleaning, this would be a right nice place!" She seemed pleased with the small house.

Jerome and Richard exchanged a glance, both thinking she must be crazy.

"You got to be kidding me," Richard said as he wiped his finger across the wooden table and looked at the buildup of dust now collected on it. "This place is a total dump."

"I wouldn't want my worst enemy to live here," Jerome jumped in.

"If it was cleaned up, it would be better than where me and my mom stay," June replied, her lower lip quivering as she shuddered at the obvious judgement she felt coming from them. Just then June realized that she might never see her mother again. She lowered her head as tears filled her eyes and started running down her cheeks.

"What's wrong?" Jerome put his arm around her shoulders. "Everything will be all right, and we're going to do everything we can to get you to a safe place." He had no idea what he'd said to upset her, but it was beyond clear that they'd said something to hurt her feelings, which was the last thing they wanted to do.

"I is sad cause I ain't never gon' see my mom again," June sniffled.

"Hey, hey, there now," Jerome said, trying to comfort her. "Never say never; you'll see her again."

"Once you get to a safe place and get established, you can work on getting your mother to you," said Richard gently.

At their comforting words, June looked up with a little smile and wiped the tears away. The promise of reuniting with her mother and starting a new life warmed her heart.

Jerome picked up a chair and dusted it off with his hand. "I think we should stay here until it gets dark before moving on," he suggested.

"You won't get any complaints out of me," Richard said as he grabbed another chair, also dusted it off, and sat down. June found a rag and dusted off the table, pushed a chair over, and dusted it off as well. The three sat down and ate the last of their food, feeling at ease despite their surroundings.

Richard wiped his mouth with his sleeve after he swallowed his last bite. "Well, that's it, no more food, water almost gone, and here we sit in this dusty shack. It can't get any worse than this."

June looked up. "I like this house. This would be right nice place for me and my mom."

"Are you kidding me?" Richard asked, looking at her like she had lost her mind. "There is no running water, no electricity, no bathroom, and no central heat or air-conditioning. This place ain't fit for man or beast!"

June was very confused. "What you mean running water and what is electricity? What is a bathroom? Is that a special room for taking a bath, because that sounds wonderful."

Jerome and Richard were just as bemused as she was. She continued. "What is central heat? What is air-conditioning?"

Jerome leaned back in his chair, looked over at Richard, and started laughing, realizing how different their lives were, and how much modern comforts had changed people's expectations.

"Let me see how you explain all that," he said, putting his hand under his chin thoughtfully.

"I got this, I got this," Richard said, rubbing his hands together.

June, with her unending thirst for knowledge, sat on the edge of her seat with her eyes focused on Richard, excited about what she was about to hear. Richard paused for a moment to gather his thoughts on how he was going to explain something that what appeared to be the smartest person of this time would not understand. He could see the excitement on June's face.

"Let's start with electricity. Electricity is something you use to create light and heat for the house, except you don't need a fire to do it."

"Is it like candles and wood?" June asked. Jerome dropped his head and started snickering.

"You ain't no help," Richard said, looking over at Jerome. "Let me put it this way…it is a power that creates light, heat, cold, and does a lot more to make life easy. In the summer, it will help make your house cool, and in the winter, it will make your house warm, and at night, it will give you light."

June had a concerned look on her face. "That power sounds like witchcraft. If there is a power that can make light and heat without candles or wood, it ain't no good for you. Mama says you is got to be careful because there is evil out there that can take over your spirit and control you."

"Just because we don't understand something don't make it evil," Richard said as he stood up. "Most people don't understand electricity, but we do know without it we wouldn't have a lot of things we enjoy."

June kept her eyes on Richard. She did not understand what he was talking about, but it did fascinate her. "I don't expect you to understand all of this, no one around here can," Richard said. "There are things Jerome and I know that people could not imagine in their wildest dreams."

"Like what?" June asked with a look of anticipation.

"Let me see." Richard paused for a moment. "Would you believe that Black folks and White folks can marry each other where we come from?"

June's mouth dropped wide open. She looked over at Jerome.

"It's true," Jerome confirmed as he sat there, enjoying watching the excitement come over her.

"Tell me more," June asked as she rested her chin in the palm of her hands with her elbows on the table. She was enthralled, witchcraft or not.

"There is so much I don't even know where to start," said Richard.

"It don't matter, I just wants to hear," she said with a big smile.

Jerome could not believe how someone could be so excited about learning, something he just took for granted. He was starting to understand why Mrs. Wilkins loved teaching and how disappointed she was when no one cared. As he looked at June, perched on the edge of her seat with anticipation, sadness came over him, knowing that she would not have the opportunity to see and do all the things that he had taken for granted.

"Hurry, hurry!" June said as she bounced up and down in her chair.

"Okay, okay," Richard said with a smile as he got caught up in the moment of her excitement. "Where we come from, there is no slavery. Black folks can own land, businesses, and do all the things White folks can. Blacks and Whites go to school together and Blacks have the same opportunities that Whites have."

Richard paused for a moment as he thought of how Mrs. Wilkins would talk to him over and over about the importance of learning. Richard shook his head. "A lot of young Blacks don't even care about learning. They go to school, wasting their time, their teacher's time, and sometimes they make it hard for the students who are there to learn." As he was talking, regret crept into his voice.

June sat straight up in her chair, not believing what she heard. "You say they can learn and they don't want to?" she asked. "I do anything to learn…anything," she said, a hint of contempt creeping into her voice.

They had something that she wanted so badly and they took it for granted. They were starting to realize the weight of the responsibility they bore in their education. Richard looked over at Jerome. The two could sense the shame that each was feeling. They knew what she was saying could have been directed at them.

June's expression turned to sadness, knowing what she wanted seemed so out of reach. She was hungry for knowledge. She wanted to learn to read and write. She wanted the knowledge she saw in Jerome and Richard and the people she saw every day who came to the big house. Frustrated and sad, realizing how much she didn't and couldn't know, she laid her head on the table. "I is tired; I gon' get me some rest."

Silence fell over the small, shabby house. Jerome and Richard knew better than to speak up. They were feeling heavy feelings, and neither wanted to talk about it. They knew they'd taken so much for granted, they were desperately missing home, and they were both hurting for having upset June, whom they were growing to feel very protective over.

CHAPTER 9

Jerome woke up and for a moment he did not know where he was. After he gathered his composure, he tapped Richard on the shoulder.

"Wake up, man, we got to go," he whispered urgently.

Richard sat up, still groggy from sleep. "Boy, do I ache," he complained, stretching his arms and legs. "I don't feel this bad after a hard day of practice."

The commotion Jerome and Richard were making as they moaned and stretched woke June up.

"Is it time to go?" she asked, yawning and rubbing her eyes.

"Yeah, it is. We got to make a move," replied Jerome. Jerome then kicked Richard's chair to reinforce the urgency of his request.

"I'm up, I'm up," he replied as he sat up and leaned his head way back, rolling his stiff neck around in circles for a moment.

After a few minutes of grumbling and stretching, the three were ready to move on. Jerome grabbed the canteen with the little water they had left, and they headed for the front door. Outside, they could see that the sun had set below the horizon. There was a late evening breeze cooling things off.

"Well, I guess we better get a move on," Jerome said, looking around to survey the surroundings. He then took a deep breath and led the way. They started walking at a fast pace, rushing to get to the safety of the high brush.

After several hours of walking in the darkening light, they could see a small town in the near distance. The three paused, looking down at the town.

"Now what?" Richard asked, looking at Jerome and June. "We can't just go walking down there."

"I think this is the best time to walk down there," Jerome said. "It's still dark and by now, the streets should be empty."

"We got no papers; if we get caught with no papers, it won't be good." June looked down at their clothes, realizing that they would stick out if they were caught in the town and they wouldn't have a good explanation for why or how they had gotten there.

"It's just a chance we'll have to take," Jerome said as he started walking toward the town. Not having any other choice, Richard and June followed close behind.

When they entered the town, the streets were quiet and empty as the daylight slowly darkened into night. They stayed out of the open, walking close to the buildings or places where they could duck into and hide if needed.

As they progressed through the streets, Richard tapped Jerome on the shoulder, pointing toward a building. "Look, there is a stable up ahead. Maybe we can rest in there until we figure out our next move."

"That might not be such a bad idea," Jerome replied, evaluating their options. "Hopefully no one is in there, because we have got to get off these streets before someone sees us."

They reached the stable and looked around to make sure no one saw them as they went in. Jerome opened the door slowly and peeped in while June and Richard kept watch. He did not see anyone, which gave him great relief. They walked into the deserted stable, looking for a place they could hide just in case someone did come in and surprise them while they were there.

"Look up there," Richard said, pointing at the loft. "If we go up there, we would be out of sight if someone comes in."

Richard climbed up the ladder that led to the loft, followed by June first and then Jerome. The loft was full of old hay but not much else, and so the three found a spot and tried to make it as comfortable as possible.

Tired and hungry, they lay in the prickly hay, not saying a word, all lost in their own thoughts. Neither of them knew what their next move might be. The initial rush of this time period for Jerome and Richard and life outside of the plantation for June—had worn off, and now the exhaustion brought on by survival was setting in.

After a while, June sat up. "What we gon' do come daybreak? Folks gon' be around, so what we gon' do?" she said, worried that this could be the end of their journey. She'd never imagined that they'd make it this far, and now that they were here, the uncertainty of the situation was proving to be deeply unsettling.

"Not sure," Jerome said. "We got this far, something will come up. We just have to believe that." He knew that June was just as uncertain as he was, but he also wanted to reassure her, and perhaps reassure himself in the process.

"I don't know," Richard said, shaking his head. "June's right. Come day, when there are people around, I'm sure someone will be coming here, and then we're going to be trapped. Maybe we should just go around this town and keep moving," he suggested.

"Go where?" Jerome asked. "We don't know where we are or where we're going. We have no food and no water left. We won't last out there."

Silence fell between them. Jerome continued, "And if we did make it to the next town, then what? We'll be in the same situation. We might as well figure these things out now before moving on."

Jerome crawled over to the part of the wall where there was a hole, which gave him a view of the main street that headed into town. "Hey guys, looking through this hole you can see everything. Come morning we'll be able to see what's going on and what we'll have to deal with. We should just rest tonight and in the morning, we can check things out before we make any moves or decisions."

With no better options, they all agreed that would be the best plan. The three returned to their spots in the hayloft. Exhausted from the long day, they quickly fell asleep.

Morning came quickly, and the three were awakened by a commotion down in the street. Jerome, wide awake with the sounds, rushed over to the hole in the wall and looked out. He could see people gathered around what appeared to be a group of slaves with their hands bound.

Richard came over to assess the situation. "What do you see?"

"It looks like a slave sale is about to take place." Richard took a look through their viewing hole.

"Damn, that ain't even right," he said softly and then turned around and leaned his back against the wall.

"Now what we gon' do?" June asked in her quiet, panicked whisper, looking over at Jerome and Richard. Just then they heard a loud cry from the street.

"No, Massa, please don't take him away from me, please, Massa," they heard a woman cry.

Jerome looked out the hole and Richard peeped out a small crack that was next to it. Kneeling and pressed against the wall, they could see a pregnant Black woman on her knees in the street with her arms around the leg of a Black man.

"Please, Massa, please, Massa, don't take my husband, we gon' have a baby," she continued desperately. The man just stood there with his head down while a White man pulled the lady away from him. They put the man in the back of a wagon and rode away.

The White man held the pregnant lady as she screamed, "Leon, Leon, no, Leon!" over and over until the wagon could no longer be seen.

Jerome turned to Richard, disgusted. "How did Black people take this abuse day in and day out?" he asked. "I guess we don't know how lucky we have it."

"I'm glad you feel lucky," Richard said, "because I don't feel so lucky stuck in this loft."

"You know what I mean, man. In our time, we don't have these problems. This is straight messed up."

"All I know is that we are stuck in this stable with no food, no water, and no plan to get out." Frustrated, Richard then grabbed a handful of hay and threw it.

Just then the front door of the stable opened, and they all instinctively froze, trying not to make any sounds or movement. Jerome put his finger to his lips. He started moving closer to the edge of the loft to try to see who had come in. As he crawled trying to get closer to the edge, his hand landed on a loose board, which made a small squeak. He stopped moving, hoping the person who came in did not hear it.

"Who's up there?" came the sound of a deep voice from below. "I knows you is up there. Best come on down."

"Damn," Jerome said quietly under his breath. At that moment they looked at each other and they knew they had no choice but to come down from the loft.

The three climbed down slowly. Standing there waiting in the middle of the stable was a middle-aged Black man wearing an old shirt, pants, and a straw hat.

"What y'all doing up there? Is you on the run?" the man asked.

After leaning over and brushing his pants off, which gave him a small amount of time to think of something, Jerome looked up. "We are just passing through and needed a place to rest, so we stopped in here."

Richard said to the man. "We didn't mean any harm; we just wanted a place to rest before moving on."

June stood there looking at the ground, not saying anything.

"Ain't seen no coloreds that look like you two around here. Where is you from?" the man asked.

Jerome looked around and then walked closer to the man to whisper. "You can't let anyone know, but we're on a mission to get the girl to a safe place up north, and our organization can use your help."

"You must be the three they was looking fo' the other day." The man seemed surprised to see the three standing before him.

"Was it two White men?" Richard asked.

"Yeah and they were plenty mad," the man confirmed. "They say is I seen two strange nigger boys with a nigger gal and I say no suh. They say if'n I is lying, I would be in a heap of trouble because you is runaway slaves. Then Massa say if I see anyone, I better let him know."

"That's not true!" Jerome exclaimed. He pointed at Richard. "Have you ever seen slaves that look like us, dress like us, or talk like us?"

The man pushed his hat back on his head before responding. "You is right about that. I ain't never seen slaves that look like you two around these parts."

"What's your name?" Jerome asked the man standing before them.

"My name is Elijah." His master owned the stable and several other businesses in the town. Some of the slaves worked in the businesses, while the rest worked on the plantation, which lay just a short distance away. Elijah was good with horses and had been around them all his life, which was the main reason his master had purchased him.

"Look, Elijah, we have to get this girl to a safe place up north, and we could really use your help," Jerome said firmly.

"What can I do? I is a slave myself," Elijah responded.

"This is what you can do," Jerome suggested. "Don't tell anyone we are here. We need something to eat now and then we'll need some food and water to take with us. We also need you to find out what direction to go that would take us up north. Could you do that for us?"

Elijah took his hat off and started rubbing his head nervously. "I don't know," he said hesitantly. "If Massa fine out, it won't be good for me. Maybe y'all should leave now, and I won't say nothin."

"Now what we gon' do?" June asked as she started to cry. "They gon' fine us and kill us. That what they gon' do."

Richard walked over to Elijah, and asked him, "Did you see what went on out there in the street earlier?"

"I did, and it brings back bad memories of what was done to me," Elijah responded sadly, the hand holding his hat sinking down to his side.

"What happened?" Richard asked, not having to try to look concerned.

"My old Massa sold me away from my family 'bout ten or twelve year ago. Ain't seen my wife or younguns since," Elijah said, his eyes misting as he remembered his family.

"I know that must be tough," Richard said, holding his arm out to rest on the man's shoulder.

"Yeah, some days are worse than others. I have two girls; they be 'bout y'all age now. I don't think 'bout them much anymore—it hurts me too much," Elijah said, his voice breaking with emotion.

"That's even more reason why you should want to help us!" Jerome said. "Helping a girl to freedom should make you feel good, knowing that you have two girls and you would want someone to help them if they needed it."

Rubbing his chin, Elijah was clearly torn about what he should do. He knew that if he was caught helping them, he'd be in serious trouble, but he remembered the look on his wife's face when they'd been separated, and his heart ached.

The three travelers looked at him with anticipation, knowing he was their only hope to get out of this town as free folk. They knew if he turned them in, things would not end well for them. Elijah thought about how his master hadn't bought his family, and he resented him for that. In his own way, he felt that by helping them get away, he would be getting back at the people who had ruined his family.

A big grin came over Elijah's face. "I'll do it!" he said with eagerness. "I believe it will make me feel good if'n I help someone get to freedom."

The three exhaled, not realizing they'd been holding their breath. A look of hope spread across June's worried face.

"I'll works on getting what ya need," said Elijah. "Y'all best get back up in that loft so you is out of sight. Go on now."

They clambered back up in the loft, relieved, knowing they had someone willing to help them continue on their journey to freedom.

CHAPTER 10

ow that Elijah had made a commitment to help the three scared adolescents he'd discovered, he knew a mistake could cost them their lives and maybe cost him his. As he sat there contemplating whether he had made the right decision to help them, he wondered why they had picked the stable out of all the possible places to hide. He considered his previous dreams of being a free man, and found himself torn between their foolish unpreparedness and impressed with their courage.

After he thought about it for a while, he concluded that they were sent to him by some larger force so he could help them. Confident in his newfound purpose, he then started thinking about what he needed to do to get them safely on their way to freedom.

"Hey," Elijah called softly and tapped the ladder that went up to the loft to get their attention.

There was a slight rustling of hay from above. "Yeah?" Jerome asked, looking down.

"I is gon' get y'all somepin to eat. Stay out of sight, and if someone comes, don't make a sound," Elijah cautioned.

"Will do," Jerome said as he lay back down.

Elijah left the stable, mumbling, "I is got to get them on their way or I is gon' be in a heap of trouble." Elijah hadn't made it as far as he had without a good head on his shoulders. He'd learned early on to keep his head down, be agreeable, and stay out of the spotlight.

Elijah headed to the café in the square, which was owned by his master. This is where he would get his meals while he was working in the stable, and where he thought he might be able to acquire some rations for them. Emma, one of the slaves who worked in the kitchen, would meet him at the back door to give him his meals. They usually would chat for a few minutes before he headed back to the stable. Emma liked Elijah, and she knew that even after many years, he was still hurting from being separated from his family.

As Elijah approached the back of the café, he felt a nervous energy surging through him. He had always tried to toe the line and do what was expected of him. He had never wanted to cause any trouble, but now, he thought of his children and felt a slight inkling of hope somewhere inside of him.

"Hey Emma, I is needin' yo' help with something," he said quietly when she came through the back to greet him.

Emma was a sturdy woman whose cooking kept people coming back to the café regularly. "Sure, what is it?" she said with a smile.

"You can't let anyone know what I is 'bout to tell you," Elijah said nervously.

"I won't," Emma said with a concerned look on her smooth face.

"I have three runners in the stable and they is needin' my help."

"Is you crazy?" she exclaimed. "If someone find out you is helping runners, you is gon' be beat for sure or somethin' far worse." She'd seen a fair amount of runners in her time, and running wasn't something she ever wanted to do.

"Don't you think I knows this? But they needs my help and right now they needs some food. Will you help me?" The urgency in Elijah's voice surprised her.

Emma paused for a moment to calm down. She patted Elijah on

the shoulder, and replied, "Sure, I'll get them some food to eat."

Emma went back into the kitchen and quickly packed some food, then hurried to the back door before someone saw her. She knew there would be questions if someone saw her packing that much food for Elijah. She opened the door and glanced around to make sure no one was watching before handing him the food.

"Thanks, Emma. I really am grateful," he said with a smile.

She looked into his eyes, then put her hand on his cheek and in a low, soft voice said, "Be careful, now, you hear."

"I will," he said and then turned around and quickly headed back to the stable carrying the food she'd packed.

Elijah opened the stable door carefully and hurried in with the food tucked under his arm. Jerome, Richard, and June, not sure if it was Elijah, did not move or make a sound. The three lay still, tense, waiting to see if he had returned.

"Is y'all up there? I is got some food for you," rang a voice.

When they heard Elijah's voice, there was a small but still audible sigh of relief from all three. "Yeah, we're up here," Jerome said as he leaned over the edge of the loft. Elijah handed him the food and Jerome thanked him profusely. Elijah could see the appreciation on his face, which made him feel good.

As the three sat up in the loft and ate the food that Emma had packed, Elijah sat below, also eating and thinking about what his next move would be in order to get them on their way out of town without being seen. He knew he had to come up with something and quick because the longer they stayed around, the greater their chances of getting caught, which would not be good for any of them.

Elijah finished eating and was ready to start his day in the way he did every day, but he knew that this day would be different. He looked up at the loft, calling, "Is y'all okay up there?"

"We're fine," Jerome said. "Happy and stuffed. Thanks for the food, man."

"I got some things to do, so y'all just stay up there, and if someone comes in don't make a sound."

After they had eaten and Elijah had worked for a while, the stable door opened. Jerome, Richard, and June could hear the squeaky hinges, and they could see the light from the sun that filtered through the opening. They stayed quiet and out of sight, trying to make out what was being said.

A loud and deep voice resonated throughout the stable. "Elijah!"

"Yes, Massa?" Elijah said as he rose from his work and hurried over to the man who had come through the stable door.

"I got some gentleman coming in with a couple of horses to sell, and I want you to look them over real good, you hear?"

"Yassuh, I'll look them over real good. Where is they coming from?"

"Never you mind that, boy; you just look them over real good and let me know if they are worth my investment. I don't want to be wasting my money on no-good horseflesh."

"Yassuh," responded Elijah obediently. The man then turned around and walked out quickly, slamming the door behind him.

"Who the hell was that?" Richard asked, leaning over the edge of the loft.

"That my massa, Massa Edward Hall. He gets high strung sometimes, like a horse that's been corralled too long," responded Elijah.

"I could not deal with that every day," Richard said, shaking his head.

"Well, I ain't got no choice. He my Massa," said Elijah.

"Have you come up with any plans to get us on our way?" Jerome wasn't trying to rush the kind man, but he also wasn't planning on sticking around the barn any longer than he had to.

"Don't know yet," Elijah said, pushing his hat to the back of his head, "but I plan to have somethin' before dark. The way I figure, you'll be on your way by nightfall."

"Good, because I don't know how much longer I can sit up here,"

Jerome said and then he flopped back onto the hay. He was bored and nervous, but his boredom was currently winning the battle against caution.

"How's the girl? I ain't heard much from her," Elijah asked.

Richard looked back to where June was asleep on the hay. Her breathing was slow and even, and he realized he hadn't seen her so restful since they'd met. "She's laying down resting, probably the best rest she has had in a long while," he responded.

"That's good. She gon' need the rest. You should get some rest too because you gon' have a hard way to go once you leave here," Elijah suggested.

"Yeah, I guess I'd better," Richard said before crawling back to his spot to lie down.

Time went on, seemingly not moving at all, as Jerome and Richard lay down, both lost in their own thoughts. June had stayed asleep and Elijah continued his work when suddenly the stable door opened.

Jerome reached over and put his hand on June's mouth, just in case she was startled by the sudden influx of sound and light and made a noise that would draw any attention from below. June woke up, eyes wide, and Jerome put his finger to his mouth indicating not to make a sound. He then pointed down to let her know that there was someone in the stable. When June understood what was going on, he took his hand away from her mouth.

"Bring them in," Edward Hall said to the men leading the horses who were coming in behind him. "Elijah!" he called, blinking in the change of the light from bright daylight to the dimness of the barn.

"Yassuh!"

"I want you to take real good care of these horses. The gentlemen and I are going to lunch to talk business." Edward's voice was commanding.

"Yassuh, I is gonna take real good care of them, Massa," replied Elijah.

Edward Hall leaned over to Elijah and whispered so that the men couldn't hear. "I want you to look the horses over from top to bottom, you hear?"

"Yassuh, I is gon' look them over real good, suh."

Edward Hall walked back over to the men, patting them on the back as he passed, heading toward the door. "All right, gentlemen, let's go eat and talk business." The three walked out of the stable and headed down to his café.

Elijah took the horses and put them in the stable boxes and started looking them over. They were large and strong, snorting and whinnying softly as Elijah led them into their pens.

"Oh, these look like real nice animals," Elijah said to himself as he patted one of the horses. Jerome came down the ladder and walked over to where Elijah was looking over the horses.

"Nice horses, I guess," Jerome said, with a puzzled look, knowing he didn't know the first thing about horses.

"What is you doing down here?" Elijah exclaimed. "If someone comes in and sees you, it won't be good for either one of us."

"I know, I know," Jerome said. "Those two are asleep and I just had to get up and stretch. Being cooped up there is driving me crazy." Jerome had always been a restless child. One of the reasons he'd taken so well to basketball was that the activity gave him the opportunity to run off his excess energy. Despite being terrified, confused, and more surprised about his surroundings than he'd ever been in his life, he found that his restless energy was starting to get the better of him.

"If someone comes, I will make sure they don't see me," he assured Elijah. Jerome then put his hands on his waist and bent backward, then side to side. "Now, that feels good," he said, glad to be able to move freely again.

Elijah looked at the other horse. "Yeah, sir, these are some mighty fine animals. Massa gon' be real pleased with them," he pronounced proudly.

"How come you know so much about horses?" Jerome was in awe. He'd never been around horses, and was surprised by how large and strong they seemed.

"Oh, I been around them all my life. My massa before Massa Hall raised them, and ever since I was a little boy, I have loved being around them," Elijah said. There was a gleam of appreciation in his eyes. He clearly respected and maybe even loved the horses he cared for.

"When I was a little boy, I dreamed of owning my own ranch, like the one I was raised on. Raising and training my own horses was my dream. One day me and Jim—that was Massa's son, 'bout the same age as I is—we was out watching the trainers train the horses and I told Jim, 'When I grow up, I gon' own my own ranch.' He started laughing and said, 'You silly nigger, slaves can't own no ranch.' He then hollered to the trainers, 'This nigger said he gon' own his own ranch when he growed up,' and they all started laughing. I said, 'I is. You wait and see.' Then I ran off and all I could hear was them laughing." Elijah paused, the light in his eyes now gone. He looked sadly at the horse, patting it softly.

"I ran to my dad, who was working in the stables. I was crying. 'What's wrong?' he said. I told him what Jim said, and I could see his face change from concern to sadness. He took me and put me on his lap, and what he said next changed my life completely. He told me we is slaves and we can't own anything, that massa owns us and it's time I understand that. I was 'bout eight or nine, and my life was never the same after that." Elijah's hand, which had been patting the horse, stopped, and Jerome noticed that it was shaking slightly.

"It must be tough, knowing the thing you want most in this world you will never have the opportunity to get," replied Jerome quietly. He felt a heavy weight in his stomach, thinking of a younger Elijah, gleaming with childhood enthusiasm. Then he said determinedly, "I have got to get back home. I cannot live in a place where people control your every move."

"You mean where you is from ain't got no slaves?" Elijah inquired. He'd realized that these children seemed foreign, but he hadn't realized that they didn't live with the concept of slavery.

"That's right," said Jerome. "Ain't no slaves and if a Black man wants to own a ranch, he can. Hell, if a Black woman wants to own a ranch, she can."

"You mean Black women folk can own a ranch? Not even White women folk around here can own a ranch." Elijah was stunned.

"Black women, White women, any woman can own anything a man can," said Jerome.

"It sounds like where you is from would be a right nice place to live and raise a family," said Elijah, surprised. "If I lived there, I'd for sure still be with my family." Elijah lowered his head and spent a moment thinking about his wife and children. Jerome's restlessness had been stilled by the weight of Elijah's revelations about his past. He respectfully stood in silence, waiting for Elijah to speak.

"Tell me some more good things about this place you is from?" Elijah asked softly. He was curious about the travelers but more curious about the place they'd come from, which seemed completely imaginary to him.

"Let me see." Jerome paused to think about it. "There are so many things we take for granted. I guess you just don't know how good things are until you are in a place where you don't have them. Black folks can go to school, own businesses, own homes, even eat in the same places that White folks eat and even be served by Whites," he said, thinking of the things he'd experienced since he'd found himself in this time and place.

"I don't believe that," Elijah said. It seemed impossible. "The day White folk serve Black folk around here, hell gon' freeze over." He laughed, thinking about being served lunch by his master.

"I bet you and yo' friend take advantage of all the good things you have like yo' learning. I wish I had some formal learning like reading and writing. But I guess being a slave I ain't got much need for that."

Jerome felt ashamed, knowing he was wasting and taking for granted his education. He thought of how he and Richard had laughed about their lessons and how he'd been eager for each school day to end.

Elijah and Jerome could hear loud talking and laughing headed their way. Elijah stood up straight and still, listening.

"That's sounds like Massa; you better get back in the loft before they get here," he urged.

Jerome quickly headed up the ladder to the loft. As he made his way up the ladder, the noise woke up Richard and June.

"Somebody coming, hold it down," Jerome said in a low voice as he gingerly picked his way back to his hiding place.

When the stable door opened, Jerome, Richard, and June kept quiet and still.

"Elijah!" rang the loud voice as the light poured into the stable, dust motes floating in the air.

"Yeah, Massa?"

"Did you take good care of the horses like I told you to?"

"Yassuh, and they are some mighty fine animals," Elijah said calmly, turning his attention back to the horse.

Edward Hall knew that Elijah was telling him that the horses would be a good purchase. He looked over at the two men and said, "Let's go and complete this sale. I know you want to catch the evening train."

"Yes, the South is fine, but I can't wait to get back up north," one of the men said.

"Elijah, I want you to take the wagon and go to the café and get two cases of my fine wine and take them to the train for these gentlemen. Emma will have them for you. Now, when you hear that whistle blow, you have fifteen minutes before the train leaves, so you make sure you get that wine on the train before it leaves, you hear?"

"Yassuh, I'll make sure I is there on time with the wine," responded Elijah.

"Thank you, sir, that's real nice of you," one of the men said.

"Don't want you to go back telling them northerners that we didn't treat you right down here." Edward Hall chuckled.

"We have been treated with the utmost respect since we have been here, and we are grateful for your hospitality."

"All right, gentlemen, now that that's settled, let's go and take care of this deal," Edward said.

After they left the stable, Elijah knocked on the ladder. "They is gone."

The three leaned over the edge of the loft.

"Good, I didn't think they would ever leave," Richard said.

"I is got a plan that is gon' get you on your way," Elijah said with a big smile, rubbing his hands together.

"Now we talking! What you got?" Richard asked.

"Well, Massa said to take the wagon over to the café to get the cases of wine and take them to the train. Now, what I is gon' do is have y'all covered up in the back of the wagon. When I take the wine to the train and unload it in the freight car, y'all can get in the freight car and hide. When the train leaves, you be headed north." Elijah was pleased with himself. He'd always considered himself a compliant man, and this act of insubordination was wild and wonderful all at the same time.

"Sounds simple enough. I hope it works that way," Richard said with uncertainty in his voice.

"It is that simple; I is gon' go to the café and get the wine and have Emma pack y'all some food, then come back here. When the train whistle blows, it gon' be leaving in 'bout fifteen minutes. We head to the train and when I load the wine in the freight car, y'all get in. Few minutes after that, the train be leaving with you on it." Elijah was pleased with himself for the plan and was optimistic about the opportunity.

"Well, let's pray that it works," Jerome said as he looked up and closed his eyes for a moment. This was a dangerous situation. This chance could be the best thing that had happened to them since they'd arrived here, but this could also lead to a terrible outcome.

As time went on, the three sat up in the loft, waiting impatiently while Elijah continued to work below.

"I is hoping we be leaving soon 'cause I don't think they is gon' stop looking fo' us," June said as she tapped her foot and bit at her nails nervously.

Jerome put his hand on her shoulder. "It's going to be all right. We're going to get on that train and be on our way headed north and everything is going to be okay."

Richard grabbed a handful of hay and threw it into the air, watching the pieces float back down. "I'll believe it when I see it," he said skeptically.

Elijah hollered up to let them know that he was going and to be ready when he got back. He hitched up the wagon and headed to the café. As he made his way to the café, he looked up. "Lord, please let this plan work and be with them as they head north."

Elijah pulled the wagon to the back of the café, got down from the perch, and knocked on the back door. Emma opened the door, smiling to see Elijah. "You is here to pick up the wine."

"Yes, I is," confirmed Elijah.

"Follow me," she said.

As she turned to walk, Elijah grabbed her by the hand. "I is got a plan for the runners, Emma. They is gon' be on that train when it leaves," he said, perhaps even happily.

Emma checked to make sure no one was around before she asked Elijah, "How is you gon' do that?"

"They is gon' be hiding in the wagon when I take the wine to the train. When I load the wine in the freight car, they is gon' hide in there," he said, his voice excited.

Emma was surprised. She'd never seen Elijah like this before, and she was enthused by the care he was showing for the strangers he'd told her about.

"They gon' need some food and water…can you get that for them?" he asked.

"I'll get it, but you better be real careful," she said.

"Don't worry, Emma, I is." He handed her the canteen for the water.

As Elijah was loading the wagon with the cases of wine, Emma quickly filled the canteen with water and grabbed some food for the runaways and put it into a sack for them to carry with them.

"Here, this is all I could get," she said when Elijah returned.

"Thanks." Elijah quickly took the sack and canteen and put it in the back of the wagon. "I thanks you fo' everything you did."

"You just be careful now," Emma replied.

Elijah smiled at her, then headed back to the stables. He pulled the wagon in front of the stables just as the whistle from the train sounded. Elijah ran into the stables, calling, "Come on, y'all, we is got to go. The train is gon' be leaving soon."

The three came down from the loft as Elijah grabbed a horse blanket to cover them up when they got into the wagon. Elijah looked out the door to see if anyone was around. "Come on, y'all!"

They got into the wagon, and Elijah covered them up, then got into the driver's seat and headed for the train.

Elijah pulled the wagon near the freight car. "Be quiet, here comes someone," he said under his breath without looking back.

"Hey, boy! What is you doing over here?" called a voice.

"I is got some freight that needs to go on the train for Massa Hall," replied Elijah, struggling to stay calm.

The man walked over to the wagon and looked it over. "What you got, boy?" he asked as he went to grab the blanket where they lay huddled together, barely breathing.

Elijah hopped out of the wagon before the man could remove the blanket.

"No suh, not that, it's the two crates in the back. Is you gon' help me haul them up?"

The man took his attention away from the blanket to respond

sharply to Elijah. "You is one dumb nigger if'n you think I is gon' help you. So you best get it loaded. We gon' be pulling out in a minute. Close that door when you finish loading, you hear?"

After issuing his directive, he turned around and walked away.

"Yassuh, I'll close it up real tight," Elijah assured him as he moved away from the wagon.

Elijah exhaled a sigh of relief and looked around to make sure no one was watching. He pulled the blanket back.

"Get up in there quickly; we ain't got much time," he said urgently.

They jumped out of the wagon and climbed into the car. Elijah loaded the wine crates and then handed them the canteen of water and sack of food.

"I is gon' have to close the door and it gon' be dark in there, but when the train gets out of town, you can open it to get some air and light," he said, smiling proudly.

"Thanks for everything you did for us," Jerome said.

"Yeah, thanks," Richard said sincerely.

June hugged him firmly around his neck and whispered in his ear, "Thanks fo' savin' our lives."

"God bless y'all," Elijah said and slowly closed the door. He got in the wagon and watched as the train slowly pulled away. He then lowered his head and whispered. "God be with them as they continue their journey. Keep them safe and show them mercy." His heart was full, and he thought of his wife and children as the train grew smaller in the distance.

CHAPTER 11

The train had been in motion for a while before Jerome felt it was safe to open the door to let some light and air in. When he opened the door, a welcome breeze came through.

June sat up as she felt the cool air rush through the train car. "Oh, that feels good," she said. The breeze seemed to embrace her body and filter through her hair. Jerome looked back at June sitting on the floor of the car, and for the first time he saw her in a different light. He suddenly felt an attraction toward her that he hadn't before. He knew he had to quickly dismiss that thought, because falling for her would only complicate things and take his focus away from what needed to be done. They needed to focus on finding freedom and making their way back home.

"Now, that feels good," Richard said as he, too, sat up. "I thought I was going to die up in here; this heat is hot as hell."

"That breeze do feel good," Jerome said, moving away from the door. "We have got to plan our next move. We've been lucky so far thanks to all the help we've gotten."

"Plan what?" Richard asked. "As long as this train gets us far away from those guys chasing us, I don't see any problem."

"Well, let me see," Jerome said, rubbing his chin in thought. "We are two Black guys that will stand out no matter where we go, helping a slave girl run away. We have no money, little food, and we are hiding on a train headed somewhere, but we don't know where, and when we get to this somewhere, we sure won't know anyone. Need I go on?"

"I guess if you put it that way, we do have a few details to work out," replied Richard, uncertain.

June looked up. "I just hope we gets far away so Billy don't find us. He plenty mad 'bout now."

"I know that's right," Richard said. "After that whipping we put on him, he can't be too happy. I know it is eating him up that he can't find us." He laughed.

"I can see him with his boys, sitting around the fire talking about we should have found those niggers by now. He is steaming every time he thinks about what we did to him." Richard started laughing and gave Jerome a high-five.

June, with a puzzled look, not understanding what they had just done, raised her eyebrow in their direction. "Y'all do some strange things where you is from," she commented.

"That's just one way we express ourselves where we come from," Jerome said.

"Yeah, it's called a high-five," Richard said.

"High-five? Why is it called that?"

"Well, let me explain it to you," said Richard. "See, you hold your open hand up high in the air and slap the other person's open hand high in the air, causing your five fingers to slap their five fingers, and that's why they call it high-five."

"It sho look silly to me," June said, smiling and shaking her head.

"All right, we need to get down to some serious business," Jerome said. "I believe that when the train gets near the next town, it will sound the whistle, letting people know that the train is coming. We should then get ready so when the train stops, we can jump off if no one is around."

Richard asked Jerome, "Why would we jump off this perfectly good train when the next stop is not where we want to be?"

"Because they might be loading or unloading freight from the car, and we don't want them to see us in here," Jerome said thoughtfully.

"When they finish, we can get back on," added June.

"I suppose that makes sense," Richard said. "But we better hope no one's around so we can get off without being seen."

"You're right, Rich, if we see there are people around and we can't get out, we'll have to hide in here and hope no one finds us," said Jerome.

"Well, I don't know about y'all, but I'm hungry. We can cross that bridge when we get there," Richard said as he grabbed the bag of food.

"How you know they gon' be a bridge to cross?" June asked.

"That's just an expression," Richard said. "It means I will worry about that when we get there."

"Why you don't just say that then?"

"Yeah, Rich," Jerome said, snickering as he grabbed the bag of food from Richard. June got up and crossed the car to sit down between the two.

"I be real confused if'n I had to go where you is from," she declared.

As they sat there and ate, they watched the panoramic view unroll in front of them as the train moved down the track. After they finished eating, they sat back and continued enjoying the view.

The motion of the train made June sleepy, and she yawned and leaned her head on Jerome's shoulder, and in a few moments she was fast asleep.

Richard looked over at her sleeping figure. "All right, JT, you better be careful. She might be falling for your big head."

"Nigga, please," Jerome said. Deep down he hoped it was true because he knew he was falling for her. He'd never met someone so curious and strong and found himself surprised by the attraction that he felt.

Richard said, "I think I'm going to do like June and get me some sleep." He then leaned against a crate and closed his eyes.

"I guess I could use a little nap myself," Jerome said as he crossed his arms and put his head down. Before long, all three were fast asleep.

After several hours, the train approached a small town. The whistle blew and the sharp sound woke them up.

"I think we've been asleep for a while; it's starting to get dark," Richard said as he got up and went over to look out the door.

"Do you see anything?" Jerome asked.

"Looks like a small town up ahead," Richard said.

"Well, let's get ready," Jerome said as he went over to the door to look for himself.

Not knowing what to expect, the three waited patiently as the train approached the station. Jerome slid the door mostly closed but kept it open just enough so that he could see out. They could hear a loud screech from the wheels as the train came to a jerking stop. Jerome kept a lookout to see if anyone was approaching.

"Do you see anyone?" Richard asked.

"Looks like some people are getting on the train, but no one is headed this way," Jerome responded. "I believe they are just picking up passengers at this stop."

"Maybe we should just stay in here," Richard suggested.

"Fine by me, I didn't really want to get out anyway," Jerome said.

The three stayed silent, huddled in the darkness of the train car. A few moments later, the whistle blew and the train started moving.

"Looks like this was just a passenger pickup stop," Jerome said, with a sigh of relief. The little town disappeared as the train moved forward down the track, and after a time, Jerome felt that it was safe to open the door of the car. "I think we are safe for now," he said as he moved away from the door and sat down.

"Where is we gon' be headed?" June asked, looking over at Jerome and Richard.

"Yeah, where are we going?" Richard asked.

"I think we should go to Illinois. You know that is a free state," suggested Jerome, racking his brain for any knowledge of American history that might help them in this moment.

"Looks like someone was paying attention in Mrs. Wilkins' class," Richard said with a smile.

"You mean there is no slaves in this Illinois?" June asked. "I be free and be able to do things like White folk," she said, cautiously, with a look of eagerness on her face.

"Well, I don't know about all that," Richard said slowly, shaking his head, "but at least no one will own you. You will have a lot more opportunities than you do as a slave."

"That's the truth," Jerome said. "You will have the opportunity to learn how to read and write, even get a job and earn some money. It won't be easy, but it'll be freedom."

"I ain't never had no money. I won't even know how to count it," June said fretfully. "Slaves ain't got no need for money." She dropped her head down.

Jerome put his finger under her chin, lifted her head up, and looked her straight in the eyes. "Now that you won't be a slave, you have to stop thinking like one." He then put his arm around her. "Don't worry, a smart girl like you will be reading, writing, and counting money in no time."

She gave him a big smile after those words of encouragement, and he felt a warmth spreading through his chest. It felt good to be able to reassure her.

The train continued moving down the tracks, and since there was nothing for them to do, June continue to pepper them with questions.

"How long do you think it gon' take us to get to this Illinois?" she asked.

"Don't really know," Jerome said. "We don't know how far this train is going or how long we will be able to stay on it." His optimism was tempered with an extreme amount of caution.

"When we get to this Illinois, where is we gon' stay, since we ain't got no money and we ain't gon' know nobody?" Now that they could breathe a bit, the future seemed full of unknowns to June, who hadn't really had time to think of any of this before.

"We'll just have to figure that out when we get there," Richard said.

June smiled and in a mimicking voice and gestures, trying to look and sound like Richard, she asked, "So, we gon' cross that bridge when we get there?"

All three looked at each other and started laughing, the moment of levity welcome.

"I think at the next stop, we need to get off and find out where we are and where this train is headed," Jerome suggested.

"So we're just going to get off this train and walk up to someone and start asking questions? Man, I don't think that's going to work." Richard stood up. "I can see it now; two strangely dressed Black guys with a slave girl, no papers, no money, in a slave state. How's that going to play, man? That's going to go over real well."

"Well, we're going to have to do something," Jerome responded. "We need to find out where we're going."

"I got it," Richard said. "We can have June go up to one of the passengers or even the conductor and find out where this train is going. She won't look as suspicious as we do."

June started shaking her head nervously. "I can't just walk up and talk to some strange White folk, no suh."

"You'll do fine," Jerome said. "We'll tell you everything you need to say."

"Yeah, don't worry," Richard said. "You'll know exactly what to say." He looked over at Jerome and in an unconvinced voice he asked, "Now, what's she gonna say?"

"Yeah, what is I gon' say?" June asked, nervous but also eager to be helpful.

"Don't know yet, but it will all be worked out before we get to the next stop," Jerome said with a look of certainty, but he could see that his response did not convince Richard or June.

A few moments passed, and suddenly, Jerome jumped up. "I know exactly what she can say!" Richard and June turned their attention to him as he paced back and forth in the train car. "June can go up to the conductor or the porter and say her master is inside and he wants to know where the next stop is and how long before the train gets there."

"I see," Richard said, moving his head up and down as he processed the suggestion. "That will let us know if we're going in the right direction."

"There you go," Jerome said. He held his hand up for Richard to give him a high-five. Jerome looked at June; he could see that she was not comfortable with this.

"Don't worry, June, you can do this," he said confidently.

She smiled but the smile could not hide the expression of worry that she displayed.

The train continued moving down the track, and they started to settle down for the night. At this time, things were peaceful and the only thing they could hear was the noise of the train wheels rolling down the track.

Since things were quiet and peaceful, June began to think about her mother and the only home she had ever known, which was the plantation she grew up on. She thought of the good times she had had with her mother, the times they would sit around at night, talking endlessly in the quiet, still night. She thought of the times her mother would be in the big house cooking and singing, especially during the holidays or when there was a party at the big house. She could see how her mother took pride in her work and how happy she was when she was cooking and working in the kitchen.

Everyone had always complimented her on her cooking, which gave her a sense of pride and usefulness. June remembered how she would sit at the table when she was a little girl and watch the joy her mother would express as she cooked and ran that kitchen. Those memories gave her mixed emotions of happiness and sadness, knowing she probably would never see her mother or experience those good times again. The feeling was bittersweet. She knew her life would be greatly different from this point on. She then turned her head away to hide the tears that came suddenly as she cried alone in silence.

CHAPTER 12

As the train approached the next stop, the sound of the whistle woke them, bringing a new set of challenges with its sharp blast.

"Oh, I feel like I've been laying on rocks all night," Richard groaned as he sat up. He started rubbing the back of his neck, trying to get feeling back into it.

Rubbing her eyes and yawning, June sat up. "Is we where I is free yet?" she asked, looking around hopefully.

"Not yet." Jerome stood up, stretching, trying to get full circulation in his body again after lying in the same position for so long. "I believe we still have a ways to go before we're in a free state," he said, struggling to remember the geography and history lessons he'd been taught in school.

Jerome went over to the door and looked out. The town they were approaching was much bigger than the one they had just left. He slid the door closed, allowing a small opening to see out and let some light in so he could continue to peer out. "Let's get ready," he said, looking back at Richard and June. "It's almost time to make our move."

It took a few moments for them to compose themselves, each of them filled with worry, fear, and a glimmer of hope at the possibility of freedom. They stood patiently as the train began to slow down, holding on to the sides of the train car. The train began to jerk and the sound of the train whistle screamed again while the train moved closer and closer to the station. Moments later, even though it seemed as though hours had passed, the train came to a stop.

Jerome opened the door and took a quick look to make sure no one was around or looking their way. "Let's go," he said. They then jumped out, making their move before anyone noticed them. They knew they only had one chance.

They ran between two buildings where they would not be noticed. Since it was early in the morning, there was no one around, which was a good thing.

"I don't think anyone saw us," Jerome said as he peeped around the corner of the building they were huddled against. They then moved behind some old boxes and crates that were on the side of the building to stay out of sight.

Jerome put his hand on June's shoulder and asked, "Are you ready?" She shook her head yes, followed immediately by a nervous look. "All right, tell me what you're going to say."

June paused for a moment, took a deep breath in, and then let it out slowly.

"Take your time," Jerome said, encouragingly.

June dropped her head and closed her eyes, pausing for another moment before looking up. "I is gon' tell him my massa is inside and he want to know where is the next stop and how long 'fore we get there." She exhaled.

"Perfect!" Jerome said. June smiled. Hearing that from Jerome gave her the confidence she felt she needed.

Jerome looked around the corner again and saw the conductor greeting people as they left the train. He turned back to June. "All right, June, it's time. The conductor is greeting people as they get off the train; head over there and say just what you said to me."

June started slowly walking toward the conductor, keeping her head down and whispering under her breath what she was going to say.

Richard looked over at Jerome. "Do you think she can do it?" he asked.

"Man, I certainly hope so," Jerome said as he bit his bottom lip.

June reached the conductor as he was greeting the last person to leave the train. She stood there with her head down, fumbling with her fingers.

"What you want, girl?" the conductor said in a harsh, cold tone.

June kept her head down and spoke quietly. "My massa is in there and he wants to know where is the next stop and how long 'fore you get there," she said in a soft, subservient tone.

"Your master sent you over here to talk to me?" he said with a surprised look.

"Yassuh," she said, looking down and making sure not to make eye contact.

"Well, girl, you tell him this train is leaving in about fifteen minutes and headed to Jonesboro, Illinois. We'll be arriving sometime late tomorrow morning. Now you get," he said as he pushed her away from him, causing her to fall to the ground. "You tell your master I said don't ever send a nigger gal to ask me any questions," he said, seeing her quickly trying to collect herself.

"Did you see him push her down?" Jerome started to move toward June, but Richard grabbed him by the arm, stopping his progress.

"What you gonna do, kick his butt?" he whispered sharply.

"That's messed up," Jerome said, snatching his arm away from Richard.

"The only thing you gon' do is get us lynched if you go out there," Richard warned.

June got up, while Jerome and Richard watched with concern. She smiled as she brushed the dirt off her clothes. With a puzzled look Richard turned to Jerome. "Why is she smiling? She was just knocked down."

"I don't have a clue," Jerome said, shaking his head, just as confused as Richard was.

June made it back to Jerome and Richard with a big smile. "I did it, I did it, just like you said I could!" Her joy showed.

"I knew you could do it." Jerome gave her a big hug.

"Why did he push you down?" Richard asked.

"He didn't like me talking to him," she replied, still proud of herself.

"That's so messed up; that's no reason to push you down," Jerome said.

"I had worse done to me by White folk," she responded. "They funny like that; I don't understand it."

"Well, what did he say?" Richard asked.

"He say the train gon' leave in fifteen minutes and it gon' to a place called Jonesboro, Illinois, and gon' get there late tomorrow morning. Is that where I gon' be free?"

"Illinois is a free state now; we just got to get there," Jerome said.

Richard peeped around the corner of the building at the train platform, then looked back at June and Jerome.

"We got to get back on that train, and we don't have much time," he said with urgency in his voice.

"I know," Jerome said. "But we need to find some water to take with us and food if we can. 'Til tomorrow is a long way to go without it."

"Yeah, you're right, we do," said Richard. "The problem is we left the canteen on the train, so we need to come up with something quick. The longer we wait, the tougher it's going to be to get back on that train without being seen." He was trying to remain calm, but a bit of panic was beginning to well up inside of him.

The three were hunkered down behind the boxes and crates, trying to figure out their next move, when they heard a wagon approaching. Making sure not to be seen, they watched the wagon slowly roll by. There was an old White man on the wagon with an old corn pipe in his mouth. He pulled the reins back, stopping the wagon in front of the building. From their position they could only see the back the wagon. The man got out of the wagon and walked into the building. They could hear the front door of the building open, then close.

"I think he went inside," Jerome said as he stood up. "I'm going to check this out." He walked over and looked carefully in the back of the wagon. "Hey, there's fruit and vegetables in here," he said in a low voice.

Jerome jumped in the back of the wagon and grabbed some apples and carrots and put them in a sack that he saw on the floor of the wagon. He quickly jumped out and went over to where Richard and June were waiting.

"I got some apples and carrots for us to eat!"

"We still need some water," Richard said.

"I know. Let's get back to the train, and we can figure out what to do there," Jerome said. Not having water wasn't ideal, but carrots and apples could tide them over if necessary, and getting on the train was more important.

They checked to make sure no one was around, and then they made a dash back to the train.

"I think we made it without being seen," Richard said, catching his breath after the sprint.

"Looks that way," Jerome said as he took another look to make sure.

Richard picked up the canteen and tossed it up and down in his hand as though it were a basketball. "What about the water?"

Jerome looked over at June. "It's going to be up to you to go back and get some water. There is probably a water pump somewhere around the building. Don't spend a lot of time looking for it; if you don't see it, get back here quick," he directed. June nodded her head yes.

Uneasy about going out there again, she took the canteen from Jerome.

"You'll be fine," Jerome said. "They've already seen you, and if someone asks what you're doing, tell them you're getting the water for your master."

He glanced out the door to see if it was clear. "Time to go; remember to make it quick." He helped her down from the car and closed the door behind her, leaving a small opening so he could see.

June went to the side of the train station, her body tingling with nervous energy. No one was around but an old Black man sitting in a wooden chair sleeping. Everyone was in the train station, either getting their tickets or waiting until it was time to get on the train.

"Excuse me, suh," June said to the old man.

He raised his head and slowly opened his eyes.

"What you doing wandering around here?" he asked in a scratchy, rough tone.

"I is looking for some water," she said timidly.

"Pump 'round back, but you best get it and git from 'round here. These White folk crazy," he warned her.

"Yassuh," she said, grateful to know where to go.

She went around to the back of the building and quickly filled the canteen with water, then headed back to the train. Walking at a fast pace, June continued looking back behind her, making sure no one was following her. When she made it back to the train, she started banging on the door, desperate to get back in, adrenaline coursing through her small body.

"I is back," she said. Jerome opened the door and quickly helped her in.

"Did you get the water?" Richard asked with concern.

"Yeah," she said with a big smile, raising the canteen up.

"Well, I guess we're set," Jerome said. "Now, once this train starts moving, I'll feel a whole lot better."

He then went over to the door and took another look. A few moments later he saw the conductor walking along the platform. "All aboard!" the conductor shouted.

Jerome could see the passengers coming out of the station and getting on the train. "I guess we're getting ready to leave," he said as he watched the last of the passengers climb on board.

Moments later the train started slowly moving, the whistle sounded, and the wheels began to turn, jerking them forward.

"We're on our way," Richard said as he settled in for the long, hard ride.

Jerome kept looking out of the cracked door until the station was out of sight. When the train was well into the open country, Jerome opened the door to let the breeze and light in. "I guess we can relax for a while." He went over and sat by Richard and June.

"I guess the next time we stop, I gon' be free," June said, with a small smile.

"We certainly hope so," Jerome said.

"When I is free, what y'all gon' do? Try and get home?" she asked, suddenly uncertain again as she thought about the future.

"That's right." Richard sat up from where he'd been leaning against the wall of the car. "We're going to get our butts back home. This place is wild."

The reality of being free in a strange place and not knowing anyone was starting to sink in for June. A wave of anxiety crashed through her.

"Where is I gon' stay? Who gon' be with me?" June asked with concern.

"We'll make sure you are taken care of before we move on," Jerome promised.

"If y'all can't get back home, then what you gon' do?" she asked, stating the question that neither one of them had wanted to say out loud, but had definitely both thought.

"Don't say that, please don't say that," Richard begged, shaking his head.

"You know, man, that is something we need to think about," Jerome said, finally acknowledging that possibility out loud. "We don't have a clue as to how we're going to get back; hell, we don't even know how we got here. The more I think about it, I believe the answer is back at that big tree where this nightmare began."

Richard looked at Jerome like he had lost his mind. "You can't be serious. There is no way in hell we can go back there," he said incredulously.

"At one time you thought it was a good idea."

"Yeah, I did, but June convinced us that it wasn't, and now I think we made the right decision. After what we did, if we got caught, they would string us up for sure. You do remember what happened to that man when he got caught?"

"I'm just saying the answers may be where we started," Jerome replied, but Richard cut him off before he could say another word.

"Well, you need to say something else, because I ain't hearing that," Richard said heatedly.

Jerome thought about it for a moment. "You're right, going back there would be crazy. I'm just reaching for anything right now, trying to make some sense out of this whole thing. I guess we should just concentrate on getting June to a safe place and then we can figure out what we need to do."

"Now I hear you," Richard said.

They both took a deep breath. They hadn't had a moment to breathe since they'd realized where and when they'd found themselves. Survival had become the only goal. How, where, and when had stopped mattering.

"If y'all can't get back, maybe y'all can stay and teach me reading and writing," June suggested. "Maybe you can open a school and help other Black folk learn reading and writing." She knew they had something that so many didn't have, and she yearned to be able to do that.

"I don't think so," Richard said. "We got to get home so we can continue with our lives. All our family and friends are there, and I'm sure they are worried about us." As he spoke, Richard saw the look on June's face turn from excitement to sadness. At that moment he knew that had been an insensitive thing to say, knowing she had left everyone she knew and loved behind for a chance at freedom. He knew it was something she would have to live with for the rest of her life.

"Damn," Richard said under his breath. "Hey, June, I'm sorry. I know it was not easy leaving your mother and friends, and I should be more sensitive to that."

Without saying a word, June dropped her head. Jerome put his hand under her chin and raised her head up. "Richard is right. We don't belong here, and we do need to get back to where we belong. I know you feel that you will be all alone, but we will make sure you're in good hands before we move on," he said.

"Before you know it, you'll be meeting new people, making new friends, and a number of opportunities will be available that you would not have had as a slave. With all the new things you'll be doing, you'll forget all about us," Jerome continued, encouragingly.

"I will never forget you and Richard and all that y'all is doing fo' me." She had tears in her eyes, but the idea of being free to make her own choices and live her own life brought a bright feeling into her chest that chased away the fear of the unknown and the sadness of the loss of her family.

"Okay then, give me a big smile," Jerome said. June smiled, but it was bittersweet, clearly the result of mixed emotions. Excited about her new life and all it would bring, but also sad knowing she may never see her mother and friends or Jerome and Richard again. It was a lot to feel all at once.

"All right, guys, enough of the gloom and doom," Richard said. "It's time for you to be excited, because by the time we get to the next stop, you'll be free. So, let's talk about what you want to do once you become a free person."

"Yeah, I is gon' be free," June said, smiling and slowly moving her head up and down. She stood up in the train car and started spinning around in circles and singing, "I is gon' be free, I is gon' be free." The joy was overtaking the fear and sadness, and the possibility of a new life suddenly felt more exciting than terrifying.

A few moments later, June was dizzy and breathing hard from all the spinning, so Jerome helped her sit down. "Now, don't kill yourself before you're free," Jerome said with a smile.

"That's right," Richard said. "Then we would have done all this for nothing!"

At that, the three looked at each other and started laughing.

Jerome and Richard could see a childlike enthusiasm in June. She was like a child on Christmas Eve who could hardly wait for Christmas day.

"Well, go ahead, tell us what you want to do once you're free," Richard suggested.

"Well, there is so many things I want to do, but school learning is the first thing," she said excitedly. "I want to learn reading the most. When I was in the big house cleaning, and Miss Ann was reading to the little kids, I would slow down cleaning so is I could listen. When Miss Ann was reading, it made you feel like you is there. When I learn reading, I gon' read everything I can so is I can feel like I is in different places and feel like I is seeing lots of things. And then I want to teach others school learning because I think it is the most important thing, and everybody should have school learning." Her eyes glistened with possibility.

"Man, this girl has a hunger for learning like you wouldn't believe," said Jerome.

Richard shook his head. "I guess when you can't have something, you want it that much more. Now, you look at us; we have all the opportunities and resources to learn anything we want, and we don't take it serious, but we should."

"Hey, Rich, did you ever think we would agree with the things that Mrs. Wilkins was saying?"

Richard shook his head in understanding. "Ain't that a trip?"

June put her hands up and shouted, "I can't wait to be free!"

Jerome told June, "Now you may be free, but White folks will still let you know that you are not equal to them. You will still be treated like a second-class person."

At that, June looked very puzzled. "What do you mean, second-class person? What that is?"

"That means you're not equal to White folks. There are still things you will not be able to do because you're Black," Jerome explained.

"Ain't that the truth," Richard agreed.

"Where you is from, you is free and equal. You said you can do everything White folk can do. If I is free, why can't I do everything White folk can do?" June genuinely didn't understand what they were saying.

Jerome looked at June. "There are things you need to know. You may be free, but there are laws that only allow you to do certain things. The laws are set up to keep you from being equal. But even if you're not equal now, with knowledge you have power, and with power you can influence change. Over time, the change in laws will bring you closer and closer to being equal."

"So, where you is from, you is equal but we is not?" she asked.

"That's true, the laws where we are from do say we are equal, but there are other ways they keep us from being equal, and in a lot of cases, we help keep ourselves from being equal."

"Why would you keep yourself from being equal? If I had a chance to be equal, I would do everything I could," she said, determinedly.

"Well, one way we help keep ourselves from being equal is by not getting a good education," Jerome said thoughtfully. "Remember, with knowledge comes power, and with power you can influence change. That is why you need to make sure you learn everything you can so you can have power."

"Listen to you," Richard said, with a surprised look on his face. "If I didn't know better, I'd swear I was listening to Mrs. Wilkins."

Jerome paused for a moment. "I guess this experience has helped me understand why Mrs. Wilkins tries so hard to make us understand the importance of education."

"You know what's funny, JT?" Richard asked.

"What's that? Because I haven't seen anything funny lately," Jerome responded. "Think about this. The teacher we dread seeing the most, and the one we think is out to get us, is the one who cares the most about us."

"Man, that's true, and if I ever get back, you'll see a change in me," Jerome said.

"What do you mean *if* you get back? Don't you mean *when* you get back?"

"You're right, I feel you. *When* we get back," Jerome said, holding his hand up for Richard to give him a high-five. "When I get back, I promise you will see a different JT."

CHAPTER 13

The train had been moving for several hours, and they had settled in for the long ride ahead. The day had slipped into late afternoon when Jerome sat up, looked in the bag, and grabbed an apple.

"Want one?" he asked, holding the bag up to June and Richard.

"Yeah," Richard said. "We have nothing else to do, might as well eat." Richard took an apple and passed the bag to June, who also took one.

"This time tomorrow, we should be off this train," Jerome said.

"No time too soon for me," Richard grumbled. "If I never see the inside of a freight train car again, it won't be too soon."

"What you mean, man? We niggas got our own private car, and you can't beat this," Jerome said, laughing as he put his hands behind his head and leaned back against the rough wall of the car.

"Nigga, please," Richard said, who didn't see any humor in Jerome's comment.

June, listening to their conversation, was confused at what she was hearing. "Why you got so mad when Billy and that man with the wagon called us niggers? We *is* niggers."

Jerome and Richard looked at each other, both baffled by her comment.

"Explain that," Jerome said, looking at Richard.

"What's with that question, June?" Richard asked.

"Well, you just called each other 'nigga,'" she said, mimicking Richard's tone, "but when Billy and the man in the wagon called us niggers, you got so mad. I don't understand, because we is niggers."

Richard paused for a moment to gather his thoughts. "Well, let me put it this way. First of all we ain't niggers. When White folks call us niggers, it is meant with the utmost disrespect, and we do get mad."

June looked at Richard, confused, then over at Jerome for clarification, hoping he could explain it to her so that it made sense. Jerome shrugged as if to say, "I can't explain it any better."

"If it's so bad, then why do you call each other nigger?" she asked.

Richard paused to think about how to respond. He knew the answer he gave would never justify using the word nigger. Deep down inside he knew Blacks shouldn't even be using that word, not after the significance it held when used as a weapon by Whites.

"Well, let me put it this way. Blacks can call Blacks nigger, but Whites can't call Blacks nigger. That's just the way it is where we're from."

"I is so confused by how you do things where you is from," she said. "You mean Blacks can call each other nigger, but get mad when White folks call Blacks nigger even though Blacks is niggers. That is so confusing. Why would you get mad at people for calling you what you is?"

Richard knew she did not know the history of the word as he knew it to be. Still, the words she said pierced right through him. *Why would you get mad at people for calling you what you is?* Those words were the dagger that cut through his closed mind and allowed him to see the word for what it really was: a hurtful racial slur to stigmatize Blacks to make them feel inferior to Whites. Richard was speechless at his realization. He looked over at Jerome, who could not say anything either, apparently lost in his own realization of the term. He knew when they used the word, it was not meant to be in a negative way.

He also learned from Mrs. Wilkins' class that the word had certain characteristics, which were all negative. Lazy, ignorant, dirty, and worthless were a few meanings of the word that was used to describe Blacks. He also knew that at times they portrayed themselves that way, such as doing dirty and stupid things and being lazy in the things that they needed to do, such as their education. By acting this way, it made them look worthless.

Jerome looked at June, moving his head up and down in a yes motion. "June, you have opened our eyes to so many things that we are doing wrong, and so many things that we just take for granted. The things you have made us aware of in this short period of time should change our attitude in the way we think and do things, and I thank you for that."

June smiled, uncertain as to what she had done, but grateful to have been of assistance. "I is not sure how I did that but you is welcome."

She made them feel ashamed for using the word. June had made them realize why they should not use that word, not even when they talked to each other. Not knowing that the word had such a long history of negativity behind it, she made them realize that no matter what the context of the usage, deep down the meaning of the word would never change. It would always be engraved with negativity. It also made them realize that they needed to change their behavior to ensure that they are not acting like the negative meaning of the word.

Jerome sat up. "Well, that was a deep conversation that makes you really think."

Richard said, "When you have a chance to see things from someone else's point of view, especially someone who has not been influenced by the environment we're from, it makes you see things much clearer."

Jerome looked Richard straight in the eye. "I see why Mrs. Wilkins gets so frustrated with you. She is trying to teach you, but your hard head just don't want to learn."

"Sad, sad," Jerome said, snickering under his breath.

"Nig— Oops." Richard caught himself before he completed the word. "Boy, please, you got to be kidding me. You're the one who does things to frustrate Mrs. Wilkins, and my dumb butt is always following behind you."

June said to Jerome, "Sounds like you make a good leader. You should make sure people is following you fo' the right reasons."

Jerome smiled. "Sounds like you would make a good teacher," he said.

"You really think so?" June asked, smiling back at Jerome.

Richard looked at Jerome, then at June. He could see that they were staring into each other's eyes.

"You two are full of crap," Richard said, shaking his head.

Jerome broke eye contact and looked over at Richard. "Don't hate because I'd make a good leader, and June would make a good teacher, and your dumb butt will only make a good follower," he said smugly.

"Hey, hey," Richard said, looking at the two of them. "Do you know how hard it is for someone with my leadership and teaching skills to sit back and let someone else lead and teach? But me being the unselfish person that I am, I do it to give other people the opportunity to get where I am."

The three started laughing.

Jerome rubbed his hands together. "Now that we're not so serious, let me tell you some other things we say."

June looked on, excited because she enjoyed hearing about the things where they were from. A lot of it did not make sense to her but she enjoyed hearing them talk about it anyway.

Jerome looked at June, anticipating her reaction to what he was about to say.

"When we see something that looks good, we say that's bad, and when we see something that looks bad, we say that's bad too."

Jerome and Richard waited for her reaction. June looked at Jerome, and her expression went from excitement to puzzled. She then looked at Richard. "Is that true or is he teasing me?"

Richard laughed. "It's true. What's good is bad and what's bad is bad."

"Oh, my Lord! Is you serious? I is never heard nothin' like that. Everybody knows bad is bad and good is good. How is somebody gon' know you think something is good when you say it's bad?"

"That's easy," Jerome said, laughing. "If I say something is bad and it's good, people will know that I think it's good, and if I say something is bad and it's bad, people will know I think it's bad." He stated it as though it were simple.

"I don't know," June said, shaking her head. "If something is good you should just say it's good. You sure do and say funny things where you is from."

Richard yawned and stretched. "You two can sit up and talk about what's good is bad or whatever. I'm going to lie my big head down and get me some sleep. Maybe when I wake up, this whole nightmare will be over. If not, maybe we can have dinner sent in since we have our own private car."

"I see you got jokes," Jerome said.

"Wake me up when dinner comes," Richard murmured. He then turned his head away from them and closed his eyes.

"Do you want to take a nap, June?" Jerome asked.

"No, I is wide awake. I want to hear more about where you is from," she said.

"There is so much I can tell you and most of it would be hard for you to believe," Jerome said.

"I want to hear it anyway," she said as she pulled on his arm like a little kid trying to get his attention. She was desperate to learn every-thing she could.

"Okay, okay," Jerome said, laughing at how eager she was. "I guess I'd better tell you before you snatch my arm off. Let me see," he said as he thought about where to start. "I would love for you to see and experience the things where we're from. I could take you downtown and show you the tall buildings, some fifty stories high, some even higher. We could go to the movies! You could even come and watch me and Richard play basketball and see how we school them fools out there."

June looked at Jerome. She could see how excited he was as he talked about everything that was familiar to him. What he was saying did not make much sense to her, but she enjoyed listening as she had done when Miss Ann would read to the children back on the plantation.

"I would love to see what you is talking about," said June. "What is a building with fifty stories? What is movies and you play basketball and school fools? They have schools for fools where you is from?"

Jerome started laughing. "I guess I need to explain the things I'm talking about. I have to remember that this is all foreign to you."

June sat patiently as Jerome tried to find the words to explain the things he had mentioned. "Well, let me start with the buildings with fifty stories. A story in a building is a floor, and each floor is a story."

He could see from the look on June's face that she did not understand. "I thought a story was what Miss Ann would read out of the book to the children."

"That's another use of the word story, but you can also use story to mean floor."

June had a look of confusion as if to say, "None of what you are saying makes any sense."

"I got it," Jerome said, snapping his fingers. "Didn't the big house where you worked with your mother have an upstairs?"

"Yes, I helped clean up there sometimes," she said.

"Okay, the buildings I'm talking about have fifty or more upstairs, all stacked on top of each other, so the building is really tall."

June was stunned; she could not believe what she was hearing. With her mouth wide open in surprise, she had a look of amazement. Jerome took his finger and put it under her chin, closing her mouth.

"How is you gon' walk up all them steps?" she asked. "I knows you get tired by the time you walk way up there."

"To tell you the truth, most people won't walk up that many stairs," he answered.

"Then how is they gon' get way up there?"

"Well, there is something called an elevator that you go in that has a button for each floor. Whatever floor you want to go to, you push that button and the elevator will take you to that floor, like a big lift."

"How does it do that?" June asked in disbelief.

"It uses a long cable that pulls the elevator up and down to the floors. I guess you would have to see it to really understand," Jerome said, realizing that so much of what was familiar to him was completely outside of the realm of anything she could comprehend.

"What about movies and basketball? Tell me about that," June directed enthusiastically.

"You know how you said Miss Ann would read stories to the children?" Jerome asked. "When she reads, you see the story in your mind. A movie is people acting out what you see in your mind. You see pictures of them acting on a big white screen. And basketball is a game we play. You run back and forth and try to get a ball into a hoop with a net hanging below it. When we win by scoring the most points, we say, 'We schooled you.'"

Jerome could see none of this made any sense to her by the look on her face.

"I don't understand, but it don't matter. Slaves ain't got no time fo' movies or playing games; we're too busy working. If we don't get our work done, we gets beat and that's our life. Sounds like where you is from is a nice place to be," she said.

Jerome sat in silence for a moment. He realized that no matter how bad his life had been, it could not compare to how bad life is for a slave. Realizing that if a people can endure the life of slavery, they could achieve anything, especially if there are opportunities available.

He began to understand the value of learning about the past that Mrs. Wilkins tried to instill in her class daily.

"You won't have to worry about that anymore," he said, attempting to soothe her. "When we get off this train, you will no longer be a slave. You will be able to enjoy some of the good things life has to offer."

"You think so?" June said, excited again by the prospect of new experiences outside of what she had known.

"Sure, no one will own you, and anything is better than that."

"I want to go to school and learn everything I can."

"Knowing you, I can see that happening," Jerome said, shaking his head with a slight grin.

As the train went around a tight curve, it caused Richard to roll over, waking him up.

"What's going on? What happened?" he asked groggily. After a few moments he realized where he was. "Ah man, I was having a good dream, and I woke up to this nightmare. I was dreaming I was home at the dinner table getting ready to eat some of Mom's good old spaghetti; then I woke up to this. You've got to be kidding me. I didn't even get to eat any spaghetti in the damn dream," he said, clearly frustrated.

Jerome reached in the bag and grabbed a carrot and tossed it to Richard. "Room service sent this up while you were asleep," he said.

"Real cute," Richard said, taking an aggressive bite of the carrot. Jerome and June looked at each other and started laughing. "I see you two got jokes," he said, then took another bite of the carrot.

"How long was I sleep?" Richard asked as he rubbed the back of his neck, trying to remove the stiffness that came from lying in an awkward position.

Jerome looked at June. "Would you say it's probably been about a couple of hours?"

"That's 'bout right," she said.

"I was asleep that long and I didn't even get to eat the spaghetti. That sucks," Richard said, clearly not satisfied with the carrot replacement.

Jerome licked his lips. "You need to stop talking about that spaghetti. You're starting to make me want some."

As time went on, the three sat up and talked about everything. June asked many questions, and they answered them as best as they could. They laughed and joked, which made the day go by much faster. As the evening settled in, they became quiet, each lost in their own thoughts. All they could hear was the sound of the train as it went down the tracks. The steady and continual sound of the train wheels rolling down the tracks relaxed them, and before long all three had fallen asleep.

CHAPTER 14

The train whistle sounded loudly, emitting one long whistle followed by two short ones, which woke them up. Jerome got up and went over to the door of the car and looked out.

"What do you see?" Richard asked, yawning as he stood up.

"Is I free?" June asked, excitement apparent in her voice.

Jerome looked back at them. "You can see that this is a much bigger town, and as far as I know, you are free, June."

"I is free," June said in a low, soft voice. "I sho wish my mama was here with me."

Richard put his hand on her shoulder, both looking out at the landscape surrounding the train. "You make her proud by doing something good with your life, and someday you will see her again."

She smiled, comforted by Richard's statement. "Yeah, someday I is gon' see her again."

"Let's get ready to get off this train," Jerome said as they approached the station.

"Not a moment too soon," said Richard, straightening his clothes.

"When we get off this train, where we gon' go? What we gon' do?" June asked in an uneasy voice.

"Not sure," Jerome said. "I guess we haven't thought that far ahead. I'm just surprised we got this far. Thank God for the help we got along the way."

"That's the truth," Richard said. "Let's hope it continues a while longer."

Jerome looked at the two, concern apparent on his face. He knew that they weren't in the clear yet. "You can bet there will be more crap for us to deal with when we get off this train," he said.

"It can't be any worse than what we already been through," Richard said, shaking his head.

As the train moved closer to the station, they waited patiently to get off after what had been a long and trying ride. Jerome opened the door wider, then looked over at Richard and June. "When the train stops, we need to get off quick and hopefully before anyone notices us, just like before."

The train slowly came to a complete stop, and the three jumped off. Jerome shut the door, and they quickly walked away from the train, not stopping to look back.

"It feels good to get off that train and on solid ground," Richard said as he took a deep breath of fresh air.

As they stood a short distance away from the train, not sure what to do or where to go, they noticed that there was a Black man nearby watching them. He was nicely dressed and well-groomed, making them aware of the fact that they were unwashed and rumpled from their journey.

He headed their way, and Richard looked at Jerome. "Here comes the welcome wagon."

June watched him come toward them. "Maybe he can help us," she said hopefully.

Jerome said, "Not everyone offering help has good intentions."

"What you mean?" she asked.

Jerome leaned over and whispered in her ear, "I'll explain it later."

The sharply dressed man came closer, and Jerome leaned over to Richard and whispered, "Oh, he is sharp and ready to prey on who he thinks are naive niggas from the South, but we ain't the ones."

"That's the truth," Richard said.

"Good day," the man said by way of greeting as he gave June a big smile.

"Hi," she said in a giggly voice. Jerome grabbed June by the hand and pulled her back and stepped up to the man.

"What's up?" Jerome said, nodding his head up, then looking him straight in his eyes. The man seemed confused by his question.

"What you want?" Richard asked. They were clearly protective of June, who had far less experience in the world than they did. They might not have come from this time, but they were aware of the predatory nature of those who would prey on the weak.

"I saw you all get off the train, and I don't think you were paying customers," said the man. "The law don't take kindly to people who cheat the railroad."

"So what are you, the railroad police?" Richard asked.

"No, no," the man said, with a slight smirk. "Don't get me wrong, I'm here to help you. I see runaway slaves come through here all the time, and when they get here, they're hungry and they don't know where to go."

"What makes you think we're runaway slaves and what makes you think we need your help?" Jerome asked.

"Now, you two don't look like slaves. As a matter of fact, I ain't never seen niggers that looks like you two, but I do know she is. I have seen enough slaves come up here to know one when I see one, and like I said, I'm here to help."

"I is hungry," June said, looking imploringly at Jerome and Richard.

"See now, the young lady is hungry. At least let me take you where you can get something to eat," suggested the man.

Jerome looked at Richard. They knew his intentions were not good, but they felt they had no choice at this time.

"All right, let's go," Jerome said reluctantly.

"By the way, my name is George Washington Talbert," said the man. Jerome and Richard were trying not to laugh. "Yeah, yeah, I know. My mom named me after the first president. When she was pregnant with me, she had a crazy vision that someday there will be a Black president. According to her vision, he's even going to be from this state. A nigger president from Illinois…ain't that the craziest thing you ever heard?" He laughed at the impossibility.

Jerome looked at George. "Never say never."

"You must be crazier than my mama if you believe these White folks gone let a nigger be president," replied the man. Jerome and Richard smiled.

George held his hand out to shake theirs. "What's your names?"

"They call me JT," Jerome said as he slapped his hand.

"They call me Rich, and this is June," Richard said as he slapped his hand. George looked down at his hand, confused at the hand slap.

"That's a high-five," June said with a smile.

The three of them followed George. June was fascinated by what she saw. There were Black people walking around and interacting with White people in a way she had never seen. To see Blacks and Whites talking and interacting that way was something she could have never imagined. The only interacting she had seen or experienced with Whites was in a subservient position.

"Well, here we are." George grabbed the reins of the horse that was hitched to the carriage. "Hop on in," he said, smacking the wooden bench of the carriage.

Jerome and June sat in the back of the carriage, and Richard sat up front with George. "Giddy up," George said as he snapped the reins. The wagon began moving away from the train station.

As they moved slowly down the main road, June was like a little child taking in everything see saw. She tapped Jerome on the shoulder. "I never believed I would see colored folks free like White folks."

Jerome looked around but did not say anything. June could tell his attention was somewhere else.

"Is you okay?" she asked.

"Yeah, just trying to figure out what his intentions are," he replied.

"What did you mean? Back there when you said everyone offering help intentions is not good."

"He's helping us because he wants something. I just don't know what," Jerome replied.

"Maybe he just wants to help us like the others did," she suggested.

"No, not this one. He's up to something, I know it. This hustler is trying to hustle us, but I have news for him. We ain't the ones."

"Hustler, what that is?"

"In his case he's trying to take advantage of someone because he thinks they don't know any better. If anyone asks you who we are, just tell them you don't know anything about us; we just showed up and helped you escape," he said, trying to formulate a plan.

"Okay," she said, confused and not understanding his reasoning.

They continued until they reached an area of the town where the Black people lived.

Richard looked back at Jerome, inclining his head toward the neighborhood. "Looks like we're in the hood."

June asked Jerome, "What's the hood?"

"It's the area of town where mostly poor people live, and in this case, it looks like poor Blacks."

"Hold up," George said as he pulled back on the reins, stopping the carriage in front of a big house. "Here we are."

June, with a surprised look, asked, "Is this your house? Black folks have big houses like this?"

"No, I just work here," said George.

"And what makes you think your boss is willing to help us?" Jerome asked.

"Because that's what she do," he replied.

"I bet she does," Jerome said under his breath.

They all got out of the carriage and walked up to the house. George opened the front door. "Come on in," he said, motioning through the door.

June looked all around the entrance, amazed at what she saw. The house décor of fine furniture was something she believed only White people could enjoy. There was the sound of a piano playing a soft melody. Black men and women sat around, leisurely enjoying each other's company. There was the same ambiance she saw in the big house on the plantation when there was a party. The difference was that on the plantation, only the White people were enjoying themselves and the Blacks were working.

George led them into the area where the piano was playing. There were others sitting around, talking and listening to the music. "Why don't you all have a seat in here and listen to Cole play the piano while I go and get the boss lady," he suggested.

Jerome nudged Richard. "Now I see what's going on. I can't believe it took me so long. In our time he would be the pimp that sits at the bus stop and waits for the naive runaway girl to get off. He knows she has nowhere to go, no money, and he promises to make all her dreams come true. He thinks June's that girl." Jerome was clearly upset about that, and was concerned about June's safety more than his own at that moment.

"Well, what about us?" Richard responded.

"I'm sure they will try and find a way to get us out of the picture," replied Jerome.

The three sat down, uneasy in the house despite the offer of comfort. They continued to wait. Jerome and Richard were talking while June listened to the music and watched the people. There was a lady sitting by herself who drew June's attention. She had never seen a Black woman as beautiful as her, and all she could do was stare at the woman. The lady smiled at June. Embarrassed, June quickly looked away and dropped her head.

Moments later, George and a woman walked over toward where

they were sitting, and the three of them stood up. June kept her head down, nervously fiddling with her fingers.

"Well, who do we have here?" the woman asked.

Taking the lead, Jerome responded first. "They call me JT."

"Just call me Rich," said Richard.

The lady looked at June, who didn't say anything and still had her head down. She put her hand under June's chin and raised her head up gently. "Well, who is this?"

"My name is June," said June meekly.

"You sure are a pretty little thing," said the woman kindly.

"I knows you is being nice by saying that, but I thanks you anyway," said June politely.

The woman stretched her arms out. "I know beauty; just look around. Beauty is my business, and if I say someone is pretty, you can bet I mean it."

That comment made June feel good. She raised her head and made eye contact with the other woman still sitting across the room from them. The lady smiled, and June smiled back.

"Well, everyone around here calls me Mama D, and I run this establishment." The woman smiled proudly as she gestured around the room.

"What kind of establishment is it that you run?" Jerome asked.

"I'm in the entertainment business, but enough talk for now. You all look like you could use something to eat," she said abruptly, avoiding any further questions about her business.

"Now you're talking," Richard said as he rubbed his hands together.

"Just go down the hall. The door on the left is the kitchen. Tell Ida Mama D said to fix you something to eat."

"Let's go," Richard said enthusiastically as he led the way.

After the three were in the kitchen, Mama D told George, "With some training, that girl will make a good addition, but the two guys look like nothing but trouble for us." Mama D paused for a moment, and then continued in a low voice. "There is something about them two that is different. They look different, dress different, and they even talk different. They're not from the South, that's for sure. If we can get her away from them, she will be no problem."

George shook his head. "That is easier said than done. I don't know what their connection is with her, but they are very protective of her."

"Since they are so protective of her, I will just have to find a way to get them on my side," she said thoughtfully.

"Good luck with that," George said.

"I didn't build this establishment without knowing how to persuade people to do what I want," she said, determination evident in her voice.

"If anyone can do it, you are the one," George said with a smile. He knew there was no changing her mind once it was made up. "So, what's our next move?"

"We'll let them finish eating, then we'll find out if they know anyone here. If not, and they probably don't, we'll let them know how tough it will be without knowing anyone and without any place to go. We'll get them depending on us and then we've got them." The plan was simple. It was exactly as Jerome had predicted, more than meets the eye and never something for nothing.

"I guess that's why you're the boss, because you have an answer for everything," said George. He clearly knew what it took to earn her approval and keep it.

"Like I said, I didn't build this establishment without knowing how to persuade people to do what I want."

Jerome, Richard and June sat at the kitchen table as Ida prepared something for them to eat. Ida looked over at the three, knowing that this was her chance to learn as much as she could about them. "Are you all new in town?"

Richard said, "Yes, and we are very hungry." Jerome would have laughed had the situation not been so perilous.

"So, where are you from?" she asked as she continued to prepare their food.

"We just got in from Louisiana and hungry we are."

Ida said with a smile, "I take it you are hungry."

"Whatever gave you that idea," Richard said with a slight chuckle that betrayed his annoyance with the line of questioning.

Ida placed the food on the table, and the three started eating like it had been a while since they had eaten a decent meal. Ida stood there and watched them for a moment. This scenario was something she had seen on many occasions. It would usually be just young girls, though. Seeing them bring in young males was something new to her.

"Did you come in on the train?" she asked, curious about this new development and wanting to know more.

"Yes, we did," Jerome said without looking up, as he continued eating.

"I bet George was waiting when you got off the train," said Ida.

Jerome stopped eating, sat back in his chair, and looked up at Ida. "Are you trying to tell us something?"

Ida glanced around the room, then leaned on the table over them. "You be real careful, now. Everything ain't what it seems around here," she said in a low voice.

Jerome sat there tapping his fingers on the table as Richard and June continued eating. A few moments later, he got up and walked over to Ida, who was cleaning dishes by the sink. "So, what kind of place is this?" he asked.

She nervously looked around. "I've said too much already. If they find out I've been talking to you about this place, it will be trouble for me."

"If there is something you think we should know, you need to tell us," Jerome said urgently.

"I don't want any trouble with Mama D. No good will come from messing with her," she said nervously.

"I know you're concerned or you would not have warned us to be careful, and I know I'm putting you in a tough spot, but if there is something you think we should know, please tell us. Me and Rich can handle ourselves, but June is real important to us, and we don't want anything to happen to her," Jerome implored.

She paused for a moment. "You have to promise me that no matter what, you will not let Mama D know you heard this from me," she said, looking around again.

"Anything you say will stay between us, I promise," Jerome said sincerely.

She walked over to the door and looked down the hall to see if anyone was headed their way; then she walked back over to Jerome.

"This place is nothing but a fancy whorehouse. They prey on young girls by telling them all the things they want to hear, making promises to them that they never intend on keeping. Before you know it, they are trapped in a lifestyle that they cannot get out of. Believe me, that's what they plan to do with her," she said, looking at June.

Jerome hit the countertop with the palm of his hand, and exclaimed, "That's what I thought!"

Richard looked up. "What's going on?"

"This place is just what I thought it was. Let's finish eating so we can get the hell out of here," said Jerome angrily.

Ida's eyes were full of worry. "Remember what you promised," she said.

"You don't have to worry, I'll keep my promise."

"When you leave, go and find the colored mission. Pastor Edward runs it and he will be able to help you," she offered.

"Where can I find this mission?"

"Ask any colored person; they will be able to direct you. Now go finish eating. I done told you too much already," she said, ending their conversation.

Jerome sat back down and continued eating as quickly as he could.

Richard wiped his mouth with the back of his hand, then asked Jerome, "Now what are we going to do?"

Jerome put the last strip of bacon in his mouth and while chewing it said to Richard, "We're getting the hell up out of here. Now."

June looked up. "We're leaving?"

"Yeah," Jerome said as he stood up and pushed his chair under the table.

"Where we gon' go?"

Jerome shrugged. "Don't know, but I don't think this is the place for us."

June looked around for a moment. "I think this is a right nice place."

"Not everything that glitters is gold," Jerome said.

"What that mean?" June asked.

"What that means is everything that looks good to you may not be good for you, so we're out of here," said Jerome. As they headed out of the kitchen, Ida wished them good luck and told them to be safe.

Mama D and George met them halfway down the hall. "Did you get enough to eat?" she asked.

Jerome, rubbing his hands together, replied, "Yeah, we did."

"So, Ida treated you right?"

"Yes, she did. Not much for talking, but she is a good cook," said Jerome.

Mama D's facial expression changed to a more serious one. "I pay her to cook and not run her mouth," she said sternly.

Jerome put his hand out to shake Mama D's hand. "On that note we'll be moving on, but we do thank you for everything."

Mama D's serious look changed to one of concern. "Where you going? Do you have a place to stay?"

"We haven't quite figured that out yet," Jerome said.

"You know, being in a strange town and not knowing anyone can be real tough, especially for a young girl," Mama D said.

"We'll be okay," Jerome said.

Mama D snapped her fingers. "I got it! The girl can stay here and when you two get things together, you can come get her," she said, attempting to project hospitality in her offer.

"I think that would be a good idea," George agreed, moving his head up and down.

"I think we will be moving on, but again, we thank you for everything," Jerome said as he gestured for Richard and June to come on.

"Now wait a minute," Mama D said. "It don't make any sense for a young girl to be wandering around in a strange town with no place to go." She grabbed June by the hand. "Would you like to stay here until they find a place for you?"

June looked around, uncertain and nervous. "It is a right nice place," she said.

"That settles it! She will stay here until you find a place," exclaimed Mama D victoriously.

Jerome grabbed June by the hand. "Like I said, we thank you for everything, but we must be going now," he said firmly. The three headed for the front door with Jerome pulling June by the hand as she looked back, reluctant to leave.

"They'll be back. It ain't easy out there; they will be back," Mama D muttered in a low, soft voice.

"I told you it wouldn't be easy to get her away from them. There is something different about them. Those ain't your average niggers," George said, with a slight grin to let Mama D know he was right.

"Who asked you for your opinion?" Mama D snapped as she turned around and walked away. "They will be back and when they do come back, I will make them beg me to let her stay, because nobody tells me no. Nobody."

CHAPTER 15

They started walking without any money or any idea where they
were going. They just hoped that the information they had received about the mission would be the answer they needed.

As they walked, Richard looked over at Jerome and June. "Our bel-
lies are full; we're walking in a strange town; we have no money; and we
don't know anyone. Now what?"

"We need to find that mission and we need to do it with the utmost urgency," Jerome said.

They continued walking until they saw an elderly Black woman
sitting on a front porch. "Good morning," Jerome said, waving in her
direction.

The woman put her hand above her eyes to block the glare from
the sun. "I'm blessed," she responded. "Don't look like you all from
round here."

Jerome walked closer to the porch. "No, ma'am, we just got in
from Louisiana and were looking for the colored mission."

The elderly woman got up from her chair and walked closer to
them. "You're on the wrong side of town. You need to keep heading
down this road a few miles, then turn left, and that will take you to
town. When you get there, ask any colored; they can give you directions to the mission. That's a good place. They help colored folk who

come into town with no place to go," she said helpfully. "There is one place on this side of town that claims to help girls who have nowhere to go. It's that whorehouse up the road run by some lady who calls herself Mama D. Mama D, that's a joke. That lady ain't no kind of mama to those girls. Instead of helping them, she just uses them as sex objects for men who come in there all hours of the day and night," she said, shaking her head. "You best keep her away from there," the old lady said with concern as she pointed at June.

Jerome looked at June in a way to let her know that's the reason they left. They thanked the woman for her help, then headed in the direction of town. "You all be safe, you hear!" she called after them. She then slowly headed back to the porch.

"That's why you didn't want to stay there," June said to Jerome.

"I told you not everything that glitters is gold."

"You think this mission gon' be a good place?" she asked.

"Hope so," replied Richard. "It better be, because as you can see, we don't have many options."

It was early afternoon by the time they made it to town. People were walking around, taking care of their daily business. As they went further into town, June noticed that the people were staring at them.

"Everyone is looking at us," she said. Jerome could see that it made her very uncomfortable.

"Don't worry," he said. "They probably looking at Richard and me because of how we're dressed."

"Check this out," Richard said, walking with a strut. "I know what it is. They have never seen such a good-looking brother with so much swagger like me in these parts," he said with confidence. June put her hand over her mouth and started giggling.

"You sho look funny walking like that; they gon' think you is possessed," she said, still giggling. Seeing how it didn't bother Richard made June feel a little less uncomfortable.

"There is a brother over there loading up that wagon. Let's holler at him," Jerome said, heading toward the man. He started walking at a rapid pace with Richard and June walking slowly behind.

As they were walking, June asked Richard, "Why he called him brother and why he gon' holler at him? He don't know that man, and if he holler at him, he might not want to help us."

"We call all Black people brothers and sisters, and hollering at someone just means you want to talk to them," he replied.

His answer confused June. "When you really gon' holler at someone, what you do?"

"Well, I guess you holler at them," Richard said thoughtfully.

June shook her head. "It sho is confusing how you talk."

"What's going on?" Jerome said to the man who was loading the wagon. The man looked up and paused for a moment, not knowing how to answer the question.

Jerome continued. "Look here, can you tell us where the colored mission is?"

Still startled by the sudden line of questioning by the three travelers, the man pointed down the road. "You go to the end of town, turn right, walk a little ways, and you can't miss it."

"Thanks," Jerome said. Richard held his hand out, and the man held his hand out, and Richard slapped it. The man looked down at his hand, confused by the gesture. June just walked by him and smiled.

As they walked to the other end of town, people continued staring and whispering to each other. June still felt uncomfortable. Richard continued strutting and waving at the people as though he was some kind of celebrity.

After a while, they could see a large building next to a small house and church. "That must be it!" Richard exclaimed.

"Well, let's go," Jerome said as he picked up the pace.

When they reached the mission, they could see that it, as well as the church and house, was not in the best condition. But it was a sight for sore eyes, as they knew they did not want to be on the street come nightfall.

There was a woman watering flowers on the front porch of the building. "May I help you?" she asked in a kind voice.

"Is this the colored mission?" Jerome asked.

"Yes, it is," she replied, continuing to water the flowers.

Jerome hesitated for a moment, then cleared his throat. "You see, ma'am, we're new in town and we were told to come here if we had no place to stay. We were told to see Pastor Edward."

"I'm Mrs. Edward," she said with a smile. Her warm smile and pleasant voice put Jerome at ease. "Why don't you all come inside and get out of the sun?"

They followed her into the sitting area. "Please make yourselves comfortable while I go and get the pastor," she said, sweeping out of the room.

"This looks like a good place to be," June said.

Richard looked around. "The place we left is starting to look really good to me."

"You know we couldn't stay there," Jerome replied.

"I know, I know. That place may not have been gold, but that glitter sho is looking real good right about now."

Jerome grabbed June's hand and looked her straight in the eyes. "We need to get our story straight before they get back," he said urgently. June could see how serious he was and gave him her undivided attention. "You cannot tell anyone, and I mean anyone, about the things we told you about where we are from," Jerome said.

"Why is that?"

"Because people would not understand it, so it's best to keep it to ourselves for now. If someone asks about us, you tell them we just showed up there, and when we found out you needed help, we helped. That's all you tell them."

June did not understand why but agreed.

Paster Edward and Mrs. Edward walked in. "Well, who do we have here?" the pastor asked in a deep and strong commanding voice. He was much older than Mrs. Edward. The pastor was in his mid-fifties, and Mrs. Edward was in her mid-forties. She clearly admired him and looked up to him with great respect.

The three of them stood up, and Jerome shook the pastor's hand. "Good afternoon, sir, I'm Jerome, and this is Richard and June."

"Nice to meet you, sir," Richard said as he shook his hand.

Not making any eye contact, June said in a low voice, "Hello, how you doin', sir?"

"I'm doing just fine," replied the pastor. "I'm Pastor James Edward. Mrs. Edward said that you just arrived in town and you have no place to stay."

"That's true," Jerome said.

The pastor wasn't sure what to make of Jerome and Richard. He turned to June, who continued looking down at the floor. "Where are you from?"

Jerome responded, "We just got here from Louisiana. We helped June escape from the plantation that she lived on. If we didn't get her out of there when we did, she most likely would be dead today."

The pastor looked at Jerome and Richard. "You two don't look like runaway slaves," he said slowly.

"We're not," Jerome said. "We just helped June escape, and now that we're here, we have no place to stay. We would like to stay here until we figure something out, if that might be a possibility."

"We don't turn anyone away who we believe really needs help," replied the pastor. "If we allow you to stay, you will have to pull your weight around here. Everyone must pitch in and work around the mission; that's the only way it can survive."

Mrs. Edward chimed in. "And take classes; you must take classes. Most people who come here can't read, write, or do basic arithmetic. Without these basic skills, people will try to take advantage of you. So, while you are here, we will try to teach you the basics." She was clearly passionate about her work.

"Amen," Pastor Edward said. "Mrs. Edward watches over the teachings ministry at the mission." At that, June raised her head up and looked at Mrs. Edward with a smile, and Mrs. Edward smiled back.

"Well, I have some work to do at the church, but I would like to talk to you two later," he said, looking at Jerome and Richard. "There is something different about you two that piques my interest. Mrs. Edward will show you around and explain how things are done, and if you agree to follow those rules, you're welcome to stay."

They showed a sign of relief and thanked him profusely.

"Follow me," Mrs. Edward said as she led the way.

They followed Mrs. Edward around the mission. She explained how the different areas ran. They saw women working in the kitchen preparing meals. There were children in classrooms learning. Volunteers would come in and help Mrs. Edward with the teaching. She explained that the adults and the young adults their age would take classes after the workday was done.

They went out behind the mission where men, women, and young teenagers their age were working the fields and tending to the animals. She explained that they used the crops from the fields and the animals as food for the mission. She also told them that they made money from selling crops to the merchants in town, which helped run the mission.

When she finished the tour, they went back inside and sat down at the table in the kitchen area. She had one of the ladies bring them something to drink.

"What do you think of the mission?" she asked, with an expression of pride at their accomplishments.

"Very impressive," Jerome said, moving his head up and down and looking around.

"Looks like a lot of good is done around here," Richard said.

Mrs. Edward turned her attention to June. "What do you think, June? Could you see yourself here?"

June looked up, "Yes, ma'am," she said with excitement. "I want to learn schooling so I can teach others."

"That's excellent," Mrs. Edward said. "So many of our people don't have the education they need. We need more people who are willing to take on the role of teaching. One of our dreams is to have a full-time school here at the mission. Maybe someday you could become a teacher here."

"Do you really think I could teach?" June asked, clearly excited.

"With that excitement and if you're willing to work hard, I know you can," replied Mrs. Edward.

June smiled. "I will work very hard, ma'am, you'll see."

"I believe you will," Mrs. Edward said. She turned to Jerome and Richard. "Are you two as excited about learning as June?"

"No one can be that excited," Richard replied with a smile.

"Well, I think it is good that she is so excited about learning. I just wish some of the others here would be that excited." June smiled. "I think the next thing we need to decide is how you can contribute to the mission while you're here. What are some of the things that you're good at?" she asked.

Jerome and Richard sat there with blank looks on their faces. June, on the other hand, was enthusiastic and thrilled to share what she could contribute.

"I worked in the big house with my mama since I was a little girl. I is good at cleaning, cooking, and washing clothes. I can even work in the fields and tend to the animals," she said, brightening even more as she relayed her skillset. June smiled as she looked over at Jerome and Richard.

"Show-off," Richard said under his breath.

"What about you two?" Mrs. Edward asked Jerome and Richard.

Jerome replied, "Well, I ain't good at cooking, cleaning, or washing. And I sho don't know anything about working in no fields or tending to any animals."

Mrs. Edward, suprised by that answer, looked over at Richard, who shrugged and shook his hear left to right and said, "I can't do those things either." She figured young men their age must have some kind of skillset that might be useful.

"Well, what kind of work have you done?" she asked.

Jerome and Richard looked at each other, then at Mrs. Edward, and said at the same time: "We ain't never worked."

Mrs. Edward was speechless for a moment. "You mean you have never worked?"

"That's right," Jerome said.

"Never worked," Richard said, shaking his head.

This took her by surprise, knowing most young men their age were working to help their families or were even married.

"Well, I'm sure we can find you something around here to do. We can start with class tonight," suggested Mrs. Edward.

"With all due respect," Richard said, "I'm sure what's being taught we already know."

"We'll see about that tonight," she said with a smile, thinking he was just trying to get out of going to the class. Mrs. Edward stood up. "Let's get you three settled in. June, you will stay in the house and room with Sarah. You are about her age. You two will room in the mission with the other young men your age," she directed.

By the time the three had settled in, early evening had approached. People started coming in after a hard day's work. As the young men came in the room, Jerome and Richard could see the curiosity on their faces. No one said anything to them; they just looked at the two of them and whispered amongst themselves.

Meanwhile, June was sitting on the bed in her room when a young lady about her age walked into the room.

"Hello, my name is Sarah. What's yours?"

"I is June," she said in a low voice.

Sarah could see that June was very uncomfortable, so she sat by her, hoping that would put her at ease.

"Mrs. Edward told me that we will be roommates and to make sure that you were comfortable and to help you with anything you needed. She told me that you escaped from the plantation that you lived on, and things have been pretty tough," said Sarah kindly.

"Is you a runaway slave?" June asked.

"Yes, I am," answered Sarah.

"You don't talk like any slaves I know."

"I was about three or four when me, my mama, daddy, and grandmother ran. My mama and daddy died on the way here. My grandmother and I, with the help of a number of people, made it," she said, a distant look on her face as she remembered bits and pieces of the harrowing journey.

"I don't remember much about my mama or daddy or much about how we got here. My grandmother would always tell me how brave my mama and daddy were and how much they loved me. When we arrived here, my grandmother got a job at the mission cooking and cleaning. When she died a few years ago, Pastor Edward and Mrs. Edward took me in."

"Do you go to school?" June asked.

"I go to the colored school, and after school, I do my chores and then I help with the classes here," Sarah responded.

"You think you could help me with my learning?"

"Of course I will help you," said Sarah.

"I don't know reading or writing," June said nervously.

Sarah put her hand on her shoulder. "You will be reading and writing in no time!" she said supportively.

June smiled and gave her a big hug. The hug surprised Sarah. It really made her feel good that someone wanted to learn. She felt most of the people at the mission who were her age and older did not care for the classes. She believed that they only went because it was part of the agreement to stay at the mission. She could see that June really wanted to learn, and she was excited for the chance to help her.

Sarah stood up. "Is there anything you need me to do to help you get settled?"

"I ain't got nothin' but what I is wearing."

"Don't worry, we look about the same size, and I have plenty of things you can wear," Sarah offered generously.

June smiled. Sarah walked over to the closet and pulled out a dress and held it up, considering it and June. "This looks like it will fit you," she said, offering the dress to June.

June jumped up excitedly and took the dress and held it up to her and looked at Sarah. "This is the prettiest dress I is ever saw," June said.

Sarah smiled. "Now, let's get you cleaned up and into that dress before supper."

Jerome and Richard sat talking about what would be their next move when they noticed everyone leaving. One of the young men stopped and looked back. "You two better come on. It's supper time, and when they close the kitchen, you won't get nothing to eat until morning."

Jerome and Richard stood up and walked over to the young man. "They call me JT and this is Rich," Jerome said by way of introduction.

"My name is Isaac," replied the young man.

"I guess we would be sitting here hungry if you didn't say something," Jerome said, shaking his head.

"It takes people around here some time to warm up to strangers. Everyone around here has had it pretty tough in one way or another," said Isaac.

The three started walking to the dining area. "By the way, if you don't mind me asking, where you from? You look different than anyone we have ever seen at the mission. I don't know if you noticed when everyone came in the room how they were staring at you two," said Isaac.

Richard replied with a smirk, "That's an understatement."

"We're from a different place and time, and we just helped a young lady escape from a plantation in Louisiana," Jerome said, not knowing how Isaac would take his answer.

Isaac looked at them, confused and not sure what to make of the comment. His attention soon shifted to the sight and smell of the food. "It has been a long day, and now it's time to eat. See you around," he said with a salute. He left the two of them standing in the doorway as he headed to the food line.

Jerome and Richard stood there looking around to see if June was in there. Everyone looked like they had a long, hard day. Richard asked Jerome, "Is this what we have to look forward to if we can't get home?"

"Don't even think like that," Jerome said. "We have got to get home."

After looking around for a few moments, they didn't see June so they went and got their food and then sat down to eat. For the first time in a long while, they felt safe and comfortable, sitting and eating, not worried about someone coming after them. Jerome glanced up and saw June coming into the dining area.

"Rich, is that June?" Jerome asked with a dazed look.

"Damn," Richard said. "That can't be the same girl that came here with us. And who is that fine sister with her?"

"I don't know," Jerome said. "But we're about to find out because they are headed this way."

"Hi guys!" June said, smiling as she stood tall and proud in the dress she was wearing. "JT, Rich, this Sarah. She let me wear this beautiful dress," she said, beaming.

"Hello," Jerome said. Then he turned his attention back to June.

Richard jumped out of his seat and pulled the chair out for Sarah. "Would you like to sit down?" he asked, giving Sarah a big ear-to-ear smile.

Sarah smiled back. "I think we should get our food first, but thank you."

As Sarah and June walked away, Richard said, "Hurry back, we'll be waiting."

When June and Sarah were out of hearing distance, Jerome pushed Richard on his shoulder. "Man, that girl had your mouth wide open."

"I thought I was going to have to roll your tongue back in your mouth the way you were looking at June," Richard responded.

"Yeah, right, she's like a little sister," Jerome said defensively.

"Tell that to someone who don't know you," Richard said.

Not able to hold it in any longer, Jerome started laughing. "She sho do look good, though."

Richard looked up. "Chill, here they come." They both stood up and pulled out the chairs, and the two young women sat down.

After eating for a few minutes, Sarah asked, "Are you two excited about the classes like June? They will be starting in here right after supper."

"Personally, I could do without them," Richard said.

"You can learn a lot from Mrs. Edward," Sarah said.

"Well, I is ready," June said. "And Sarah helps with the classes and she gon' help me with my learning."

Richard smiled. "In that case, I will be in the front row."

Sarah smiled, then asked Jerome, "What about you?"

"I'll be there only because I have to," Jerome said reluctantly.

"You can learn a lot from Mrs. Edward too," Sarah repeated.

"Yeah, yeah, we'll see," Jerome said, not enthused about the whole idea of going to the class.

CHAPTER 16

Supper finished and everyone was waiting for class to start. Mrs. Edward walked in and put some books on the table. "Good evening," she said, with enthusiasm and eagerness in her voice. "I hope everyone is ready to learn something new today. You know that knowledge is the key to success."

Jerome looked over at Richard. "She sounds just like Mrs. Wilkins. We go all the way back in time and there is a Mrs. Wilkins here. You got to be kidding me," Jerome said, shaking his head.

Mrs. Edward held up a small book. "Who wants to read from the book today?" she asked her students. Everyone looked around but no one would volunteer. While Mrs. Edward was trying to persuade someone to come up and read, Sarah was passing out papers with the alphabet. Sarah handed a paper to Richard.

He looked at the paper incredulously. "ABCs, are you kidding me?"

"You should appreciate the help Mrs. Edward is giving you," Sarah said in a quiet but scolding voice.

Richard handed the paper back to Sarah. "I don't need any help with ABCs."

Sarah snatched the paper. "Mrs. Edward, this young man will read since he thinks he don't need any help with the alphabet." Sarah then handed Jerome a paper. He took the paper and laid it on the table. "I see someone appreciates the help," Sarah said, then continued passing out the papers.

Jerome leaned over to Richard and whispered sarcastically, "Well, that's going to help you get in good with her."

"Come on up," Mrs. Edward said, excited that someone wanted to read.

Jerome leaned over and whispered so only Richard could hear. "Go on up, Mr. Professor, and read from the first-grade book."

Richard stood up, whispering, "I see you got jokes." Jerome started laughing as Richard started walking to the front of the room.

Mrs. Edward handed him the book, and he opened it and stared at it for a moment before looking up to see that all eyes were on him. Mrs. Edward walked over and put her hand on his shoulder and leaned in so only he could hear. "Just do the best you can. I'm here to help you."

He looked over at Sarah, who had a look of smug satisfaction on her face, thinking she had embarrassed him. Richard closed the book and put it on the table, then picked up another book. Unbeknownst to him, it was a book that Mrs. Edward would read whenever she had a spare moment.

Richard started reading from the book, and after he'd begun, surprised looks and whispers came from everyone. Richard read several paragraphs, then closed the book and put it back on the desk. At that moment Mrs. Edward realized he did not need to be in the class. She had Sarah take over the class and told Jerome and Richard to follow her. Richard looked at Sarah as they headed out of the room, and she just looked away.

"Well, I guess you two don't belong in the class," said Mrs. Edward once they were in the hall. "I suppose reading is no problem for you either," she said to Jerome, assuming correctly.

Jerome shrugged. "I do all right," he responded.

"I'm going to have to find something more suited for you two," Mrs. Edward said thoughtfully. "Maybe you can help with the classes like Sarah."

"That's a good idea," Richard said with a big smile, knowing that would give him a chance to be close to Sarah. "I love learning and I love sharing what I know." He sounded enthusiastic, but Jerome knew the real reason behind his enthusiasm for the task.

Mrs. Edward looked at Jerome. "What about you? Do you think you would like to help with the classes?"

"Naw, teaching ain't my thing, that's Rich. He's the brain," Jerome said, in no way interested in teaching anyone anything.

"Well, the pastor did want to talk to you both. Let's go to his office as he may have some ideas," she said kindly, escorting them toward Pastor Edward's office.

When they entered the pastor's office, he was sitting at his desk reading. Mrs. Edward knocked on the door. The pastor looked up. "Come in," he said brightly.

"Here are the two young men you wanted to see. I thought I would bring them over here because they are too advanced for what I'm teaching," Mrs. Edward explained. "Richard has shown an interest in helping with the classes, but we still have to find something for Jerome to do. I guess I'll get back to my class and let you gentlemen work that out," she said, sweeping from the room and heading back to her students.

"Sit down," the pastor said, pointing at the chairs that were in front of his desk. He was quiet for a moment, leaving them to take their seats and sit nervously in silence. After a long pause, he looked up at them. "I need you to be truthful with me. You say you're from Louisiana but you're not slaves. You say you helped the girl that was with you escape from the plantation she was living on."

"That's correct, sir," Jerome said. "There was someone that needed help, so that's what we did."

"That was a noble thing you did, helping someone knowing that if you got caught, you could lose your life and now you can't go home. What about the loved ones you left behind? You know what you did might put them in danger," said the pastor thoughtfully.

Jerome and Richard looked at each other, not knowing what to say. They knew the pastor would not believe them even if they told him the truth. They could see he was becoming very suspicious of their story. "We don't have anything or anyone that we are tied to in Louisiana," Jerome said, hoping that the pastor would not ask any more questions.

Tapping his finger on the desk, the pastor paused for a moment. Jerome and Richard exchanged a glance, not knowing what to think. The pastor stopped tapping and looked up. "What you two did for the young lady was a good thing," he said, finally. "If you ever want to share anything, I'm here."

A sigh of relief came over Jerome and Richard. They knew that if he kept asking questions, they would have a hard time answering without telling him the truth, and it certainly did not seem like the right time for the truth.

"Mrs. Edward told me that you two don't have much in the way of working skills, but she seems to be impressed with what you know in the way of education. I guess she thinks you can help her with the classes," said the pastor. He was a wise man and he knew that he wasn't going to get the boys to tell him what he wanted to know without scaring them off. He knew it was best to let it be for the time being.

"Yes sir," Richard said excitedly, his face visibly brightening.

The pastor looked over at Jerome. "You don't seem as enthused as your buddy," he said.

"Teaching ain't for me. Besides, don't they have schools they can go to?" Jerome asked, resenting that yet again, school was the task at hand, a task that he despised.

"Most of the kids have never been in a school. They can't read, write, or do basic arithmetic. Here at the mission, we try to teach the basic skills so that when they leave the mission, the transition to a traditional school won't be so overwhelming," explained the pastor.

Jerome shook his head. "That seems like a lot of responsibility."

"Well, you have to do something to stay at the mission," replied

Pastor Edward. "If you don't want to help with the classes, we can have you out there in the fields or working with the animals."

"This teaching thing might not be so bad after all," Jerome said, knowing he did not want to work in the fields or with the animals.

The pastor took on a more serious disposition. "Mrs. Edward takes her call to teaching very seriously. She must see something in you two if she is willing to have you help. I just hope you don't disappoint her."

"We won't, you just wait and see," Richard promised.

"You should head back to the class to see if there is anything she needs you to do before you call it a day," suggested Pastor Edward. The boys thanked him and left his office.

As they headed back to the class, Jerome looked over at Richard. "Man, you seem to be taking this teaching thing pretty seriously."

"You know I like learning and teaching," said Richard.

"I guess I better learn to love it or the pastor is going to have my butt out in those fields or with those stank animals," said Jerome grudgingly. Richard started laughing. "I don't think that's funny," Jerome said, giving Richard a long, hard stare.

"Sorry, my bad," Richard said with a half grin spreading across his face. "I can just see you out there chasing chickens and milking cows."

"Ha, ha, very cute," Jerome said, knowing Richard was right.

They walked back into the class, where everyone was working. Some were doing basic arithmetic while others were writing words that were displayed on the board. Mrs. Edward was walking around helping where needed while Sarah was working with June, who seemed to be very excited.

Mrs. Edward looked up and waved the two of them to come up to the front. "Did the pastor come up with anything for you?"

Richard, looking very pleased with himself, said, "We're going to help with the classes."

"That's great," Mrs. Edward said with a look of satisfaction. She looked over at Jerome. "You still don't look too excited about this."

"Like I said before, teaching ain't for me, but it's either teaching or being out in the fields, or even worse, dealing with the animals, and I most definitely don't like neither one of those options," he said honestly.

Mrs. Edward gave Jerome a light pat on the shoulder. "You'll see that there is great satisfaction in teaching," she assured him.

"I'm just satisfied that I don't have to work in the fields or with those animals," Jerome said with a slight smirk.

"I think you two are going to work out just fine," she said with a big smile. "I will meet you here tomorrow morning right after breakfast and let you know what you will be doing."

"Sounds good," Richard said while Jerome just shook his head.

Mrs. Edward dismissed the class, and everyone left except June and Sarah, who were still working. Jerome and Richard were sitting in the back waiting for them to finish. Moments later, Sarah declared that was enough for the day. The girls got up to leave and were surprised to see Jerome and Richard waiting for them. June ran to them, excited to share what she had learned. She showed them what she had learned like a first grader after the first day of school.

Jerome took a real interest in what June was saying, while Richard turned his attention on Sarah, who was smiling and genuinely happy for June. She could see that June cherished everything she had learned that day.

Seeing his opportunity, Richard walked over to Sarah and apologized for the way he acted. Sarah smiled and accepted his apology. Jerome and Richard then walked them back to the house. Richard and Sarah walked together while Jerome and June followed a few feet behind them, both couples deep in their own conversations.

Jerome and Richard headed back to the mission once Sarah and June went inside. "I see you worked it out with Sarah," Jerome observed.

Richard rubbed his hands together. "Yeah, you know the girl can't stay mad at the player," he said with mock bravado.

Jerome gave Richard a playful shove. "You know your full of it."

Richard shoved him back. "You know you full of June," he retorted.

"I told you, she is like a sister to me."

"Sister my foot, let one of them Mandingo brothers roll up on her and I bet she won't be like a sister then."

"Now you know they don't have a chance," said Jerome.

"Now listen to you. I thought so."

"You better worry about Sarah. Fine as she is, she probably already has somebody."

"If she does, he'd better watch out because Rich is on the scene now." Rich's spirit remained jaunty, despite their playful teasing. It seemed that everything was looking up for them at the moment.

They made it back to the mission and sat out on the porch enjoying the cool breeze. "Now what?" Jerome asked Richard.

"We could be playing basketball instead of sitting on this porch not knowing if we will ever get home. I can't imagine this being our life. We've got to figure something out." Richard had a look of defeat on his face and frustration in his voice. "Our problem is we don't even have a clue on how to get home."

"We would have a fighting chance if we only knew where to start. Man, this is frustrating," Jerome said, shaking his head.

Isaac walked up to where they were sitting on the porch. "You two are the talk of the mission. People don't know what to make of you, and when they saw you walking Sarah and that new girl back to the house, the talk really started," he said.

"Talk about what?" Richard asked, immediately defensive.

Isaac turned to Richard. "One thing they were talking about is you walking with Sarah, because everyone knows there is a boy that goes to school with her that is sweet on her. Another thing you should know is that he's from a well-off colored family, and they donate a lot to the mission, so you'd better be careful," he said.

"Careful of what?" Richard asked with a concerned look.

"I'm just saying you trying to talk to a girl that one of the biggest donor's son likes could be trouble for you," said Isaac.

"Whatever," Richard responded.

"I guess I'm going to call it a day. I've got lots of work to do tomorrow," Isaac said, heading toward the door. He then looked back. "What kind of work do they have you doing?"

"Teaching the kids," Jerome said, clearly not thrilled with his new line of work.

"So while we are out breaking our backs you two are going to be inside teaching?" asked Isaac incredulously. "I can see that will go over well with everyone."

"You let anyone who has a problem with it know that they can come talk to me," said Jerome defiantly. Jerome then held his hand out for Richard to slap it.

"I don't have a problem," Isaac said, tapping his chest, "but some might."

"Like I said, they can come see me." Jerome then looked at Richard, and his tough talk turned into insecure talk. "The least of our problems are the guys in this room. We will be teaching kids tomorrow and what do we know about teaching?"

CHAPTER 17

Early the next day, Richard was up bright and early, excited about teaching. Jerome noticed the shift in his energy and shook his head. "If the fellows could see us now; JT and Rich teaching. They would have a big laugh," he teased.

"They would really have a big laugh if they could see you chasing chickens or out in the field with your straw hat and a hoe in your hand. And I don't mean like the ones you walk around the school with," he retorted.

"That ain't even funny," Jerome said as they headed out of the room for breakfast.

Jerome and Richard walked into the dining area. Jerome could see June working in the kitchen area. She was smiling and seemed to be enjoying her work. Jerome smiled as he watched her. "She is going to be all right," he said to himself. He looked over at Richard, who did not hear a word he had just said because he was just looking all around the dining area. Jerome tapped him on the shoulder. "She's probably already on her way to school."

"What you talking about? I'm just looking for somewhere to sit," Richard said defensively.

"Sure, you can tell that to someone else because I know better," Jerome said as he pushed Richard in the direction of the breakfast line.

June saw Jerome and Richard from across the dining room, and she waved and ran over to them. She put one arm around each of their necks and pulled them close to her for a hug. "Thank you fo' bringing me here. I is real happy here," she said, and they could see her eyes shining with joy.

"We are happy for you," Jerome said. Richard was clearly not paying any attention to what June was saying. Jerome elbowed him in the side.

Richard returned his attention to them, saying, "Yeah, yeah, whatever," as he continued to look around. "June, I don't see your friend. Is she working in the kitchen with you?"

"No, she gon' to school." June smiled at Richard, "You like her!" she exclaimed as she made the realization.

"She's all right," Richard said, trying not to act too excited, but Jerome could have sworn he saw a bit of a flush creeping up Richard's cheeks.

"Well, she talked a lot about you."

"What did she say?" Richard asked, suddenly so eager that his attempts at playing it cool had evaporated.

"We will talk later. I got to go back to work," June said, stepping away.

"Wait, wait, tell me what she said," Richard pleaded, curiosity eating at him.

"We will talk later," June repeated as she headed back to the kitchen area.

"Damn," Richard said, disappointment flooding through him.

"Boy, she got you whipped."

"Please, this is Rich," he said as he headed to the breakfast line. Jerome started laughing and shaking his head as they walked.

Breakfast was ending and everyone started heading out to start the daily jobs. Mrs. Edward came over to where Jerome and Richard were sitting. "Good morning," she said in a cheerful voice. "Are you ready to get started?"

"Yes," Richard said, both excited and eager. Mrs. Edward looked over at Jerome, waiting for his reaction.

"I suppose so," Jerome said with no enthusiasm.

"Well then, let's go get started. The little minds await," she said, smiling at the two of them.

As they headed to the room where the children had their morning classes, Mrs. Edward remembered she had left something in the office. "I need one of you to come with me to the office and help me get the study materials."

"I'll go," Richard said.

"Jerome, if you go down this hall, the room where the children are is the second door," she said, pointing in that direction. Mrs. Edward and Richard headed to the office, while Jerome slowly walked down the hall, not looking forward to dealing with a room full of little children.

Jerome walked into the room, and immediately all eyes locked on him. There were twelve children between the ages of seven and ten sitting at two tables. All of the children were sitting up straight, with their hands folded and big smiles on their faces. Jerome could not see what they had to smile about. They were living in a mission; some of the children had no shoes and their clothes were tattered. But their eyes told a different story than the one you could see from their outside appearance. Their eyes gleamed with hope and joy, and it was an unfamiliar feeling for Jerome to experience, given their circumstances.

Jerome stood there looking at the children, not knowing what to say or do. For the first time, he did not have a comment or something funny to say that would deflect the attention away from the real situation. He could see the hunger for knowledge in their eyes as they sat there patiently. He started to understand why Mrs. Wilkins put her heart and soul into teaching. It was for children like these, eager to learn and possessed with a thirst for knowledge. All she ever received on a daily basis was a room full of problems and disappointments, and he knew he was the one who gave her the most dissatisfaction and frustration with her work.

At that moment he started to feel bad for Mrs. Wilkins. He then made a promise to himself that if he ever got back, he would apologize to her and the class for his disruptive and disrespectful behavior. At that moment, he decided that he wanted to be part of the solution and not a part of the problem. Seeing these children made him realize why Mrs. Wilkins stressed the importance of learning about our past. Children just like these are the ones who fought and struggled, giving him and his friends the freedom and opportunities that they took for granted.

He took a deep breath. "Good morning, class, my name is JT." He hoped he had sounded more confident than he felt, but he felt that he was off to a good start.

In unison all the children said, "Good morning, JT."

One little boy raised his hand. Jerome pointed at him and motioned for him to stand up.

The boy stood up tall and straight. "Is you gon' be our teacher?"

Jerome paused for a moment, then smiled. "Yes I am. All right, let's get aquatinted," he said, rubbing his hands together. "Everyone tell me your names."

Each child stood up and said their name, and Jerome said good morning and repeated that name so that he'd remember.

"Now that we've got that out of the way, let's talk about what you want to be when you grow up." Jerome stood there waiting for their answers, thinking they would say doctor or lawyer…something he thought most children their age would say. No one said anything. They just sat there, confused. He then realized these children in their short lives probably had no reason to think about growing up. Life had been real tough on them, and they had not seen many Black role models, if any, achieve success outside of the realm of certain lines of work.

After a few moments, one hand went up. Jerome pointed at the little boy. "Do you know what you want to be when you grow up?" Jerome asked, eager to hear his answer.

The little boy stood up. "I want to be White."

Jerome was confused by his answer. "Why would you want to be White?"

The little boy paused for a moment, then dropped his head. "'Cause life would be better."

"What gave you the idea life would be better if you were White?" Jerome asked.

"My daddy did."

Jerome was shocked by his answer. "Why do you think your daddy gave you that idea?"

"He always say to my mama when White folks treat us bad, if we were White they would not treat us like this," said the boy, looking back up at Jerome.

Jerome stood there speechless because he knew that what the boy said was true. Being White had its privileges, especially in this time. He knew that he had to teach these children to learn all they could, because education would open doors and give them opportunities no matter the time period in which they lived.

Mrs. Edward and Richard walked into the room. All the children said, "Good morning, Mrs. Edward."

"Good morning, children. This is Richard and he will also be teaching you." All the children said good morning to Richard.

"Just call me Rich," he said.

"Now children, these two young men will be teaching you. I want you to listen to them and learn all you can. Remember, knowledge is something no one can ever take away from you. Now I want you to have a good day." She then looked at Jerome and Richard. "I'll be back later to see how things are going."

They spent the first part of the morning figuring out the levels of the children. Then they split the children into two groups. They could see that each group was way behind for their ages, as related to their own understanding of their modern education, and they felt this was the best way to give them the attention they needed.

Jerome worked with one group and Richard worked with the other. By mid-morning both groups were diligently working while Jerome and Richard walked around the tables helping where needed.

It was around noon and Mrs. Edward came into the room. "Lunch time!" she said, and all the children started clapping and hollering, eager for a break. "Children, you know what to do," she said. The children got up and pushed their chairs under the table and lined up by the door. She then looked at the children as she walked down the line. "You may go," she said. They walked quickly down the hall, headed for lunch. Mrs. Edward, Jerome, and Richard followed close behind.

All the children received their lunch and sat down to eat, chattering amongst themselves. Jerome, Richard, and Mrs. Edward were sitting at a table nearby. Jerome and Richard were eating and Mrs. Edward was drinking a cup of coffee. "How did things go this morning?" she asked.

"Great," Jerome said, excited, feeling a renewed sense of purpose. "The children are so eager to learn and hungry for knowledge. They really are a great bunch of kids." Mrs. Edward and Richard looked at each other with their mouths wide open, stunned and unable to speak. "What?" Jerome asked, holding his hands up.

Mrs. Edward smiled. "This can't be the same young man from a few hours ago who wanted nothing to do with teaching, can it?"

"Yeah, where is the JT I know?" Richard said, looking all around as if the real Jerome was somewhere else in the room.

"Funny," Jerome said. "I guess I do enjoy teaching children who are eager to learn. When you look at their faces, you can see in their eyes that they are hungry for knowledge, and you just want to teach them everything you know."

Mrs. Edward gave them a mystified look. "I don't know what to make of it, but there is something very different about you two. I just hope it is a blessing for what we are trying to do here."

Jerome and Richard looked at each other, then put a spoonful of food in their mouths, not saying anything.

Mrs. Edward finished her coffee. "I need to get back to my work. If you ever feel the need to talk to someone about anything, the pastor and myself are always available. Remember we are here to help if we can," she said kindly, but her offer was very clear that she was hoping they'd reveal their secret, whatever it was.

"We appreciate that," Jerome said.

Mrs. Edward got up and said goodbye to the children and headed back to work while Jerome and Richard gathered all the children and headed back to the classroom.

They continued working with the children for several more hours before the school day ended. When the children left, Jerome and Richard started straightening up the area. "This teaching thing ain't too bad," Richard said.

Jerome replied, "Anything is better than working out in the fields or with those animals."

"You know you enjoyed working with the kids," Richard said.

"Actually, I did," Jerome said. "But when you teach every day, you must enjoy it."

"When have you ever taught anyone anything?"

Jerome smiled. "I school every day on the basketball court." He laughed, then balled up a piece of paper and took a jump shot at the trash can. "All day," he said, looking back at Richard after the paper went into the trash can.

CHAPTER 18

Jerome and Richard were sitting in the room when the others started returning from a hard day's work. They could feel the tension and hear the remarks and comments everyone was making. The other young men looked beat and tired from working all day out in the sun.

Richard said, "Damn, looks like we have a bunch of haters."

"That it does," Jerome said, "but you can bet I don't feel bad. If we didn't have the education we have, we would be walking in here looking just like them." Jerome paused for a moment. "I guess Mrs. Wilkins was right when she said education will give you better options when it comes to job careers."

Isaac walked over to where the boys were sitting. "Hey, don't mind them; it was a hard day out there. They just don't think it's fair that they work hard all day, and when they walk in the room, they see you two looking like you haven't worked at all."

"Trust me, they are the last thing on my mind," Jerome said nonchalantly. "I have bigger things to worry about." Then, he said loud enough so they all could hear, "If they don't like their situation, don't get mad at others; do something to change it."

"Damn," Richard said, "you sound just like Mrs. Wilkins. I guess you were paying attention to some of the things she said."

"How could you not? She said them enough times," Jerome said, rolling his eyes and shaking his head. He tapped Richard on the shoulder. "Man, let's get out of here before I say or do something that I'll regret."

As they headed out of the room, Jerome looked back. "Hey, Isaac, I'll holler at you later."

Isaac was puzzled. "Why you gon' holler at me? I didn't say nothing; that was them," he said, pointing at all the other guys in the room.

Jerome started laughing. "I mean we'll talk later."

When Jerome and Richard left the room, everyone started giving Isaac dirty looks. "Don't get mad at me," he said, "I just told them how you all feel."

Jerome and Richard were sitting on the front porch when Mrs. Edward walked up.

"How was the first day?" she asked.

"It was all right," Jerome said.

Richard said, "Teaching went well, but I think some of the guys in the room aren't happy with us."

"Why is that?"

Richard hunched his shoulders. "I guess they don't think we're working hard because we are not out there doing what they do."

Mrs. Edward responded uneasily, "Do you want me to talk to them?"

"No, we'll handle it," Jerome said.

"Okay," she said. "We cannot have tension in the mission, especially not tomorrow."

"What's tomorrow?" Richard asked.

"Oh, that's right, you don't know." Mrs. Edward was a little embarrassed that she had not informed them. "Tomorrow is the mission's open house. Some of the influential and wealthy colored and White folks will be here, so we need to put on a good impression because the mission counts on their donations. Those donations are a big reason why we can stay open, so everything needs to run smoothly."

"Since you two are teaching, you will have to put on a good impression." She then looked Jerome and Richard up and down. "You will have to get cleaned up and put on some clean clothes. Since you are teaching, I'm sure that there will be a lot of questions coming your way. One of the areas the donors look at is the teaching we are giving the children. If we impress them in that area, they will most likely donate more." Her concern for the children and the mission was evident.

Jerome stood up and stretched his arms out. "These are all the clothes we have. What you see is what you get."

Mrs. Edward paused for a moment. "I think the pastor may have some clothes that he no longer can fit into that you two can wear. I can have one of the ladies take them in if needed."

They went to the house and tried on a couple of suits that the pastor no longer wore. They did need to be taken in a little. Mrs. Edward had one of the ladies come by and fit them into the suits. She told Mrs. Edward that she could have them ready to try on some time after dinner.

Dinner started and everyone was sitting down and eating. Jerome could see June working in the kitchen area. Richard was looking around to see if Sarah was there. A few moments later Sarah came into the dining area. Richard stood up to greet her immediately.

"Hey Sarah," he said, with a big smile, "you can sit with us if you'd like."

"I'll be right there," she said.

Richard sat down, grinning from ear to ear. He then grabbed his chicken leg and took a big bite.

Jerome shook his head. "Boy, you're pitiful."

"You got some nerve," Richard said. "I see how you look at June."

"Yeah, but at least I ain't drooling every time I see her," retorted Jerome.

Richard slapped the table. "Ah, so you do like her! I knew it, you can't fool me."

"Calm down," Jerome said in a low voice. "Here they come."

Richard looked up and saw June and Sarah walking their way with their dinner. Richard sat up straight and wiped his mouth to make sure he wiped away any crumbs. When the girls arrived at the table, they all ate and talked about the day.

After they finished dinner, they sat and talked for a while longer before June got up from the table. "I got to get back to work. We got a lot to do fo' the big day tomorrow," she said.

"I'll go with you," Sarah said. "Since there won't be any class tonight, because of the big day, I'm sure Mrs. Edward will have me helping anyway."

After June and Sarah left, Isaac came over and sat down. He tapped Richard on the shoulder. "I see you like Sarah."

"What makes you think that?"

"Boy, please," Jerome said, "even Stevie Wonder can see that."

"Who is Stevie Wonder?" Isaac asked.

"He knows what I'm talking about," replied Jerome, still looking at Richard.

"You two have some of the strangest sayings." Isaac turned his attention to Richard and took a more serious tone. "You do remember what I told you about the fellow that likes Sarah?"

"What about him?" Richard asked.

"His father is a big donor to the mission, and the word going around is that he likes Sarah and thinks his son and Sarah will marry someday."

"What's that got to do with me?" Richard asked.

Isaac stood up. "All I'm saying is if it comes down to one of the biggest donors or someone living at the mission, who do you think they will choose?"

"Whatever," Richard said dismissively.

"Just something to think about," Isaac warned before he walked away.

Jerome looked at Richard. "You might want to be cool tomorrow."

"I'm gonna be cool, but that don't mean I won't talk to Sarah if I want to."

"All I'm saying is we don't need to be kicked out of this place, because we definitely don't have anywhere else to go. Where else are we going to go where all we have to do is teach kids their ABCs and we have a place to stay and food to eat? Until we find out how to get home, we don't need to mess this up."

Richard paused for a moment. "You're right, I'll be cool."

At that moment, Mrs. Edward walked up. "Here are the suits and a couple of shirts; you two need to try them on to make sure they fit. If they don't fit, please get them back to me right away so I can have the changes made." Jerome and Richard took the suits from Mrs. Edward and headed to the men's living area to try them on.

They walked into the room, where everyone was talking, laughing, and joking. When everyone noticed them, things got quiet. Jerome and Richard walked over to their area and tried the suits on. Moments later, Isaac came into the room and saw them with the suits on, each making sure that they fit.

"Damn, where did you get those suits?" he asked enthusiastically.

Jerome made a move like he was modeling. "I know I look good in this," he said, looking down and admiring his new clothes.

Richard pulled Jerome by the arm and moved in front of him. "Now, I look good," he said as he pulled back one side of the suit coat and put his hand in his pocket, then took a few steps turn around, and struck a pose.

A loud and slow continuous clap echoed throughout the room as one of the young men in the room walked slowly toward them. Jerome, Richard, and Isaac looked up. Jesse was his name. He was the tough guy in the room, and no one messed with him. Everyone was afraid of him, so they always followed his lead. If he said to do something, they pretty much did it.

"What do we have here?" he asked, as he continued to slowly clap. "It's the two guys that walk around here like they are all high and mighty, thinking they're better than everyone in here."

Isaac walked up to him and put his hand on his shoulder. "Hey, Jesse, they haven't done nothing to you. Why don't you leave them alone?"

Jesse pushed Isaac's hand off his shoulder, then gave him a hard look. "You need to back off," he warned.

Isaac put his hands in the air and backed away slowly. He looked at Jerome and Richard. "You two are on your own," he said in a low voice.

Jerome walked up to Jesse and looked him straight in the eyes. "What's your problem, man?" he asked.

Jesse looked back at the others in the room to include them. "Our problem is you come in here and think you're better than us," he said.

Richard walked up to Jerome. He knew Jerome was not one to back away from a confrontation. "Remember, you told me to be cool. You need to do the same thing here."

Jerome dropped his head and paused for a moment, looked up at Jesse, then at the others in the room. "Look, everyone, we don't think we're better than anyone in here. If you think about it, we're all in the situation together. We don't have anywhere to go. If we did, we would not be living in this mission." Jerome raised his hand. "Is anyone staying here because they want to, or are you staying here because you have nowhere else to go right now?" Jerome looked around for a moment, and no one had raised their hands. "Okay, it looks like we're all in the same situation."

Jerome could see the tension in the room start to ease up. He now felt he could get through to them. "What we need to do is to help each other so we all can better our situation. Everyone in here has a skill that they could share with someone. Richard and myself just happen to have education, which we are willing to help anyone with. Pastor Edward and Mrs. Edward noticed that and want us to help teach the kids because that is what we know and what we are good at. Believe me you, if we had to do what you all do, you would be dragging us in here before the day is halfway over," he said, smiling at the thought. Everyone started laughing, and even Jesse cracked a smile.

Jerome clapped his hands. "Now, what we need to do is make sure this open house is successful. This is our home for now, and when we get to the point where we don't have to stay here any longer, we want to make sure it's available for those who will be coming after we leave. That is our responsibility to Pastor Edward and Mrs. Edward."

At that point everyone seemed to have calmed down. Even Jesse shook Jerome's hand. Jerome surprised himself. He knew there was a time that if someone came up on him like that, he would be fighting without even trying to resolve the situation with his words. He had learned that if you reason with people, the outcome can be a positive one.

CHAPTER 19

When morning came, everyone hit the floor running, and everything seemed to be moving in fast motion. Jerome and Richard walked into the dining area and could see Mrs. Edward directing every move. Everything looked intense but under control.

Mrs. Edward looked up and motioned for them to come over. "Are you two ready for today?" she asked as she glanced around, keeping an eye on everything that was going on.

"We'll be ready when the time comes," Jerome said.

"Everything starts around noon, so when you finish breakfast, you need to go to the classroom and make sure it is in order. I want everything to be just right when the guests come through," directed Mrs. Edward.

Jerome gave Mrs. Edward a look of confidence and a smile. "Don't worry, we got this," he said as he gave Richard a shoulder shove in the direction of the breakfast line.

Jerome and Richard sat down with their breakfast. They noticed very little conversation going on around them in the dining room. Usually during breakfast, the room was filled with the sounds of everyone talking, but today everyone seemed quiet and tense.

"Let's eat and get out of here, Jerome," Richard said. "Mrs. Edward is walking around bugging everyone."

Jerome looked over at Mrs. Edward. "She is about to lose her mind and drive everyone crazy," he agreed. They quickly ate their food and left before she had a chance to come over where they were seated.

When they walked into the classroom, Richard asked Jerome, "Now what?"

Jerome shrugged. "I guess we put some of their papers on the wall, straighten up the tables and chairs, and we'll be done."

"Sounds good to me," Richard said as he started pushing the chairs under the tables, straightening up the room for the guests. Ten minutes later Jerome and Richard were standing at the front of the room, looking at what they had accomplished.

Jerome brushed his hands off. "I guess we're done," he said.

"Looks good to me," Richard said. They sat around the room and talked for a while before heading back to the dining room to see if they could help with anything else at the mission.

When they walked in the dining area, they could see how it was being transformed from a plain, serviceable room to a place of elegance. The old tables they ate at daily now had beautiful coverings on them. Several of the tables were filled with different pastries while other tables had punch bowls and fancy coffeepots ready to be filled.

They could see June, Sarah, and several other women cooking, cleaning, and setting things up while a few men were arranging the tables and chairs. All the while, Mrs. Edward was directing the work, barking out commands as if she was a drill sergeant.

Seeing the organized chaos, Jerome looked at Richard. "Man, I think we should get out of here. Mrs. Edward done gone crazy."

"Well, let's go," Richard said. They both quickly headed for the door before she could spot them.

As they walked quickly down the hall, in the direction of the classroom, they saw the pastor headed their way. "Morning, gentlemen," he said.

"Good morning," they both replied.

"Have you all seen Mrs. Edward?"

Jerome pointed in the direction of the dining area. "She's in there, and I don't think you want to get in her way," he suggested.

The pastor, rubbing his chin, smiled. "I almost forgot how she gets before an open house. I think I will head back to my office." The pastor quickly turned around and headed in the opposite direction.

"Look at him go. Now that's a pastor on the move," Richard said, laughing, amazed at how fast the pastor had gotten around that corner.

"We need to get a move on so she don't spot us either," Jerome said as he headed in the same direction the pastor had gone. Richard looked back in the direction of the dining area and then followed quickly behind Jerome.

They walked back in the classroom and pulled out a couple of chairs and sat down. "Now what are we going to do?" Richard leaned back in the chair, looking up at the ceiling.

"I guess we wait in here until it's time to get dressed for the open house."

Richard sat up suddenly. "How do they take it? There is nothing to do. There is no TV, no video games, and no basketball. How are we going to get along without basketball?" he fretted, suddenly consumed with the boredom of a carefree adolescent.

"Let's just hope we can find a way home," Jerome said in a not-so-enthusiastic voice.

"But what if we can't? We could be stuck here."

"I guess if we can't find a way home, we'll have to face the reality that we might be stuck here and we'll just have to make the best of it."

Richard chuckled, a laugh of futile frustration. "Best of what? There's nothing here to make the best of."

"Well, we can't stay in this mission forever." Jerome sat up and started moving his head up and down as if he had an idea.

Richard had seen that look before. "What do you have in mind?"

"Think about it. With the things we know and our hustle skills, we could come up with something that could make us some serious money," suggested Jerome.

"What the hell do we know about making serious money?" Richard asked, shaking his head uncertainly.

Jerome stood up and Richard could see how excited he was. He started pacing back and forth. "We know everything that will become successful from products to services. We can pick from anything we want, and we know it will work because we know how it will work."

Richard sat there, unmoving, with a skeptical look. "It don't matter what we come up with; we ain't got no money."

Jerome looked at Richard with a big smile. "Guess who's coming to dinner?" Richard stared at Jerome, confused. Jerome stood there, still displaying his big smile. "All the rich and successful people in the town will be right here at this open house. After today, we will know who is who and who has what."

It was Richard's turn to put on a big smile. "I see where you're going," he said.

Just then, Mrs. Edward walked into the room. "There you are," she said, as though she hadn't known where to find them.

They were surprised, caught in the act of plotting, with guilty looks on their faces. Jerome mumbled, "We just finished and were about to be on our way to look for you."

Mrs. Edward looked around the room, not saying a word. Jerome and Richard stood there waiting patiently for her to say something. She finally looked at them. "Good idea to put their work on the wall so everyone can see what they have been doing in the classroom. Good job. Now you need to go get cleaned up. Things will be starting soon, and I need you to be ready to greet the guests."

"We'll be ready, Mrs. Edward," Jerome said.

"When you're ready, come and see me. I'll be in the dining area." She turned around and walked out. A feeling of relief swept over them as she left.

They headed back to the men's living area to get dressed. They washed up, cleaned off their Jordans, and got dressed. Richard examined himself. "Not bad," he said.

Jerome looked down at his Jordans. "These black Jordans don't look too bad with this suit. When I get home, I think I'm going to start a new trend: black Jordans with a suit."

"It don't look too bad," Richard said, looking down at his Jordans. They turned to each other and gave each other a high-five.

"Now let's go and show them how two twenty-first century brothers roll," Jerome said as he pulled on his coat collar. They headed out the door with plenty of swagger in their step.

They walked into the dining area. There were only a couple of women still doing some final touchups. Mrs. Edward was sitting down, having a cup of coffee. They could see a calmness about her, and she looked like the lady they had come to know.

"Damn," Jerome said, surveying the area. "Is this the same place we eat at?"

Richard replied, "You wouldn't think so if you didn't know better. Look at Mrs. Edward; she's back to normal."

They walked over to Mrs. Edward and stood there before her, not saying a word, posing as if they were models auditioning for a job. She looked them both up and down. "Well, aren't you two quite the handsome ones," she said, a little shocked at how well they had cleaned up.

Jerome cleared this throat and held his arms out. "You know this is how we roll."

Mrs. Edward said, "I don't know what that means, but roll on." The three laughed and the they sat down.

Mrs. Edward took a sip of coffee, then pushed her cup up on the table. "Now, when the guests arrive, I want you two to mingle and just talk about the things you are doing here and what you want to accomplish with the children. Also, please discuss how you will be helping with the adult classes."

Jerome and Richard agreed with her plan. Neither of them had any idea of future education goals, but both felt as though they could work their new plan into the conversations while keeping the guests entertained.

A few moments later, Pastor Edward walked up to the table. "Well, hello," he said as he pulled out a chair and sat down. The pastor clapped his hands together. "Now, how can I help? What can I do?"

"There is nothing you need to do, dear," Mrs. Edward said. "Everything is under control. You should go get ready; the guests will start arriving soon."

"Are you sure?" he asked, trying to look concerned.

Mrs. Edward put her hand on his. "I'm sure. I just want you to be ready when the guests start to arrive." Her outwardly calm demeanor betrayed the possibility of great anticipation and anxiety beneath, but only because the boys had seen her stressed and demanding earlier in the day.

The pastor got up and pushed his chair under the table. "I guess I will go and get ready then, dear. Thank you for all of your efforts today. By the way, you two clean up real nice."

They nodded their thanks. As the pastor was leaving, Richard leaned over to Jerome and whispered, "You see how Pastor made it look like he wanted to help?"

"Now that was a smooth move," Jerome whispered back.

Mrs. Edward smiled as he walked away. "He always seems to be nowhere around until all the work is done." She paused for a moment. "That might be for the best because he probably would be too bossy, too demanding, and just drive everyone crazy." She shook her head, then took a sip of coffee.

Jerome and Richard were shocked by what they had just heard, especially after seeing how she had been acting all morning. They looked at each other in surprise, not daring to say a word.

The appointed time finally arrived, and it seemed that everything was set up for the open house. Jerome and Richard were standing around in the dining area, where everything was to start. There were a few of the women around to help serve and a few of the men there to help wherever needed.

"Look at us," Richard said. "If Mrs. Wilkins could see us now, she would be so proud of us that she would be crying."

Jerome replied, "And if the fellas could see us, they would be laughing so hard they would be crying."

"Ain't that the truth," Richard said, shaking his head and laughing.

"Now it's time to get serious," said Jerome. "Our mission today is to find out who has the big money and who we think can help us. We need to keep our eyes watchful and our ears alert and get as much information as we can."

"Then that is what we shall do," Richard said, with an affected air of sophistication, as he held his hand out and Jerome slapped it.

Pastor Edward and Mrs. Edward entered the room, looking like they should be walking down a red carpet. The pastor was standing tall and walking like a proud peacock while Mrs. Edward was looking around to make sure there was nothing that needed a last-minute touch. June and Sarah walked in behind them. Both Jerome and Richard were speechless. They had never seen two young ladies looking quite so beautiful.

Jerome tapped Richard on the shoulder to get his attention. "Remember, be cool when it comes to Sarah and that guy who likes her."

"Don't worry about me". The way June looks tonight, you'd better be worried about some well-to-do guy rolling up on her."

"Come on, man, that's the last thing I'm worried about." Richard could see that Jerome's face did show some concern.

At that moment, the four of them walked over to where Jerome and Richard were standing.

"Things are about to get started," Mrs. Edward said. "Sarah and

June are going to be helping where they are needed." Jerome and Richard could not take their eyes off them. Mrs. Edward, noticing their distraction, cleared her throat to get their attention. "All right, gentlemen, let's remember our purpose today. The pastor and I are going to look around to make sure everything is in order. If people start to arrive, just make them comfortable and let them know that we will be starting shortly."

The four sat down at a table. "You two look stunning," Jerome said to June and Sarah.

"I second that," Richard said. He held his hand out, keeping his eyes primarily on Sarah, while Jerome slapped it. June and Sarah giggled.

"You two don't look too bad yourselves," Sarah said boldly.

June sat up, tall and proud. "Sarah is so kind, she let me borrow this here dress. Ain't it beautiful?"

"Yes it is, and so are you," Jerome said, gazing at her.

"I ain't beautiful," she replied, suddenly feeling very shy. "You is just saying that so as to make me feel good. I is just a dumb, plain slave girl with no book learning." She dropped her head down, ashamed at her brief feelings of pride.

Sarah reached out and put her hand under June's chin, raising her head. "Remember what I told you," she said gently.

"Yes," June said in a low and soft voice.

"Let me hear it," Sarah said supportively as she looked at June with a smile of encouragement.

June smiled back. "You said that I is to think good things about myself, and good things will happen to me."

"That's right," Sarah said. "And if these two handsome gentlemen say good things about you, it must be true." June smiled a real smile as she looked over at Jerome and Richard, whom she trusted and respected. Her posture improved immediately, and Jerome felt relief flood through him at the sight of her change in perspective.

CHAPTER 20

The room was starting to fill up with the affluent members of the community, both Black and White. Sarah was greeting everyone as they walked in, with June close by her side watching everything she did. Pastor Edward and Mrs. Edward were walking around, making small talk with everyone. It was starting out to be a great open house.

"These are the people we have to get to know," Jerome told Richard. "They are the ones that are going to take us from poverty to riches if we end up staying in this time period."

"Doing what?" Richard asked. "We still have no idea what we're going to do."

"That will come," Jerome said as he looked around, trying to figure out who he would approach first.

Isaac came running over to where Jerome and Richard were standing. All out of breath, he tapped Richard on the shoulder and then pointed at the entryway.

"There's your competition," he said, breathing hard.

Jerome and Richard looked at the entryway, and there stood a distinguished-looking, fair-skinned, middle-aged Black man. By his side stood a very sophisticated fair-skinned woman who could very likely pass for White. Standing close to them was a young man around their age who seemed to be giving Sarah a lot of attention.

Isaac said, "That's who you have to compete with: smart, good-looking, and rich." He patted Richard on the back and walked away, shaking his head.

Richard stood there looking at the entryway, not saying a word. "Hey, hey," Jerome said, tapping Richard on the shoulder. "Remember our mission, man. We need to find out who's who. You need to stop looking over there; ain't nothing you can do about that now."

"You're right," Richard said. "I need to get my head in the game."

"Now you're talking; let's do this." Jerome then held his hand out for Richard to give him five.

Jerome, rubbing his hands together, said, "I'm going to talk to pretty boy's pops. He looks like a big dog around here."

Richard pointed to the opposite side of the room where others had gathered. "I'll work that side."

Jerome walked up to where the gentleman was standing with his wife. "Hello, my name is Jerome Thomas. I'm one of the teaching instructors who works with the children and will be helping with the adult classes," he said, holding out his hand to shake the man's.

"I'm Mr. Samuel Barton, and this is my wife Mrs. Frances Barton," the man replied, smiling at Jerome.

"How do you do," Jerome said to Mrs. Barton, smiling respectfully.

Mrs. Barton was surprised at how young he looked to be teaching and not in school. "So you teach the children here?"

"Yes, ma'am," he replied.

"You don't look much older than my son Christopher, who is around here somewhere," she said, looking around.

Mr. Barton said with a chuckle, "You find Sarah and you'll find that boy."

"Sarah is a fine young lady," Mrs. Barton said, "and the way she is helping the young slave girl is most commendable." Mrs. Barton paused for a moment. "There is talk around that two young men helped her escape from Louisiana. Would you happen to be one of those young men?"

"Yes, ma'am," Jerome said proudly.

"That was very commendable and brave. It must have been very difficult making that journey," she said.

"Yes, it was, but thank God we made it," Jerome responded.

"Now she will have the chance she deserves." Mrs. Barton looked at Jerome with a smile. "I can see that you really care for this girl."

Jerome paused, then nodded. "I guess I do, ma'am."

Mr. Barton's face took on a profoundly serious expression. "The reason we donate to this mission is because we know it helps a lot of people. Some of them have escaped from slavery and have nowhere to go. We have been very blessed and feel it is our God-given duty to give back and help where we can."

While talking, Mr. Barton glanced down at Jerome's shoes, commenting, "I have never seen such foot attire." Jerome raised his pants leg up to give Mr. Barton a better look. "The shoes have Air Jordan written on them. What does that mean?"

"I'm glad you asked," Jerome said. "Let me tell you the story of the shoe…"

"Excuse me," Mrs. Barton said. "I'm going to let you two talk and I'm going to mosey on over to where the other ladies are. It was nice meeting you, Jerome. I hope to see you again."

Jerome smiled at Mrs. Barton. "It was nice meeting you too, and I'm sure we will see each other again."

"All right, all right, now what about these shoes?" Mr. Barton asked impatiently.

"Well, sir, my partner, the other young man who helped June escape from Louisiana, and I came up with this shoe. You see, my grandfather had a problem with his feet, and wearing shoes hurt his feet so bad that at times he could hardly walk." Barton listened intently. "Before his foot problem, he was a very active man. He enjoyed working and helping in the community. He was a proud man who loved his independence. When his feet started giving him problems and he was not able to do the things he loved doing, we saw a change in his attitude," Jerome said, watching Mr. Barton's face as he explained how the shoes had come to be. "He seemed to just give up on everything. We did notice that when he was barefoot, his feet did not bother him as much, so we came up with the idea that it had to be the shoes. We brainstormed and came up with the idea of this shoe. We took our idea to a shoemaker, and he made a pair for my grandfather to try out, and it solved the problem. My grandfather loved the shoes so much that I had a pair made for my partner and myself." Jerome was quite pleased with himself and the story he'd told.

"Unbelievable," Mr. Barton said. "This could be a big moneymaker. I'm always looking for ways to make money. Did you have many of these shoes made?"

"Just the three pair," Jerome said. He did not want Mr. Barton to think the shoe was already out in the market. "Before we could have any more made, the shoemaker was found dead. Our goal was to market the shoes because we thought it would be a big moneymaker too. Before we could get things going, we ended up helping June escape, and here we are now," he finished.

"Why do you have the words Air Jordan on the shoe?" Mr. Barton asked.

Jerome had to think quickly; he knew he could not tell him the shoes were named after a famous basketball player. "I'm glad you asked that," he began. "You see, my grandfather's name was Jordan, and when he put the shoes on for the first time, he said it was like walking on air, so in his honor we named them Air Jordans," Jerome said.

"Well, Jerome, I have a proposition for you that I think will benefit us both," said Mr. Barton. "I would like to invite you and your partner to dinner tomorrow and we can discuss it."

"Sounds good, Mr. Barton. My partner and I would love to have dinner with you tomorrow."

"I will send a carriage around six to pick you two up."

"That might be a problem," Jerome said. "Since we are working here, you will have to work it out with Pastor Edward and Mrs. Edward."

"You don't worry about that. I will talk to them before I leave," replied Mr. Barton.

"Well, Mr. Barton, I think I have taken up enough of your time. I have enjoyed this talk and look forward to seeing you tomorrow," said Jerome, extending his hand.

"The pleasure was mine," Mr. Barton said as he shook Jerome's hand.

As Jerome turned around and walked away, he gave a small fist pump. "Yes," he said in a low voice.

Jerome, excited by how the meeting had gone, went looking for Richard. He saw Richard coming in the entryway of the dining area. "Where have you been?" Jerome asked.

"I've been showing some of the guests the classroom," replied Richard. "They wanted to see the class and find out what the kids are learning. You see, while you are running around doing nothing, I'm out here working."

Not saying anything, Jerome put on an ear-to-ear grin.

"What's with the silly grin? I don't think we have anything to smile about," Richard said dejectedly as he looked across the room and saw Sarah and June talking with Christopher.

Jerome saw where Richard was looking. "There you go again, getting upset about Christopher talking to Sarah."

"So you guys are on a first-name basis?" Richard asked.

"I haven't met him, but his parents told me his name, and the way they put it, he is stuck on Sarah."

June looked up and saw Jerome and Richard. She smiled and with enthusiasm waved them over. Jerome looked at Richard. "Let's go meet your competition."

"Like I really want to meet him," Richard scoffed.

"You might as well meet him since we're having dinner with him and his parents tomorrow." Jerome started heading over to where they were standing.

"What are you talking about?" Richard asked in a low, puzzled voice.

"I'll tell you about it later. Just go with it."

Jerome and Richard walked up to the girls. June gave them a big hug and with a big smile she introduced them. Richard asked Sarah, "How are you doing?"

She smiled and said, "Fine."

Christopher could see that there was something between them, and it did not sit well with him. He looked Jerome and Richard up and down in a snobbish way. "So, these are the two that everyone is making a big deal about because they helped you escape," he said critically.

June could not see that he was not giving them a compliment. "Yes, and I is so grateful fo' what they done fo' me," she said, beaming.

Sarah, however, was not pleased with Christopher's attitude and his disrespect toward Jerome and Richard, and gave him a glaring look. "If you will excuse me, I have some things to do," she said shortly, then turned around and walked away.

"Wait, Sarah," Richard said, going after her.

"Forget her," Christopher said, storming off.

June was confused at what had just happened. "Did I say something wrong?"

Jerome looked at her with a smile. "No, of course you didn't."

"So why is everybody going off like they is mad?"

"I will explain it to you later. Let's sit down. I have some good news to tell you," he said, trying to redirect her attention.

They sat down at a nearby table. Jerome grabbed her by the hand. "Christopher's father, who is a very wealthy man, wants to meet with me and Richard to talk about a business deal. If this deal works out, it should make us a lot of money and we can get you out of this place," he said enthusiastically.

"That's nice," June said as she gave Jerome a half smile.

"I thought you would be happy," Jerome said with a puzzled look.

"I is happy fo' you," she said softly.

"This would be for you too."

June hesitated for a moment. She spoke earnestly and carefully. "I like it here. I is learnin' and Sarah, she is my friend and she is helping me with my learnin'. I love working in the kitchen. When I is working in the kitchen, it reminds me of my mama."

Jerome smiled, relieved because he now understood her mixed emotions. She did not want to leave the only positive thing that she had going in her life, and she didn't want to leave a connection that she felt with the memory of her relationship with her mother. "Don't worry, you don't have to stop working or learning here, and Sarah will always be your friend. With enough money, you can have your own place and maybe we can buy your mother's freedom one day too," he said happily.

June was so stunned with what she had just heard that she put her hands over her mouth. "Do you think that could happen?"

"It's possible; all we can do is try."

June hugged him around the neck. "I love you, Jerome," she said in a low, gentle voice. Jerome, surprised and not knowing what to say, just hugged her back.

Richard and Sarah walked over to Jerome and June and sat down. "I'm sorry about how Christopher treated you, Jerome," Sarah said apologetically. "Just because he is rich doesn't mean that he has any reason to treat you the way he did."

"Ain't no one thinking about Christopher and his insecurities. Why do you think you have to apologize for him?" Jerome responded.

Sarah smiled. "That's precisely what Richard said you would say."

June looked very puzzled. "What is insecurities?" she asked, as she had a hard time pronouncing the word.

Richard looked at Jerome. "Sit back and let me explain this." Jerome leaned back in his chair and stretched his hand out to Richard as if to say, "Go for it."

Richard, with a more intellectual affectation, said, "You see, if a person has insecurities, then he has a lack of self-confidence or he has self-doubt in something."

June looked over at Sarah first, then at Jerome, more puzzled than before Richard had explained it to her. Jerome started laughing.

"If you think you can explain it better, go right ahead," Richard said as he leaned back in his chair.

Jerome paused for a moment. "Okay, let me explain it with an example. You see, Christopher likes Sarah, and he is worried that Richard likes her too. Now he is worried that Sarah may start to like Richard more than she likes him, which is making him insecure," he explained.

"Oh, I see," said June, "he is thinking Sarah gon' like Richard more than she likes him."

"There you go," Jerome said, spreading his hands out. "That is what *insecurities* means." Richard dropped his head, not wanting to look up at Sarah, who had a blushing smile on her face.

Sarah turned to June. "Looks like things are ending with the open house, so maybe we should go and help with the cleanup." They stood up, followed by Jerome and Richard. June gave Jerome a big hug and Sarah smiled as they walked away.

Richard gave Jerome a playful shove. "Man, why you front me out like that?"

"You know you like that girl, and I can tell she likes you, so I just helped you out. You should be thanking me," he said triumphantly.

Richard smiled. "She didn't disagree with what you said, and did you see that smile she gave me when she left?"

"I think she was smiling at both of us," he replied.

"That may be true, but June only hugged one of us. What's with that? Looks like you been busy."

"She was just happy because I explained to her what *insecurities* meant."

"Yeah, right," Richard said.

"Okay, enough girl talk," Jerome said. "I need to fill you in on what's going on."

"Yeah, what is this dinner with old boy's family tomorrow?" Richard asked.

"You see while you were playing teacher and having open house, I was out there making deals," Jerome said.

"What kind of deals?" Richard gave Jerome a suspicious look.

"When I was talking to old boy's pop, he looked down at my Jordans and said he never seen such foot attire."

"Foot attire?" Richard said, laughing.

"Yeah, it took everything within me not to laugh. So I told him that me and you came up with this shoe because my grandfather had foot problems and this shoe helped him. I told him that we named them Air Jordans because my grandfather's name is Jordan and he said it was like walking on air when he wore them." Jerome was nearly laughing as he relayed the story.

"He bought that crap?" Richard asked.

"Hook, line, and sinker," Jerome said. "He bought it so much that he wants to invest in the shoe and wants to discuss it over dinner. That's why we are having dinner over at his house tomorrow, so you need to be cool with home boy when we get there. You can't worry about what happened today."

"Don't worry," Richard said. "I think him seeing me sitting at his table and eating his food will be payback enough for me."

Mrs. Edward walked up to the table where Jerome and Richard were sitting and sat down. "Well, gentlemen, the open house was a great success, and you two were the talk of the day."

"Why is that?" Jerome asked.

"Everyone is impressed with what you are doing with the children.

Richard, everyone was very impressed with how you presented your mission for the children," she said gratefully.

"Thank you," Richard said.

"And Jerome, everyone was very impressed with you, especially Mr. Barton. He gave the biggest donation that he has ever given. As a matter of fact, this is our biggest donation to open house ever, and I think you two had a lot to do with this. All everyone talked about was how you helped June escape from slavery." Mrs. Edward was positively glowing.

"We are happy for the mission, and grateful for the opportunities that you've given to all of us," Jerome said as he looked at Mrs. Edward and held his hand out toward Richard, who slapped it.

"Okay, gentlemen, Mr. Barton asked if you can take tomorrow evening off because he invited you to dinner. He would not tell me what it is about, only that it has something to do with a business deal," said Mrs. Edward.

Richard looked at Jerome. "This is your deal; you explain it."

"It's too early to talk about it now," Jerome said. "Hopefully after tomorrow we will know more. All I can say is that if everything works out, it will be a great financial benefit to us, and in turn we will be able to help the mission."

Mrs. Edward stood up and gave a heavy sigh. "Well, I hope everything works out for you. Now, I'm going to go and relax for the rest of the day. You two need to go and get some rest. Looks like you have a very busy day tomorrow," she said.

Jerome and Richard smiled, and Mrs. Edward walked away slowly, tired from the long day. Jerome stood up. "Let's get out of here."

CHAPTER 21

The next morning came and everything seemed to be back to normal. Jerome and Richard made their way to the dining area. People were eating and conversing, but most noticeable was that the laughter was back, which was a far cry from the day before. June was in the kitchen area, working with a look of enjoyment on her face. It seemed as though she felt right at home. She saw Jerome and Richard and waved and smiled, then eagerly went back to what she was doing.

"Man, that girl loves to work. I have never seen anyone so happy to be working in a kitchen," Richard said.

Jerome kept his eyes on June. "She said she thinks about her mother when she is working in the kitchen."

Richard looked at Jerome, then shook his head. "Boy, she got her hooks in you. Look at you, looking all silly. I wish I had a camera."

Just then Sarah walked from the back area of the kitchen and started talking to June. Richard seemed to be in awe. "Now who looks silly?" Jerome said. Richard hunched his shoulders and they both started laughing.

Breakfast was coming to an end and everyone was headed out to their daily jobs. June and Sarah walked over to where Jerome and Richard were siting. They stood up and pulled the chairs out so June and Sarah could sit down.

"No school today?" Richard asked Sarah.

"Mrs. Edward thought it would be a good idea if I stay here and help out since yesterday was hard on everyone," she said. "After we finish here, June and I are going to work on her reading. She's really getting good."

"Before long, you will be teaching the little ones," Jerome told June.

June smiled back at him. "I hope you is right."

Jerome stood up. "Well, ladies, the little minds await, so off we go." Jerome and Richard were headed to the classroom. Richard kept looking back as he walked. Jerome turned his head straight. June and Sarah started giggling.

They made it to the classroom, and the children were sitting straight up in their chairs with their hands on the table. Jerome looked at Richard. "Mrs. Wilkins would love to be teaching these kids instead of the hardheads she has to deal with every day."

"You do know you are the head of the hardheads, right?" Richard quipped back.

Jerome's lighthearted expression took on a serious look. "That will change if I ever get home."

They worked through the day with their minds on what dinner would be like at the Bartons'. During lunch they went over everything that they thought he would ask them, to make sure that they made a good impression. When the day ended, they headed back to the room to get ready for the dinner.

Isaac came into the room and walked over to where Jerome and Richard were getting dressed. "Look at you two; you can't be going to eat in the dining area. You do know it don't look like it did yesterday," he said to them.

Richard put his hands on the lapel of his suit coat and in his snobbish voice responded, "We are dining at the Bartons' tonight, where we'll be discussing an important business deal."

Isaac said in a woeful voice, "Looks like you two are going places, and it won't be long before you'll be out of here."

Jerome could see that the look on Isaac's face was saying "Why not me?" Jerome put his hand on Isaac's shoulder. "If things work out the way we would like them to, we're going to need a righthand man. We will need someone to show us around and to help us with the ways around here, and we would like that man to be you," he offered.

Isaac's expression changed from one of woe to one of excitement. "I'm your man!" he said enthusiastically. "Now, I'm going to dinner where the plain folk eat. Good luck," he said, and headed out the door.

Jerome and Richard were waiting out front for the carriage when Mrs. Edward walked up. "Looks like you two are ready for your big dinner at the Bartons'."

Jerome looked down where the carriage would be approaching. "Mr. Barton said he would send a carriage at six, and I believe in punctuality, ma'am."

Astonished by what he was hearing, Richard looked over at Jerome. "When did punctuality become one of your characteristics? I see you got jokes."

"Well, good luck you two." Mrs. Edward walked away with a smile.

A few minutes later a fancy carriage, pulled by a magnificent horse that was stepping like it was in a parade, approached. The driver pulled the horse to a stop as he sat tall in his uniform. "This must be the Cadillac of carriages," Jerome said, holding up his hand, waiting for Richard to give him a high-five.

The driver looked down at them. "Are you the gentlemen who will be dining at the Bartons' this evening?"

"That shall be us," Jerome said grandly. They stepped into the carriage, amazed by how plush it was.

"We shall be there in approximately fifteen minutes," the driver said curtly. He snapped the reins, causing the horse to trot slowly away.

Richard was looking around the carriage and feeling the seat they were sitting on. "This dude must be a big baller."

"That's why we can't screw this up, so you need to be cool when it comes to his spoiled brat of a son," Jerome said.

Richard saluted Jerome. "I got this, I'll be cool. Besides, I want this as much as you."

They pulled up to a grand estate, something that they had only seen on television in the old movies. "Well, here we are. Let's do this," Jerome said before they got out of the carriage.

The driver looked down at them. "Just knock on the door and someone will let you in. I'll be around later to take you back."

Jerome saluted the driver; then they walked up to the door and knocked using the big doorknocker. Moments later, a sharply dressed Black gentleman came to the door.

"Good evening, gentleman," he said in his proper voice. "Mr. Barton is expecting you. Please come in." He led them into the house and to the den. "Have a seat. Mr. Barton will be with you momentarily."

They sat there, looking around the room at the fine art on the walls and the sculptures displayed throughout the room. Richard's mouth and eyes were wide. "Mr. Barton rolling like Bill Gates!"

"Lower your voice," Jerome said.

Mrs. Barton walked into the den. Jerome and Richard stood up. "Good evening, gentlemen. Dinner will be served shortly. Mr. Barton is in a meeting, but he shouldn't be much longer," she said.

"We don't mind waiting," Jerome said. "By the way, this is my partner, Richard Wilson," he said, gesturing at Richard.

"How do you do," Richard said with a smile.

Mrs. Barton smiled back. "I am doing fine, and it is a pleasure to meet you. You gentlemen relax while I go and check on dinner." She swept out of the room, leaving them waiting for Mr. Barton.

After several minutes, Mr. Barton walked into the den, and Jerome and Richard stood up again. "Hello, gentlemen. Sorry to keep you waiting. I had a business meeting that took a little longer than expected," he said.

"No problem," Jerome said, "Mrs. Barton explained everything to us. By the way, this is my partner, Richard Wilson."

"It's a pleasure to meet you, sir," Richard said as he held his hand out for Mr. Barton to shake.

"So, this is the other half," said Mr. Barton, appraising Richard.

"Yes, sir," Richard said.

"Nice to meet you," Mr. Barton said. "Let's go eat. I hate to talk business on an empty stomach."

They followed Mr. Barton to the dining room. The dining table was set up like something you would see in a magazine. Above the table was a large, exquisite chandelier that ignited the whole room with bright light that twinkled like stars as it reflected off the crystals. There were two ladies in black-and-white uniforms waiting to serve them.

Jerome and Richard sat down on one side while Mr. Barton sat at the head and Mrs. Barton sat at the other end. Richard leaned over to Jerome. "I told you Mr. Barton is rolling like Bill Gates."

"Calm down," Jerome said in a low voice, trying not to move his lips.

Mr. Barton looked around. "Where is that boy? Christopher!" he hollered. He then looked over at the two ladies. "Could one of you go and get that boy? He knows we eat dinner at this time every day and he shouldn't be late."

"Yessir," one of the ladies said, and quickly dashed out of the dining room.

Mrs. Barton said, "Calm down, he is probably doing something and just lost track of time."

Mr. Barton let out a heavy sigh in frustration. "There you go again. He is never going to learn responsibility if you keep making excuses for him," he said sharply to his wife.

Richard leaned over to Jerome. "I hope this don't mess up our deal."

Christopher came running in the dining room with his head down, tucking in his shirt as he ran. "Sorry I'm late, sir," he mumbled in the direction of his father. He then looked up and saw Jerome and Richard sitting at the table with big smiles, waving at him. Christopher looked over at his mother. "What are they doing here?" he asked.

Mr. Barton replied in a demanding voice, "I invited them and you are being rude with that attitude, so sit down so we can eat." He looked over at the ladies and instructed them to start serving.

Mrs. Barton told Christopher, "These gentlemen are from the mission. They have business to discuss with your father."

"What kind of business would someone who lives in a mission have to discuss with you?" he asked his father, condescension ripe in his voice.

Mr. Barton gave a slight chuckle at his son's abrupt question. "So now you're interested in the business? I have been trying to get you to take an interest in this business for quite some time. Now that two young men your age are here to discuss business, you all of a sudden are interested." He laughed to himself at his son's sudden interest. Christopher shook his head with a look of not caring, then took a drink of water.

Jerome leaned over to Richard so only he could hear. "I see that this spoiled brat needs to be put in his place."

"All right, remember what you told me? You need to take your own advice," Richard replied quietly and calmly.

"Don't worry, I've got this." Jerome turned to Mr. Barton. "Maybe I can explain what you're trying to get him to understand. Hearing it from someone his age may help him see it," he suggested, hoping to appear helpful.

"Good luck," Mr. Barton said as he held his hands up in frustration.

Jerome paused for a moment because he knew he had only one shot to get this right. His only purpose for saying anything was to impress Mr. Barton. He couldn't care less about Christopher.

"You see, Christopher, your father is a very successful man who is respected in the Black community as well as the White community. I observed that yesterday at the open house. It must have taken him quite some time to build that reputation, being a Black man with all the obstacles he has had to endure. Every father's dream is to leave a legacy for his son, but he has to make sure that son is knowledgeable and responsible enough to handle it. It's not that your father is always on you for no reason; he just wants to make sure his future partner is up for the task." He finished and took a sip from the water glass in front of him.

Everything was quiet for a moment. Mr. Barton lit his cigar and took a puff. "Son, this business is for you to one day take over. I just want to make sure you are ready for it."

Christopher sat there, showing no emotion. "He'll come around," Jerome said, trying to give Mr. Barton a positive thought.

Throughout dinner, Jerome and Richard were amazed at the service. They felt like they were in a five-star restaurant. The food was excellent, and the service was like nothing they had ever experienced. If it looked like they needed or wanted something, the server seemed to know it and would make sure it was there.

Dinner was coming to an end and Mr. Barton said, "After a meal like that, it makes discussing business much easier." He patted his stomach appreciatively.

"The meal was great," Jerome said as he patted his stomach and shook his head.

Mr. Barton stood up. "Well, gentlemen, let's go to my office and discuss some business." They were headed to the office when Mr. Barton looked back. "Are you coming, Christopher?"

"No sir, I have some things I need to get done," Christopher responded. He walked away with his head down.

Jerome could see the disappointment on Mr. Barton's face. He patted Mr. Barton on the back. "Don't even worry, sir, he'll come around. He just don't want to do it in front of us."

"I hope you're right," Mr. Barton responded, a look of disappointment flashing across his face.

They went into the office where Mr. Barton sat behind his desk and Jerome and Richard sat in the chairs in front of the desk. He again lit his cigar. "Like a cigar? They are imported, the best in town," he offered. They both said no.

Mr. Barton leaned back in his chair. "From what you told me about this shoe, it could be advantageous to all of us."

Jerome gave Richard a look of approval, then back at Mr. Barton. "I like the sound of that," he said enthusiastically.

"What is the next step to get this moving, sir?" Richard asked. "There is a lot that will need to be worked out."

Mr. Barton smiled. "I like him. He is all about business," he said, reaching out to ash his cigar.

Richard looked Mr. Barton straight in the eye. "This is nothing personal, just business."

Mr. Barton rubbed his chin and paused for a moment. "Well, we will have to work out a contract. I will have my people put it together. Once we agree on the contract, we will have to look into manufacturing and production. But first things first, I will have a contract drafted up and then we can go over it. I think I can have it ready in a couple of days."

"Great," Richard said. "That will give us enough time to look for an attorney."

Mr. Barton pointed at Richard. "Nothing personal, just business," he said. Then the three started laughing.

Mr. Barton stood up and shook both their hands. "I think we have done all we can do today. We will get back together when the contracts are drawn up."

They went out front where the carriage was waiting. "Thanks for everything," Jerome said, "and we look forward to hearing from you soon."

On the ride back to the mission, they could hardly contain their excitement.

"I think overall everything went well," said Jerome.

"Went well?" Richard said in an animated way. "I think it went better than either one of us expected. And the way you handled mama's boy gave us some extra brownie points."

Jerome started snickering. "Like I give a damn if he comes around. We just need him to stay out of our way so he don't mess up what we got going."

"On a serious note, we need to find a lawyer and quick. Mr. Barton is going to have the contract drawn up in a few days, and we won't have a clue what we're looking at."

"That's for sure," Jerome said as he tapped his finger on his knee trying to come up with something. Moments later he looked up. "I got it!"

"What is it?"

"We can ask the pastor. He must have a lawyer to help with the legal things at the mission," Jerome replied.

"Good idea," Richard said as he gave Jerome a high-five.

The carriage pulled up to the mission. Jerome and Richard thanked the driver and headed inside. They went into the room where everyone was relaxing and enjoying the evening.

Isaac walked up to them eagerly before they could even get all the way in the room. "How was it? Did everything work out like you wanted it to? Is that house as nice as people say it is?" he asked breathlessly.

Jerome patted Isaac on the shoulder. "Calm down and catch your breath. Everything went great and that place is not a house, it is a mansion. This place is everything you think it is and more."

Richard shook his head. "This place is unbelievable."

"So am I still going to be your right-hand man?" Isaac asked, hoping they had not changed their minds.

Jerome smiled. "Don't worry, we're going to need you. When we get a few more things worked out, we will let you in on what we are doing."

Isaac gave a sigh of relief. He shook their hands and walked away with confidence that he was going to be a part of what they were doing.

CHAPTER 22

When the next morning came, Jerome and Richard were so excited that they headed straight to the pastor's office before breakfast. They knocked on the door and the pastor waved them in. "What can I do for you two this early in the morning?" he asked, looking up from his desk.

Richard gave Jerome a slight shove as if to say, *You ask him.* Jerome looked down at the pastor at his desk. "Remember when we first got here you said that if there was anything you could do for us, just ask?"

The pastor, shaking his head, replied, "Yes, I remember. Is there something you need help with?"

Jerome could see the concern on the pastor's face. At that moment, he felt the pastor's sincerity, which made him feel comfortable in asking. "You see we need a lawyer, and we figure since you and Mrs. Edward run this mission, you must know one."

"Mrs. Edward told me that you two had some kind of business meeting with Mr. Barton. Is this why you need a lawyer?"

"Yes, sir," Jerome said.

"Mr. Barton is a very important man in the community. He would not waste his time on something he did not believe would benefit him. If he is willing to give you some of his time, he must believe in what you're offering." The pastor paused for a moment. "I do have to go into town on some business. I will stop by the lawyer's office and let him know that you would like to use his services."

"Thank you, thank you," Jerome said as he shook the pastor's hand intensely.

"Thank you, sir," Richard said. All excited and exchanged high-fives as they left his office. The pastor, not knowing what to make of that, just smiled and shook his head with a bewildered look.

They headed to the dining area to get breakfast before the meal ended. Moments later, Isaac came over with his breakfast and sat down. "So, when are you going to tell me what you got going on with Mr. Barton? Since I'm going to be your right-hand man, don't you think I need to know?"

Jerome looked over at Isaac. "Things are still in the works, but once we have all the details worked out, we will fill you in. You will have a very important part in helping us make this work."

Isaac felt good as he sat there and ate his breakfast, even if he didn't have all the details.

They finished their breakfast and headed to the classroom, where the children were eagerly waiting. Jerome and Richard passed out the morning lesson, and before long, the children were quietly working. One little boy raised his hand, so Jerome walked over where he was sitting. "Do you have a question?" he asked.

The little boy looked up at him. "How did you get to be so smart?"

Jerome could see that the little boy was very eager for his answer. He paused for a moment to make sure the answer he gave would be meaningful and useful.

"The first thing you have to do is take your learning seriously. Education is very important. It is the one thing that no one can ever take from you. You have to pay attention in class, do all your lessons, work hard, and never give up. If you do those things you will become successful and smart," Jerome said.

The little boy took everything he said to heart. "I'm going to do everything you said because I know that's what you did to get smart, and I want to be just like you." He gave Jerome a smile, then lowered his head and went back to his lesson. Jerome could see that the little boy believed every word he said. He felt like a hypocrite knowing everything he told the little boy was the exact opposite of what he did in school every day.

After the school day ended and all the children had left for the day, Jerome and Richard were straightening things up before leaving when the pastor walked in. "I'm glad I caught you," he said.

"What up?" Jerome asked. The pastor shook his head in confusion. Jerome smiled. "I mean to say, what can we do for you?"

"Isaac is heading into town with a load of produce to drop off at the local store. I told him that you needed a ride into town to meet with a lawyer. You can help him unload the wagon and then he will take you to his office, but you need to hurry. He needs to leave soon," the pastor directed.

"Thanks, Pastor," Jerome said excitedly.

Richard pushed the last chair under the table. "We're done. Let's go." They high-fived and ran out the door.

The pastor stood there with a bizarre look on his face. He whispered to himself, "I don't know about those two, but I have a feeling when they put their mind to something, they will get it done."

Jerome and Richard helped Isaac secure the produce in the wagon and were soon on their way. Jerome and Isaac sat up front while Richard sat in the back, close to the front on one of the crates. Isaac looked over at Jerome. "So you're going to see the lawyer after we unload?" he asked.

"Yeah, we need to talk to him about some business."

"Does this have anything to do with your meeting with Mr. Barton?"

"It has everything to do with it," said Richard, leaning closer. "We need some legal advice before we can move forward with our plan."

"Is everything okay? You are still going forward with everything, right?" Isaac asked in a concerned voice.

Jerome gave Isaac a pat on the back. "Don't worry, everything is going as planned."

"Oh, I'm not worried, I just wish I knew what the plan is," repeated Isaac.

"In due time," Jerome said.

When they arrived at the store, an elderly White man came out. In a prickly, scratchy voice he said, "I see you brought some help. Maybe you can get this stuff unloaded quickly this time."

"Yes, sir," Isaac said. The elderly White man then started looking over the produce and making comments of displeasure.

Richard walked over to the man. "Hello, my name is Richard." The elderly White man looked at Richard, grunted, then went back to looking over the produce.

Isaac pulled Richard away from the man. "It's best to stay out of his way," he said in a low voice. Jerome, leaning against a post, started laughing and shaking his head.

"So, you think that's funny?" said Richard in an unpleasant voice.

"My bad," Jerome said as he tried to hold back the laughter.

A little Black boy about nine or ten years old came out the door with a broom in his hand with his eyes glued on Jerome. The boy appeared to be fascinated at the way he was dressed, the way he talked, and the way he leaned against the post with poise and confidence. "What's up, little man?" Jerome said as he gave him a head gesture.

The little boy stood there in awe not saying a word. The elderly White man turned around and walked over to where Jerome and the little boy were standing. "What the hell are you doing out here? I don't pay you to stand around," he snapped. He then slapped the boy across the face. The force of the slap knocked the boy to the ground. He got up quickly holding his face, not saying a word, and ran back in the store.

Jerome turned to the elderly White man. "What the hell was that for?"

The man was shocked, at a loss for words. He had never had a Black person talk to him like that.

Isaac quickly pulled Jerome away and whispered in his ear. "Are you crazy? You can't talk to White people like that. Let me handle this."

Isaac walked over to the elderly White man. "Sorry, sir, they're new around here."

The man poked his finger in Isaac's chest. "You best explain to them how things work around here," he threatened.

"Yes, sir," Isaac said.

"Now get this stuff off this wagon and put it in the store." He turned around and headed back into the store.

"Yes, sir, right away, sir," Isaac said.

The three unloaded the wagon and put everything in the back of the store. Isaac handed the storeowner the invoice of everything that had been delivered. He looked the invoice over, signed it, and handed it back to him. When they left the store, Jerome could see the little boy looking at him. Jerome smiled with a head gesture and the little boy smiled back, then started sweeping again.

"What's with you and the boy?" Richard asked.

"He knows greatness when he sees it," Jerome said with a boastful tone.

"Well, he should have been looking at me," Richard countered.

Jerome gave Richard a shove. "Get your butt in the back of the wagon."

As they headed to the lawyer's office, everyone was quiet for several minutes until Isaac spoke up. "I didn't mean to be so tough back there, but you don't know how many people could have been affected by the way you spoke to that man."

Jerome looked over at Isaac. "He's just lucky I didn't put my foot up his butt."

Isaac shook his head. "And that would have been the biggest mistake you would have made in your life."

"Why is that?" Jerome asked, unconcerned.

Isaac shook his head in frustration. "You just don't get it."

"Get what?" Richard said from the back. "Tell us what we don't get, because all I saw was a White man putting his hands on a little Black boy. Where we come from, that White man would have got his butt kicked."

"You two can't be from Louisiana, because if you was to do what you did down there, you would be hung." Isaac gave them a suspicious look. "So where *are* you from?"

Jerome looked back at Richard, then at Isaac. "You would not believe it if we told you."

Isaac stopped the wagon in front of the lawyer's office. "Now let me explain how bad this could have been if I did not step in. Pastor Edward and Mrs. Edward could have lost their business with the store, and that income is used to help run the mission. They could have lost other business because the storeowner knows other business owners who he could influence to stop doing business with them. The little boy could have lost his job, and his family is probably depending on that money to live on. And next year at the mission open house, the donations could be a lot less. So, what you do and say just don't affect you, it affects others also."

Jerome and Richard sat there quiet for a moment. They felt like Mrs. Wilkins was giving them one of her lectures. Moments later Isaac said, "I hope this don't affect me being your right-hand man."

Jerome looked at Isaac. "Oh, it does affect it."

Isaac dropped his head. Jerome glanced at Richard, and they both smiled. Jerome said in a stronger voice, "It affects it, all right. It let us know that we need you more than ever."

Isaac's head rose. "You mean you still want me as your right-hand man?" he asked hopefully.

"More than ever," Jerome said.

Richard tapped Isaac on the shoulder to get his attention. "There is so much we need to learn about living here, and we need you to keep us straight. Don't ever feel like you can't tell us when we're doing something wrong; that is what a right-hand man is for."

Isaac smiled. "Yeah, right-hand man. I'm going to be the best right-hand man ever."

Jerome and Richard went into the lawyer's office while Isaac stayed outside with the wagon. The office was very modest and did not give the impression of much success. There was a desk, a file cabinet, and a table that had several chairs around it.

A tall, slim man stood up from the desk. "How may I help you?"

Jerome reached out to shake his hand. "My name is Jerome Thomas, and this is Richard Wilson. We're from the mission, and Pastor Edward said you would meet with us."

"Oh yes, let's sit down. The pastor said you would be coming by." The three sat down at the table. "My name is Ramon Foster. How can I help you?"

Jerome rubbed his hands together and looked over at the lawyer. "You see, we are starting a business venture with someone and we need you to look at the contract to make sure it is in our best interests. Now, we can't pay you up front, but if everything goes well with this venture, we will be able to pay."

The lawyer, rubbing his chin, said, "I don't believe I can help you without a percentage of the fee up front. You see, with expenses and all, I will need something up front."

Jerome had a disappointed look on his face. "We don't have any money, but if this deal goes through, we will be able to pay," he said, desperately.

"I wish I could help, but without something down I can't help you," said the lawyer.

Jerome stood up. "We appreciate your time."

As they were leaving Richard turned to Jerome. "You know Mr. Barton is going to have the contract ready in a few days. Now what are we going to do?"

"I don't know, we'll have to find another lawyer and fast."

The lawyer quickly stood up. "Wait," he said as he headed for the door before they could leave. "Did you say Mr. Barton?"

"Yes," Jerome said.

"He's the person you're doing the business venture with?" the lawyer asked.

"Yeah, but we need a lawyer," Jerome said, shaking his head in disappointment.

"Let's sit back down," he said as he went over and pulled their chairs back out.

The three sat down and Jerome and Richard could see a different attitude from the lawyer.

"I have been trying to get an audience with Mr. Barton for quite some time," Mr. Foster said, looking slightly embarrassed.

"Hold on," Jerome said, holding his hand up. "You will be working for us and not Mr. Barton."

"I know, I know, but if he sees what a good job I do for you, maybe I will get a chance to handle some of his business," said the lawyer.

Jerome asked, "So you will take us on without any fee up front then?"

"Absolutely, I will."

Jerome gave Richard a high-five. The lawyer seemed confused, not understanding what they had just done. He then went back to the business at hand. "When you get the contract, don't sign it. Bring it straight to me and I will go over it and explain everything to you."

"Sounds good," Jerome said.

As they left the office, the lawyer hollered, "Don't forget to bring it straight to me!"

"How did it go?" Isaac asked when they returned to the wagon.

"It went great," Jerome said as he climbed in the wagon.

"We're on our way," Richard said.

"Well, let's go." Isaac said snapped the reins, causing the horse to start a slow trot. On their way back to the mission, they passed the store where they unloaded the produce. Richard could see Christopher leaving the store. They gave each other a look of mutual displeasure.

CHAPTER 23

Several days had passed while Jerome and Richard waited impatiently for the contract from Mr. Barton. One evening, they were sitting down and having dinner with June and Sarah when the pastor came over to their table.

"Good evening. This envelope from Mr. Barton came for you two," he said, handing the envelope to Jerome.

"Thanks," Jerome said with a big smile.

"I hope it is the good news you been waiting for," said the pastor.

Sarah looked over at Jerome and Richard. "An envelope from Mr. Barton? It must be very important."

"Is you gon' open it?" June asked, eager to know what was in the envelope.

Jerome opened the envelope and slowly pulled the paper out and looked at it.

With a big grin he handed it to Richard. "It's the contract!" Richard said as he jumped up from his chair.

"A contract?" Sarah asked.

Richard boasted, "We're entering into a business venture with Mr. Barton."

June, confused, asked, "What is a contract and what is a business venture?"

"A business venture means that we are going into business with Mr. Barton, and the contract explains the conditions of the business," Jerome explained. He could see that June was still confused. He then said in an uplifting voice, "It means if everything goes right, you will be able to enjoy some of the finer things in life as you so deserve."

The look on her face was not what Jerome expected. He thought this would make her very happy. The only expression she showed was one of sadness.

"What's wrong?" Sarah asked with concern, noticing June's reaction. "This should make you very happy."

June's eyes swelled with tears. With a half smile, she said, "I is happy, but I is sad too, 'cause my mama is suffering while everything is going good fo' me."

Sarah smiled at June and wiped the tears from her cheeks. "If your mama knew how good thing are going for you, she would be very happy."

"But she don't know how good I is," June said, dropping her head. Sarah gave her a hug.

"Hey, hey," Richard said as he reached over and patted June on the shoulder. "Do you remember what I told you before we got off the train?"

"Yeah, I think so," she replied, sniffling.

"I said you will make your mama proud by doing something good with your life, and someday you will see her again. So keep doing what you're doing, and I promise you will see her again," he said reassuringly.

June looked up and smiled. She then turned to Sarah. "Can we go study? It makes me feel better when I is studying," she said.

"Sure." Sarah helped June up, putting her arm around her as they walked away.

Jerome looked over at Richard. "That was nice, what you said to June. We should make that happen."

"Make what happen?" Richard asked.

"When we start making money from this business venture, we should buy her mother's freedom," he said.

"So, let me get this straight; we should go back to the plantation we helped June escape from and walk up to the owner and say we want to buy her mother? You done lost your mind, man."

"No, we don't go back there. We hire some White guy to go down there and buy her," Jerome said thoughtfully.

"That could work," Richard said. "What do you have in mind?"

"The first thing is, we don't tell June what we're planning to do, just in case we can't make it happen. We don't need to get her hopes up, then find out we can't make it happen. I also was thinking we should ask Pastor Edward and Mrs. Edward about that rundown house not too far from theirs. We could get it fixed up for her and her mother," Jerome said.

"Sounds like you put some thought into this," Richard said.

"It has been on my mind ever since we got here. I don't think she will be completely happy until she and her mother are back together."

"So let's make it happen," Richard said, clapping his hands together.

"Let's do it!" Jerome exclaimed. "The first thing we need to do is get this business venture on the way, because without the business we can't make anything happen."

The next day Isaac went into town to pick up some supplies. Jerome and Richard rode with him to meet with the lawyer.

"So you have some information for the lawyer?" Isaac asked, hoping to get some information from Jerome and Richard.

"Yeah," Jerome said, "we hope to get this wrapped up today so we can get things moving."

"I guess when you get things wrapped up, you'll let me know what's going on," said Isaac.

Jerome looked at Richard, who was in the back of the wagon. "I guess we can let him in on what we got going on?"

"Yeah, I think it is okay to share now," Richard said, nodding.

Jerome gave Isaac a serious look. "Now, the things we talk about are kept confidential until it's time to let others know," he cautioned.

"Got it," Isaac said with a smile. "So what business are we going into?" Isaac was eager to finally hear what they were doing.

"Shoe business," Jerome said.

"Shoe business?"

"Don't look so disappointed," Jerome said. He put his foot up so Isaac could see it. "Have you ever seen a shoe like this?" Jerome moved his foot around so Isaac could get a good look at the shoe.

"No," Isaac said, shaking his head.

"No one else has seen a shoe like this either," replied Jerome. "Now with Mr. Barton as a partner, we're going to reproduce this shoe and sell them all over the country."

"And make a lot of money," Richard added.

Isaac's outlook became much more positive as he heard more and more about the business. "Whoa," he said, pulling the reins to stop the wagon in front of the lawyer's office. Jerome and Richard got out of the wagon. "When I get the wagon loaded up, I'll come back here and pick you up," said Isaac. He then snapped the reins and headed off.

Jerome and Richard walked in the lawyer's office. When he saw that it was them, he stood up quickly.

"Do you have the contract?" he asked anxiously. Jerome handed him the envelope. Eager to see what was in it, he grabbed it quickly as if to say, "I will get this before they change their minds."

"Damn," Jerome said to Richard. "He snatched that like it was going to run away."

The lawyer pulled the contract out of the envelope. Not taking his eyes off the document, he walked over to the table and sat down. "Have a seat," he said. Jerome and Richard glanced at each other and sat down.

They sat there patiently while the lawyer went through the contract. He did not say a word; he just made strange sounds as he went through each page of the contract. Some of the sounds sounded positive and some sounded negative. Each time Jerome and Richard thought it was a positive sound, they smiled, and each time they thought it was a negative sound, they frowned.

When he finished, he looked up at Jerome and Richard. They sat there breathless, waiting to hear what he had to say. "This is not a bad contract, but there are a few things you may want to consider," the lawyer said.

"We're listening," Jerome said, hoping nothing in the contract would be a deal-breaker.

"The contract gives you thirty percent, which is a little low. I think you should go for forty percent and settle for no less than thirty-five percent. Also, there is nowhere in the contract giving you a voice on how things are run with your product. If we can get those two things worked out, I believe this would be a good contract," said the attorney matter-of-factly.

"Well, what are the next steps to get the ball rolling?" Jerome asked, anxious to move forward.

"We will need to present the changes we want to Mr. Barton."

Jerome stood up. "Well, let's go to his house and get this taken care of."

The lawyer looked at him like he was crazy. "You're just going to go up to his house without an appointment?"

"Absolutely," Jerome said, grabbing the contract and heading for the door. Richard stood up and went to follow him. The lawyer sat stunned for a moment before he got up and followed them.

As they walked out the door, they could see Isaac headed their way. "Good, we don't have to walk," Richard said.

Isaac pulled up. "Y'all ready to go?" he asked.

"Yeah," Jerome said, "but we need to go by Mr. Barton's house first. By the way, this is our lawyer, Mr. Foster. He'll be going with us."

"How do you do, sir?"

"Fine, thank you," Mr. Foster said.

"Isaac will be working with us," Jerome said, climbing into the back of the wagon with Richard.

"I'm the right-hand man," Isaac said with a big smile.

The lawyer smiled back, but had a nervous look on his face, not feeling comfortable going to Mr. Barton's house unannounced.

They pulled up to the Barton house. Jerome and Richard jumped out of the back and the lawyer climbed down from the front.

"Wait for us, Isaac, we shouldn't be long," Jerome said as he led the way.

Jerome knocked on the door and waited patiently for someone to answer. Moments later the butler opened the door and asked, "May I help you?"

"We are here to see Mr. Barton," Jerome said as he took a step forward.

The butler blocked him from entering. "Do you have an appointment?" he asked sternly.

"No, we don't, but we are certain he will see us." Jerome tried to get through the door.

Mr. Foster tapped Jerome on the shoulder. "Maybe we should come back after we set up an appointment," he suggested meekly.

"We're already here. Why would we leave, set up an appointment, and then come back? That don't make sense."

"Who's at the door?" a loud voice asked.

The butler looked back and called, "There are three gentlemen to see you, Mr. Barton."

Jerome stuck his head in the door, against the butler's wishes. "It's Jerome, Mr. Barton."

"Come on in," Mr. Barton hollered as he made his way toward the front door. Jerome looked at the butler as if to say, "I told you we did not need an appointment."

"How are you doing, Mr. Barton?" Jerome asked when they shook hands. "This is our lawyer, Mr. Ramon Foster."

"How do you do, sir?" Mr. Foster asked, holding his hand out nervously.

"Fine, fine," Mr. Barton said, shaking his hand. "Let's go to my office, where we can talk."

They all sat down. Mr. Barton rubbed his chin. "Ramon Foster. I know most of the lawyers in town, but I don't believe we've met," he said.

"We met once and I offered you my services, but you said you did not need another lawyer at that time," replied Foster.

"Anyway," Jerome said, handing Mr. Barton the contract. "There are a few things in the contract our lawyer thinks we should adjust."

"Is that so?" Mr. Barton said. "And what may that be?" he asked, as he thumbed through the contract.

"Our lawyer will explain," Jerome said, tipping his head toward the lawyer. Mr. Barton put the contract down and put his full attention on Mr. Foster.

The lawyer nervously cleared his throat. "Well, Mr. Barton, we believe that thirty percent is a little low and we believe they should have some say in what is done with the product."

Mr. Barton sat there for a moment in deep thought. Jerome, Richard, and Mr. Foster sat there anxiously, waiting to hear something from Mr. Barton, who finally said, "What percentage are we looking at?"

"We're looking in the range of forty percent," their lawyer said and glanced over at Jerome and Richard to get their approval. Jerome and Richard nodded yes.

Mr. Barton let out a heavy sigh. "That's a little high seeing that I am putting up all the money and taking all the risk on this endeavor." He leaned back in his chair and paused for a moment. "I'll tell you what, I will go no higher than thirty-five percent. That's all I can do."

The lawyer looked over at Jerome and Richard with a slight smile, and they both nodded. "Good," Mr. Barton said, "I will have my lawyer make the change."

"The contract will also state that they will be involved in all decision making," said Mr. Foster firmly.

Mr. Barton, realizing that they would refuse to sign the contract without that provision, reluctantly agreed. He reached under his desk and pulled out two pairs of shoes and put them on the desk. "I'm going to need those shoes on your feet. These look like they will fit you." He then pushed the shoes across the desk closer to Jerome and Richard.

Jerome looked at Mr. Barton like he was crazy. "You want me to give up my Jordans for those shoes? You're kidding me, right?"

"Nope, we're going to dissect one pair so we can make our shoe exactly like the original, and we will use the other pair to compare with."

Jerome and Richard reluctantly took their shoes off and put on the shoes that were on the desk.

Mr. Barton stood up. "Looks like things are starting to move forward. Mr. Foster, I will have the changes completed this afternoon for you to go over. If you stop back by around two, they will be ready."

"Sounds good," he said. He looked at Jerome and Richard. "When I get the contract, I will bring it over for you to sign." They all shook hands and left with Jerome and Richard walking funny in their new shoes.

Isaac was lying in the back of the wagon when they came out. He jumped up. "How did it go?"

"It went great." Jerome held his hand up for Richard to give him a high-five. The lawyer looked at Isaac, confused.

Isaac just shook his head. "Get used to it. They are always doing strange things like that," he told the lawyer.

They dropped Mr. Foster off at his office, then headed back to the mission.

When they made it back to the mission, Isaac took care of the horse and wagon while Jerome and Richard went straight to the pastor's office. The pastor was working on some paperwork when they knocked. He waved them in. "What can I do for you two?" he asked.

Jerome asked, "Can we sit down and discuss a few things with you, sir?"

"Sure, sit down. How can I help you?"

They sat down and Richard looked at Jerome as if to say, "You do the talking."

Jerome began. "Do you know who owns the rundown house next to your house?"

"We own it. We just don't have the money or a need to fix it up right now," the pastor responded.

"With this business deal coming up with Mr. Barton, we believe we will have some good money coming in, and we would like to fix it up for June and her mother," Jerome said.

The pastor was surprised. "I thought her mother was a slave living in Louisiana," he said.

"She is," Jerome said. "We plan to buy her and bring her here."

The pastor had skepticism written all over his face.

Jerome sat up in his chair. "Please hear me out. We plan to hire some White guy to go down there and buy her. We haven't worked out all the details yet, but that's the plan. We haven't said anything to June because we don't want to get her hopes up and it don't work out. If we pull it off, it will be a pleasant surprise for her. So please don't let her or Sarah know what's going on."

"That is a very nice thing to do. I will let Mrs. Edward know what's going on," the pastor said.

"Great," Jerome said. "As soon as we get some money, we want to start working on the house."

"Sounds good. Mrs. Edward and I will do whatever we can to help."

CHAPTER 24

As time went by, Jerome and Richard talked less and less about trying to get home. Not having a clue how to get back, they turned their attention to teaching, the shoe business, and getting the house ready for June and her mother.

Isaac was put in charge of hiring and managing the crew to fix up the house. Mrs. Edward was working on furnishings and the plan to decorate the house once it was complete. Mr. Barton, with his connections, was looking into the stability of the plantation. He wanted to see if the plantation was having financial problems, which he believed would make it easier to buy June's mother.

One day, Mr. Barton sent a message asking Jerome and Richard to meet him at his home. The recreation of the shoe was complete. Jerome and Richard were given the first two pairs to try out. They wanted to make sure they felt the same way the pair they gave up had felt before production of the replications had begun. When they gave the okay, production started in earnest and things started moving fast.

They could see why Mr. Barton was a successful businessman. When he set things in motion, things got done. He also listened to their input and implemented their suggestions when he saw the benefit. He told them when their suggestions would not work and explained why.

They learned a lot about business from him, and they both respected him for that.

Isaac was headed into town to get some supplies for the house, so they rode in with him. "How are things going with the house?" Jerome asked.

"Things are going good. We are moving right along," Isaac answered proudly.

"That's good," Jerome said. "We believe Mr. Barton may have some news about moving forward on getting June's mother here, so we need you to stay on top of things."

"Don't worry, I got things under control," he said with confidence. He then snapped the reins to get the horse to move faster.

Isaac dropped them off at Mr. Barton's and then headed to get the supplies. Mr. Barton escorted them to his office. "Have a seat, I think I have some good news," he said, by way of greeting. Jerome and Richard smiled and took a seat. "I think we may have a break. The plantation where June's mother lives is having financial difficulties. That might make it a lot easier to buy her.

"I have a White gentleman who is willing to go to Louisiana and pretend to be a businessman, if the price is right," he continued. "He'll work his way into the plantation and then show an interest in June's mother to be a nanny for his two young children."

"That just might work," Jerome said.

"So, if you two agree, we can put this plan into action," said Mr. Barton.

"Let's do it," Jerome said and gave Richard a high-five.

Mr. Barton walked them to the door. "I'll get the details worked out, and hopefully we will have her mother here real soon." They shook hands and thanked Mr. Barton for all his help and headed out the door. They knew things were going to move fast once Mr. Barton put things in motion. They had to make sure the house was complete before she arrived.

They made their way to the store where Isaac was getting the supplies. They could see that he nearly had everything loaded up. There was a little Black boy about nine or ten in front of the store in raggedy clothing, wearing no shoes and begging for food. Three White boys, who looked to be about his age, were teasing him and calling him names. They chanted, "Dumb poor nigger boy, dumb poor nigger boy," repeatedly as they walked around him kicking dirt on him.

The little Black boy stood there with his head down, a look of defeat on his face, not saying a word. When Jerome saw this, he became very angry and headed over to where the boy stood. Richard grabbed Jerome by the arm. "Maybe we should leave it alone. Things are going good for us and we don't want to mess it up," he cautioned.

Jerome snatched his arm away. "That's the problem. Everyone is afraid to get involved. You go and help Isaac finish loading the wagon. I got this," he said, determined.

"Okay." Richard headed to the wagon.

Isaac looked up as he saw Richard approach without Jerome. "Oh no, here we go again." He started to walk over where Jerome was, but Richard grabbed him before he got there.

"It's no use. I tried to talk him out of getting involved, but he made his mind up, and when that happens there is no stopping him. We might as well go finish loading the wagon," he said. Isaac kept looking back as they loaded up the wagon, hoping the situation did not develop into a bigger problem.

Jerome walked in the middle and put his hand on the Black boy's shoulder. "Are you okay, little man?" he asked. The little Black boy kept his head down and nodded. Jerome then turned to the White boys. "Why are you all teasing him?"

One of the boys said, "He ain't nothing but a dumb, poor nigger."

Jerome had to take a deep breath to keep from saying or doing something he knew he would regret. "So you three are smart, rich

White boys?" he asked. They looked at each other, not saying a word. Jerome put his hand under the Black boy's chin and raised his head up. "Always keep your head up and be proud of who you are, no matter what your situation is," he told the boy. He put his arm around the little Black boy's shoulder, and they walked away. Richard and Isaac, still looking on, sighed in relief.

Jerome walked the little Black boy into the store. He looked over at Richard and Isaac. "I'll be right out." He bought the boy new shoes, a shirt, pants, and plenty of food to take to his house. When they walked out of the store, the little Black boy was in his new clothes with bags of food in his hand. He had the biggest smile on his face. The three White boys' mouths were wide open when they saw the Black boy in his new clothes and shoes. Jerome helped him into the back of the wagon.

They dropped the boy off at his house, which did not look much better than the house they were fixing up. Jerome helped the boy take the food into the house. The condition of the house made him both sick and sad at the same time. He tried not to show his disgust in front of the boy as he looked around. Jerome smiled at the boy. "Tell your mom and dad these things are compliments of the mission." The little boy smiled and thanked him as he rubbed his new shoes on the back of his pants leg to get the dust off.

On the way back to the mission, Jerome said, "I got to admit, I shocked myself on how I handled those three little punks."

"I admit you did have me worried for a moment there," said Isaac.

"Me too," Richard said. "Back home you probably would have kicked those three in the butt."

"Ain't no *probably.* I would have had those little bad butts running home to their mommies. But you know what, I believe I got more satisfaction on the way I handled it."

"And there will not be any backlash," Isaac said, shaking his head.

Richard started laughing. "Did you see the looks on those White boys' faces?" The three started laughing and mimicking how the boys looked.

After they stopped laughing at the expense of the three boys, Jerome took on more of a serious tone. "The most important thing was the look on the little Black boy's face when he came out that store in his new clothes. That was priceless," he said, feeling a surge of pride.

"Yes, it was," Isaac said, "and you handled it without causing any problems that will come back on us or the mission."

"And you made a little boy happy," Richard said.

"That's true," Jerome said, "but I don't know how long it will last. You should see the inside of that house. It's not fit for dogs to live in." He was still concerned.

"But you did give the boy and his family some happiness," Richard said.

"That's true. I told the boy to tell his parents that the food and clothes were compliments of the mission. I think when we get June's mother here, we should start an outreach program to help Black families needing help," said Jerome thoughtfully.

"Look at you, becoming quite the humanitarian," Richard said in a joking way. He snapped his fingers. "We can call it The Mission since our mission is to help Black families in need."

When they arrived back at the mission, Isaac dropped them off and then headed to the house to drop off the supplies and check on how things were moving along. As he was leaving Jerome hollered, "Don't forget we need to get this done quickly!" Isaac, not looking back, raised his hand and shook his head up and down as he rode off.

Jerome and Richard could see Sarah studying with June on the front porch of the house. Richard, astonished, asked, "Do that girl ever get tired of learning?"

"I guess not," Jerome said. "She knows what she wants and is determined to get it. I think she is going to do great things, and I believe we were sent here to help her get in a position to do that."

"You could be right," Richard said, shaking his head.

They walked up to the porch and spoke to June and Sarah. Richard asked June, "Do you ever get tired of learning?"

June smiled. "No, I is happy when I is learnin," she responded. "Mrs. Edward said if I work hard and keep learnin', I can teach someday."

Jerome smiled. "I'm proud of you, and someday you are going to make a great teacher." June smiled and blushed, then lowered her head.

"I see you two went into town with Isaac. Did it have something to do with the business?" Sarah asked.

"Yes, it did," Richard said, trying to sound and look important to impress her.

"Isaac and some other men have been working on that old house. Mrs. Edward said there is someone moving in from out of town. Do you know anything about that?" Sarah asked.

Richard looked at Jerome and they both shook their heads. Richard told Sarah, "I guess we don't know any more than you do." They quickly changed the subject before she asked any more questions about the house.

They headed into the mission to talk with Mrs. Edward to see how things were coming along with the furnishings and decorating. They felt time was running out, and they wanted everything to be perfect when June's mother arrived.

Mrs. Edward was in the dining area having a cup of coffee. "Have a seat. What can I do for you?" she asked, smiling.

"We just want to know how things are going with the furnishings and decorating," said Jerome.

"Everything is going great," Mrs. Edward responded. "I have all the furnishings thanks to all the donations we received. Isaac said he would have the place complete by the end of the week and then we can start moving things in."

"That's great," Jerome said. "Things are moving fast. Mr. Barton has a plan and if everything goes as planned, we should have June's mother here real soon."

"This is a great thing you two are doing. When you first showed up at the mission, the pastor and I were not sure what to make of you, and we are still not sure. What we do know is that the work you do with the children and the donations you have made to the mission from the money you have made from your business with Mr. Barton have been a blessing to this mission," she said gratefully.

"Thank you," Jerome said. "We are grateful to you and the pastor for taking us in when we had no place to go. We believe this mission is our home and you, the pastor, and the people living here are our family, so we are glad to help in any way we can." He smiled. "We also want to start an outreach program. Our mission is to help Black families in need. We want it to be associated with this mission."

Richard piped up, "We even came up with the name: The Mission."

"The name was Richard's idea," Jerome added.

"I like it," Mrs. Edward replied, smiling and thinking of all the possibilities it could have.

"Richard and I feel once we get June and her mother reunited, we want to give this our full attention, and we would like your help," said Jerome.

"I would love to help," she said. "You two are a blessing from God, whether you believe it or not."

CHAPTER 25

Mr. Barton moved quickly on the plan to get June and her mother reunited. He arranged for Jerome and Richard to meet with the gentleman who would be going to the plantation. The gentleman asked Jerome and Richard many questions about the people, the plantation, and about June's mother. They did not have many answers but gave him what little information they knew.

Several days after they talked, he was headed to Louisiana posing as a businessman looking at several investments in the South. After he arrived and got himself settled in his hotel room, he started putting the word out about what he was doing. He went into several businesses and introduced himself, hoping that word would get around that there was a businessman from the East looking for investments. After several days, he felt it was time to make his move.

He went down to the front desk of the hotel. "May I help you?" the desk clerk asked.

"Yes, as a matter of fact, you can. My name is Herbert Lee."

"You are the businessman looking for investments," the clerk replied. "You know, you are the talk of the town."

"Is that so?" he asked, with a surprised look, knowing that that was precisely what he wanted to hear. "Maybe you can help me."

"Sure," the clerk said eagerly.

"Could you tell me how to get to the John Williams plantation?"

"Sure, you take the road at the end of town, turn right, and follow it, and you will run into the Williams plantation. You can't miss it."

"Thank you," he said, then headed to the livery stable to rent a horse and carriage.

When he left the hotel, he could see the clerk run into the business next to the hotel. Moments later, a man ran out and jumped on his horse and headed in the direction he would be traveling. This made him believe that the rider was going to the Williams plantation to give the word that he was on his way there. Confident in his assessment, he waited about an hour before getting the horse and carriage. This would give the rider time to get there with the information.

Herbert headed in the direction of the plantation. He saw a rider headed his way and waved for him to stop. "Hello, sir, could you tell me if I am headed in the right direction to the Williams plantation?"

"Yessir, just stay on this road and you can't miss it."

He thanked the man and rode on at a slow pace. He started thinking about what he was going to say when he got there and how he would bring up that he wanted to buy June's mother.

About thirty minutes later, he arrived at the Williams plantation. As he headed down the long road to the big house, never having been down South, he was astonished at what he saw. There were slaves working all over the grounds, working in the barn, and in the far distance he could see slaves working in the fields. The young children, slaves and White children, were playing together without a care in the world. As he rode by the young children playing, he knew there would be different paths for them. As they enjoyed each other today, he knew there would come a time when that friendship would no longer be there.

He pulled up to the big house, amazed at the size of the place. Posing as a businessman from the East, he tried not to look too overwhelmed. A slave man walked up to him.

"Good afternoon, sir, Master John is expecting you," he said. "You go on in. I will take your horse and have him fed and rubbed down."

When he heard the man say Master John was expecting him, the gentleman knew he was right about the rider who quickly rode out from town.

He walked slowly up the steps of the big house, not knowing what to expect. When he knocked on the front door, a well-dressed slave man opened it. "Good afternoon, sir, I'll take your hat if you'll please follow me." He led him into the parlor. "Have a seat. Master John will be with you in a moment." He then walked away.

Herbert sat there, uncomfortable, not knowing what to expect next. From the size of this place and what he had seen so far, it didn't look like there was a financial problem. But he knew Mr. Barton had done his homework and he had to trust in that. Being down South was a new experience to him. Not understanding the ways of the South, he sat there hoping he did not get in over his head.

Moments later, a slightly overweight man with a rough exterior entered the room. "Hello, Mr. Herbert Lee. I'm John Williams, the owner of this here plantation. I've been expecting you," he said loudly. Herbert stood up and they shook hands.

"How did you know I was coming out here and how did you know my name?" he asked, trying to look surprised.

"When there is a big businessman from back East in town, news travels fast."

"So you know why I am here."

"Yes, I do, but let's not talk on an empty stomach. Let's get some good old southern cookin' in that belly, and then we can talk," Mr. Williams said.

They walked into the dining area, where it was set for a king. Herbert looked stunned at how things looked and how organized it was. There were three slave women, all dressed in white, standing along the wall waiting for instructions. There was a slave man dressed in a black suit and white shirt with white gloves who seemed to be directing everything.

They sat at the dining table, and several people came in. His wife, his sons and their wives, and his daughter and her husband made their way to the table. John introduced everyone. There was small talk as they waited for the meal. Everyone asked a lot of questions about the East. Herbert answered the questions, but the only thing on his mind was how he would bring up the subject of buying June's mother.

The food was served, and Herbert had never tasted anything so good. "This is incredible," he said honestly. "Does all the food taste this good down here?"

Everyone at the table started laughing. John said, "I'm afraid not. We have the best cook in these parts."

Herbert felt that this was his way in. "I would love to meet the cook of this great meal."

John looked toward the kitchen and hollered, "Fannie!" A short and slightly overweight Black woman came running out of the kitchen area.

"Yassuh, Master John," she said, wiping her hands on her apron.

John looked over at Herbert. "This is the best cook in these parts."

Herbert addressed Fannie. "My compliments to you. This is the best meal I have ever had."

"Thank you, suh," she said, making sure not to make eye contact.

"Your family must really enjoy your cooking."

A sorrowful look came over her face. "I don't have a family, suh. My baby June is gone."

"I'm sorry, did she die?"

"No, she ran away," replied Fannie sadly.

"That's enough, Fannie, now back to the kitchen with you," John said forcefully.

"Yassuh," she said, then hurried back to the kitchen. At that moment Herbert knew he had the right person.

After everyone completed their meal, Herbert and John went to the parlor to discuss business. Herbert explained to John that the business he worked for was looking for investments down in the South. He explained that he and several others were looking in several southern states for investment ventures. He explained that whoever the company went with would benefit greatly.

He could see that John was fascinated by the possibilities, knowing that this could be the financial help he needed. John was looking desperate. At that moment, he knew that the information Mr. Barton had given him was correct. He did not want to push too soon, so he told John that he would like to come back out and get a complete tour of his operation. They both agreed that he would come back tomorrow. He then headed back to town.

When Herbert made it back to town, he turned in the horse and buggy, then went to the telegraph office. He sent a telegram to Mr. Barton that stated, *Everything is moving as planned; should have this wrapped up in a few days; will let you know if anything changes.* He was very vague in his message because he did not know how private it would be.

When Mr. Barton received the telegram, he got word to Jerome and Richard right away. They knew things were moving right along with the house, but after receiving word from Mr. Barton, they went to the house to check.

Isaac and Mrs. Edward were arranging the furniture when they walked in.

Jerome looked around. "This looks great." Mrs. Edward smiled and then turned back around and continued to study the dining area.

Isaac walked close by them and whispered, "I must have moved this furniture a dozen times. She is acting almost as bad as she did during the open house." Remembering how that was, Jerome and Richard made a quick exit, leaving Isaac alone with Mrs. Edward.

The next day, Herbert was headed back to the Williams plantation.

All the way there, he was trying to figure out how he was going to bring up the subject of buying June's mother. He arrived without an answer, so he decided to play it by ear and bring it up when he thought the time was right.

John took Herbert all over the plantation and showed him the ins and outs of how the plantation functioned. Herbert was amazed at how many slaves it took to run a plantation. Although he did not believe in slavery, he could see how important the slave was to running a plantation. After the tour was over, they went inside to have some lunch.

John asked, "Well, what do you think of my operations?"

"I am fascinated by what it takes to run a plantation of this size," Herbert responded.

John smiled and leaned back in his chair. "Do you think this is something your people are looking for?"

Herbert gave a heavy sigh. "Let me be perfectly honest, you seem to run a tight ship, but our research shows that you may not be as financially stable as we would want in a business venture."

Herbert was hoping that talking about money would give him the opening he needed to ask to buy June's mother.

John had a desperate look on his face, and Herbert felt he was leading him right where he wanted. "Things have been a little tough, but I believe things will turn around," he said, eager to keep the conversation going.

"Well, what do you think you need to turn it around?" Herbert asked with a sincere look of concern.

"If I had some money to get me through this tough time, I'm sure I could turn this around," John said.

"Did you ever think about a loan from the bank?"

"I'm overextended and they won't give me another loan until I can show that things are stable," John explained.

Herbert felt that this was the time to make his move. "Have you ever thought about selling some of your slaves to raise the money?"

"I need each and every one of them working to get the job done," replied John.

"Not the field slaves, then how about some of the house slaves?" Herbert could see that he was pondering that suggestion. "I got it," Herbert said. "With me on the road a lot, my wife could use some help with the children and around the house. I could buy Fannie and the money I pay you could see you through the hard times. That would make me feel comfortable telling my people you have the funds you need."

John sat there for a moment, rubbing his chin as Herbert patiently hoped his plan would work. "With that money, I could get back on my feet." John paused for a moment. "Nine hundred dollars; for nine hundred dollars you have a deal."

Herbert paused, then held his hand out. "You've got a deal."

"I will have the money to finalize the transaction in a few days," he said. When he arrived back in town, he sent a wire to Mr. Barton. *My work here is complete; will turn in my report when I return. Please wire nine hundred dollars.*

When the money arrived, Herbert returned to the plantation to finalize the deal. He would not relax until the deal was complete and he was on his way back home with June's mother. When he arrived at the plantation, there was a different feeling around the place. There was an air of gloomy sadness. John took Herbert to his office to complete the transaction.

When they came out of the office, Fannie was saying her goodbyes to everyone. There were tears of sadness as she hugged everyone. She walked out the door, then looked back. "If'n my June ever come back, tell her I is fine and I love her."

She got into the carriage with Herbert. As they rode off, she looked back and waved as the tears ran down her cheeks. She did not stop looking back until the big house was completely out of sight.

Back in town, Herbert stopped at the train station to find out when the next train was headed back north to Illinois. He would not feel at ease until they were well on their way. He showed a little relief when he found out the next train was headed out in a few hours. He wired Mr. Barton to let him know when they would arrive. He then went back to the hotel, gathered his things, and headed to the train station and waited nervously for the train to arrive.

He looked over at Fannie and saw a sad, somber look on her face. He wanted to tell her that everything was going to be okay and that at the end of this journey, it would be the happiest day of her life. But he knew that he could not because he had been instructed not to tell her anything. He tried to make small talk to cheer her up, but he could see that it did not help, so he kept quiet, which made him worry even more. He kept checking the time and looking at the door as he fidgeted nervously with a hundred things going through his mind that could go wrong on their journey to Illinois.

When the train arrived at the station, Herbert jumped up and headed quickly toward it with Fannie following behind. They found their seats and he sat there, waiting eagerly for the train to start moving. When the train started moving and the town was out of sight, he relaxed as he felt the largest chance of danger had ended.

CHAPTER 26

Jerome and Richard knew they only had a few days before June's mother would arrive. The house was ready, and Mrs. Edward had planned a welcoming party for June's mother and had invited all the people who had a hand in making this reunion possible. The train would arrive the day after tomorrow around two in the afternoon. The plan was for Jerome, Richard, June, and Sarah to go into town and be the welcoming committee for the new owner of the home.

The day came and they were all dressed up to welcome Fannie. Mr. Barton loaned his driver and fancy carriage to pick her up. When the carriage arrived, Sarah looked at Jerome and Richard. "The new owner of the house must be very important for Pastor Edward and Mrs. Edward to go to all this fuss. Do you two know something we don't know?" Sarah asked in a suspicious voice.

Jerome and Richard exchanged a glance and hunched their shoulders. "We don't know any more than you know," Jerome said, trying to look clueless.

When they arrived at the train station, they waited out front. June and Sarah kept asking questions, believing that Jerome and Richard knew more than they were telling. They continued to play dumb, trying to explain that they did not know any more than they had said they did.

Several minutes later, they could see the train making its way to the station. They all were excited because no one knew what to expect. Even though Jerome and Richard knew that it was June's mother, they were eager to see how she and June would react, knowing neither one thought they would ever see the other again.

The train came to a stop and the passengers started departing, and all of their attention was on the passengers. When each passenger stepped off the train, June and Sarah tried to guess who would be the new owner. It became a game to them. Each time they got it wrong, they would start laughing. Jerome and Richard were keeping their eyes open for Herbert. They knew when he came out, June's mother would be with him.

June and Sarah were laughing and not paying attention to the train when Herbert came out. Behind him was June's mother, walking slowly with her head down. Jerome looked over at June and Sarah. "Here comes the new owner," he said, pointing toward Herbert and Fannie.

"What makes you think you know who the new owner is?" Sarah asked.

June looked up and right away she knew that was her mother. "Mama!" she cried out.

Fannie's eyes lit up in recognition. "My baby, my baby!" she exclaimed. She then dropped her bag and ran into June's arms. She put her hands on June's face, wiping the tears away as they cried in each other's arms. "Thank you, Jesus, you brought me to my baby, thank you, Jesus," her mother shouted and finally looked up. They stood there, intertwined, each crying tears of joy.

Jerome shook Herbert's hand and thanked him for everything he had done. "There is a welcoming party at the house next to the mission for everyone who had a hand in making this moment come true. We would love for you and your family to come. Mr. Barton will be there, and you can go over everything with him," he said gratefully.

Jerome then looked over at Richard and Sarah, who both had tears in their eyes, as they looked at June and her mother still embracing. Jerome walked over to Richard. "Are you crying?" he asked with a smirk.

"Nah, man, are you kidding me? Some dust got in my eyes," he replied defensively.

"Yeah, right," Jerome said as he shoved Richard.

Sarah took Richard's hand. "I love a man who can show his sensitive side," she told him.

Richard looked at Jerome and said in a low voice, "See, my plan worked."

"Yeah, right," Jerome said, shaking his head.

Sarah looked at the both of them. "This was a beautiful thing you did."

They walked over to where June and her mother were standing. Sarah put her hand on June's shoulder. June looked up and wiped the tears from her face. "This is my best friend. She is helping me with my learning. I is reading, Mama," she said proudly.

June's mother said to Sarah, "Bless you, my child," and grasped her by the hands briefly. Sarah smiled and wiped the tears from her eyes.

"This here is Jerome and Richard. They is the ones who saved me from Billy, who tried to hurt me. After that, I knew I could not stay, so they helped me escape," said June, gesturing to Jerome and Richard.

June's mother turned to them. "God bless you fo' savin' my baby. Mr. Billy and Massa were plenty mad. All Mr. Billy could talk about was catching y'all so he could set an example. I wanted to see my baby, but I knew if he brought her back, they would beat her plenty bad and do other godless things to her. I knew that they would break her spirit, and she would never be the same, so God bless you fo' takin her away," she said breathlessly.

"We could not leave her there to be abused by that man, so we did what we had to do," Jerome said. "Now, I think we need to get going."

Richard picked up Fannie's bag and they all got into the carriage.

June's mother was amazed to be riding in a carriage like that. She only saw carriages this grand when there were big parties at the plantation. She had never dreamed that she would ever ride in one.

When they arrived at the house, June and Sarah could see that something was going on from all the carriages out front. Jerome and Richard were smiling, and June and Sarah were confused. They walked into the house, and Mrs. Edward greeted them. "Welcome to your new home!" she said with open arms. You could see how proud she was of the decorated house and how the party had turned out.

"What do you mean? Is this me and my mama's house?" June asked, bewildered.

"Yes, it is, thanks to Jerome and Richard," replied Mrs. Edward, smiling.

June ran over to where they were standing, "Thank you, thank you!" She then ran over to her mother, who was standing there in shock, and hugged her. "This is where we gon' live, Mama! We really gon' live here!"

June's mother stood there shaking. She raised her hands and looked up. "Thank you, Jesus," she exclaimed. She then grabbed June and gave her a big hug.

"What's with the tears? Ain't no dust in here," Jerome said, tapping Richard in the ribs.

Richard wiped his face. "If we ever get home, you better never let the boys know about this."

Jerome started laughing. "Then you better hope we never get home," he said, clearly overjoyed.

Everyone was enjoying the open house. Jerome, Richard, June, and Sarah were sitting around talking. The ladies were in the kitchen talking with June's mother and going over cooking tips, and the men were standing around talking business.

Christopher was on the other side of the house, looking over at Sarah, not pleased at how close she and Richard had become. He did not like Jerome or Richard due to how close his father was with them. All Mr. Barton would talk about was how mature they were, how he should try to be like them, which made him begrudge them even more. He had always taken it for granted that Sarah was his girl, and now he felt Richard was threating that.

Christopher walked over to where they were. Not giving attention to the others, he looked at Sarah. "Can I talk to you?"

"Sure," she said. He held his hand out, she took it, and they went outside. Richard had a look of uneasiness and watched them until they were outside. A few minutes later, Sarah came to the table looking upset.

"Are you okay? Did he do something to upset you?" Richard stood up. "I'll deal with him."

"No." Sarah grabbed him by the arm.

Richard sat back down. "Well, what did he do?" he asked.

Sarah took a deep breath and composed herself. "He thinks he owns me. Just because he's rich, he thinks I'm just supposed to do whatever he says. He said since you three arrived, I've changed and he don't like it. So I told him just because you're rich, it doesn't give you the right to tell me who can be my friends. I told him I'm free to associate with whomever I want," she said defiantly. "He grabbed me by my arm and said if I don't stop hanging around you three, I will regret it. That's when I left."

June looked at Sarah with a worried look. "You is still gon' be my friend, right?"

Sarah smiled. "I will always be your friend."

June smiled back. "We is like sisters," she said.

"Yes, we are," Sarah said as she gave her a hug.

The guests were leaving as the open house came to an end. Mrs. Edward made sure everything was cleaned up before she left. "Well, Fannie, I will see you in the morning," Mrs. Edward said as she put the last dish away.

"Is Mama gon' be working with me?" June asked.

"Yes, she is," said Mrs. Edward.

June gave her mother a big hug. "Bye, Mrs. Edward. I is gon' come over later and get my things." June then smiled as the reality of her mother and the house finally started to sink in.

June and her mother were finally alone. They both sat there quietly, absorbing all that had just happened. Fannie stood up and walked all around, touching everything and under her breath saying, "Thank you, Jesus" over and over again.

June just smiled as she watched her mother. For the first time in her life, she could see a peace and calmness washing over her.

Jerome, Richard, and Isaac were sitting on the porch enjoying the evening breeze. Isaac said, "Everything turned out great. What you two did was a beautiful thing."

Jerome replied, "What *we* did. You had a big part in making all this happen."

Isaac smiled. "It did feel good to be a part of this happy occasion, but I do have one concern. That Christopher is trouble."

Richard stood up. "You think *he's* trouble? If he keeps pushing me, I'm going to be his worst nightmare."

"Isaac has a point," Jerome said. "I see how he looked at us when we were at the house talking to Mr. Barton, and he really doesn't like you because of Sarah. As long as he feels threatened by you, he will find a way to start trouble."

"I think you two just need to be careful and try to stay away from him."

"I'm going to be cool when I am around him, but he better not keep pushing me," said Richard.

CHAPTER 27

The next day came and everything was back to normal. When Jerome and Richard arrived for breakfast, they could see June and her mother already working. Her mother fit right in, and all the women seemed to listen to her as she gave them tips on ways to make the kitchen run more smoothly. They could see she was very experienced in her craft and were eager to learn from her. June looked on with a smile as she remembered how things were when she was in the kitchen with her mother back on the plantation.

Mrs. Edward walked over to where Jerome and Richard were standing watching the women working in the kitchen. "She is such a blessing," she said. "She came in and all the ladies took to her immediately. I also can see a different spirit about June. I can see how having her mother with her is going to make a big difference in her life going forward," she said softly.

Jerome looked at Mrs. Edward. "I'm glad everything worked out for her, because we felt responsible for taking her away. With help from everyone, we had the chance to make it right, and thank God it worked out because it could have gone all wrong."

Mrs. Edward put her hands together. "I believe God has his hands on this mission, and bringing her here, I believe, is part of his plan. That's why I feel this mission cannot fail."

She continued. "The pastor and I have been working this mission on a tight budget, praying that we have enough resources to keep it going. That's why I am so passionate about the open house fundraisers. The success of the fundraisers has kept the doors open. We also feel blessed that you two came into our lives. We believe you were sent to us by God. The money you have donated through your business has been a big blessing to this mission." She paused to take a breath. "And the work you two are doing with the children, we see great changes in their attitudes toward learning. We feel very blessed to have you here and we can't thank you enough." She smiled, gratitude lighting her face.

"We see how important this mission is for the Black community and we feel it is our responsibility to do our part," Richard said sincerely.

Mrs. Edward thanked them again and then went into the kitchen.

Jerome and Richard were sitting down eating breakfast when Isaac came over and sat down. "I'm glad you're here," Jerome said. "Now that June's mother is here, we can start working on the outreach program. This evening we three need to get together and brainstorm about how we plan to move forward on this. We can meet after dinner and start putting together our game plan," he said enthusiastically.

After breakfast, they headed out to start their day. Jerome and Richard went to the classroom, and Isaac reported to the pastor to find out what he would be doing today. After the workday ended, the three met in the dining hall.

"Well, here we are. How do we plan to make this happen?" Isaac asked.

Jerome replied, "We need to find out who are the people that need the help."

"That's easy," Richard said. "The church, most of the people who need help most likely go to the church. We need to have this outreach be a program that goes through the church."

"That's a good idea," Jerome said. "I think Mrs. Edward would be the perfect person to head it up. I will talk with her tomorrow and see if she is willing to do it."

After the meeting, Jerome and Richard went to visit June and her mother to see how they were settling in and if there was anything they needed. They knocked and June came to the door. "Come in," she said. When they walked in, they could see that June and Fannie had settled right in. June's mother was in the kitchen cooking.

Richard held his head up and took a sniff of the air. "My, my, my, do I smell pie, pie, pie?"

Fannie looked over. "Yes you do. Would y'all like to have some?"

"Yes ma'am," they said in harmony, rubbing their hands together. Fannie was real quiet for a moment as tears swelled up in her eyes. Jerome and Richard looked at each other, puzzled.

Jerome turned to June. "What's wrong? Is it something we said?" he asked, concerned. June looked at them and just shrugged.

"In my whole entire life, no one has ever said 'yes ma'am' to me. It sho feel good to be respected." She wiped the tears from her eyes. "Y'all sit on down. I is being silly."

Jerome and Richard quickly sat down. She gave them each a big slice of apple pie, and they ate it like they hadn't had anything to eat in days. Fannie looked on with a big smile, feeling appreciated for what she was blessed to do—cook. June just smiled as she watched her mother, Jerome, and Richard.

After enjoying the pie, Jerome and Richard headed back to the mission. Richard rubbed his stomach. "That had to be the best apple pie I had ever had. Can you see her back home owning her own restaurant? She would make a killing."

"Ain't that the truth," Jerome said.

"Do you think we'll ever get home?"

"Don't know, but I sho do miss the fellows," Jerome said in a sorrowful voice. "I can see myself taking the pass from you and shooting that long fade-away." He then turned around and simulated a long jump shot. "All day," he said under his breath as he stood there in his shooting position. He then lowered his head and they continued walking to the mission, not saying a word, both lost in their own thoughts.

The next day, Jerome and Richard met with Mrs. Edward about the outreach program. She had some good ideas on how to get the program up and running. She agreed that it was a good idea to run it through the church, believing it would draw more people to the church. She said she would put her ideas on paper and then they would get back together and go over them.

Later that day, Jerome and Richard rode into town with Isaac to pick up some supplies. When they walked into the store, they saw a woman pleading with the owner about credit.

Jerome looked at Richard, "Ain't that the lady from Mama D's place?" he asked.

Richard looked over. "That is her. I wonder what's going on, because she don't look too happy."

"I'm about to find out," Jerome said. "You two go and start getting the supplies. I'll be back."

Isaac shook his head and said, "Oh boy, here we go again."

As Jerome got closer, he could hear the owner and the woman talking. "I cannot extend any more credit. You haven't paid what you owe, and without a job how are you going to pay?"

"When my husband get back on his feet or I find work, we will pay, I promise," she pleaded.

"No money, no goods," he said in a harsh and unsympathetic way.

"But we have nothing, we have nothing," she said in a desperate cry. She then lowered her head and in a hopeless state walked away.

"Mrs. Ida, is that you?" Jerome asked.

She looked up. "Hi," she said with a half smile.

"Is everything okay?" Jerome asked, as he could see the worried look on her face.

"My husband and I are in need of supplies, but I can't get any more credit since neither one of us is working," she said.

"Aren't you working over at Mama D's place?"

"Not anymore—she fired me the day you all left. She believed I talked you all into leaving," she said, clearly upset.

"I promise we did not say anything," Jerome said, holding his hands up.

"I believe you, but obviously she didn't believe me, so she fired me. And ever since my husband injured his leg, he hasn't been able to work, so we have no money to buy the things we need."

"I am so sorry that happened, but maybe I can help."

"I thank you for wanting to help, but unless you have some money for supplies, you can't help."

Jerome smiled and grabbed her by the hand. "Come on, we will work this out."

Ida was puzzled but went along. They went up to the counter. "Excuse me," Jerome said. The owner turned around and when he saw Ida, a jarring look came over him.

"I told you no credit," he said shortly.

Mrs. Ida did not say a word. She just looked at Jerome, then looked down.

"I'm the one who called you, not her," Jerome said assertively.

"I'm not extending any more credit to you people," he said firmly.

"You people, what do you mean you people?" Jerome asked.

"You people come in here without any money and no way to pay and expect me to let you get everything you want. This ain't no charity."

Jerome gave Ida a smile. "He's talking about people without any money. He ain't talking about us, so you go and get everything you need." Ida looked at Jerome as if to say, "Are you sure?"

"Go, go," Jerome said, waving his hands for her to get moving. "Go and get the things you need." Jerome then turned to the owner. "This is from the new outreach program called The Mission." He went to help Ida.

Ida was walking around getting the bare minimum, feeling that she would be taking advantage if she got more. Jerome would then grab more and pile it on. Every time Ida would get something, Jerome would grab more. When they finished getting everything, they headed back to the counter. Ida looked really nervous, hoping Jerome had the money to pay for all the things they had collected.

The owner had an astonished look on his face when he saw everything they had. "I hope you have the money to pay for all this, because I meant it when I said no credit."

Jerome pulled out a wad of money. "Don't worry, just add it up and add the amount that she owes you for the credit." Ida was amazed when she saw the money, but was relieved when she knew that he could pay for everything.

Jerome helped Ida load everything into her wagon. "God bless you," she said as she gave Jerome a big hug. "Looks like things worked out real well for you."

"Thanks to you," Jerome said. "You telling us about the mission was the best thing that happened to us, and I thank you for that," he said sincerely.

"I'm glad to hear that. By the way, how is the girl that was with you doing?" Ida asked.

"She is doing great. She is working at the mission and learning to read and write. We also brought her mother from Louisiana up here," he said, feeling a stab of pride at the accomplishment.

"Well, I best be getting home. My husband is waiting."

Jerome could see that there was still a great worry weighing on her. He knew that the things she had just received would only last for so long, and without any income coming in, she would end up back in the same situation.

"I got it," Jerome said. "You can work at the mission. I'm sure they can find something for you."

"Do you think so?" Ida asked with a big smile.

"I'll talk to Pastor Edward and Mrs. Edward. You come to the mission tomorrow afternoon, and we will see what we can do."

She thanked Jerome again, then headed home singing, feeling like there was hope for her current circumstances.

Richard and Isaac were still loading up the wagon when Jerome walked up. "Well, it's about time," Richard said as he loaded a bag of cornmeal onto the wagon.

"I was doing a good deed for the lady who led us to the mission," Jerome said.

"So what was the problem?"

"Because of us she lost her job," he replied.

"She got fired?" Richard asked.

"Yeah, and she is having a hard time. Her husband hurt his leg and is unable to work, and to make matters worse, she is overextended at the store and the owner won't give her any more credit. So I got her some things and paid her debt. I told her I would talk to Pastor Edward and Mrs. Edward about giving her a job. She's coming to the mission tomorrow to talk to them."

"For what she did for us, let's hope everything works out for her," Richard said.

They finished loading everything and headed back to the mission.

The next day Ida showed up at the mission looking very nervous when she walked in. Mrs. Edward greeted her with a big smile, which put her at ease. They went into the dining area to talk. "Jerome told me what you did for them and how it cost you your job," said Mrs. Edward.

"Yes, it did, but I felt it was the right thing to do. I didn't believe that was a good place for a young girl to be, so I just did what I thought was right," Ida said honestly.

"Well, she has come a long way since that first day they showed up," Mrs. Edward replied.

"I hear she is doing very well here," Ida said.

"There she is, working," Mrs. Edward said, pointing to the kitchen area. Ida looked and saw June working and looking very happy.

"That's good. I'm so glad everything worked out for her," Ida said, pleased that she'd been able to help June escape the brothel.

"Jerome and Richard have been a blessing to this mission, which has allowed us to do many things we were unable to do before they came, so we would love to have you work here," said Mrs. Edward.

Ida, stunned for words, sat there with her mouth open.

"Can you start tomorrow?" asked Mrs. Edward, gently pushing Ida to respond.

"Yes, yes I can," she said as she shook Mrs. Edward's hand vigorously.

"Great, be here tomorrow at 7:00 in the morning and we will go over pay and what you will be doing," said Mrs. Edward matter-of-factly. Ida was ecstatic and relieved knowing that she would be able to get back on her feet. "Thank God," she said under her breath as she looked up and walked out of the dining area.

CHAPTER 28

The next day Jerome and Richard met with Mrs. Edward and talked about sending their students to a regular school. They felt the students were advanced enough and should have no problem fitting in. She trusted their judgment and felt that if they believed they were ready, she had no problem with it. Before they made a decision, they wanted to go and check the school out, just to make sure their students were not getting in over their heads. Mrs. Edward worked with the children while Isaac took Jerome and Richard to the school.

It was mid-morning when they arrived, and school was well underway. After looking in on the younger students' class, they were sure their students would have no problem fitting in. On their way out, they walked by the older students' class. Richard waved at Sarah, who smiled and waved back. He then winked at her, which made her blush. Christopher saw this and gave him a dirty look. Richard chuckled and shook his head, which made Christopher even angrier.

Jerome grabbed Richard and pulled him away from the door. "You need to leave that boy alone. You know we still need his pops."

"That's the only thing saving him. If it wasn't for his pops, I would have whooped his butt a long time ago," replied Richard.

"Yeah right," Jerome said, knowing Richard was really not the fighting type.

On their way to the wagon, where Isaac was waiting, they talked about the bad conditions of the school. "That school makes ours look like a prep school from the suburbs," Jerome said.

"Ain't that the truth," Richard said in agreement.

When they were leaving, Jerome looked over at Isaac. "Do you know where the White school is?"

"Yeah, why?" Isaac said with apprehension in his voice.

"Take us by there. I want to see how their schools are."

Isaac pulled the wagon to a stop. "You must be crazy if you think those White folks are going to just let you walk around their school."

Richard looked at Jerome, shaking his head no. "I have to agree with Isaac. Ain't no way they gonna let us just walk around their school."

"I don't know about you two. Where is your sense of adventure?"

"All right, I'm just the right-hand man. If that's what you want, I'll take you there," said Isaac.

When they made it to the school, Richard said to Jerome, "It doesn't look like things have changed in over a hundred years."

"What do you mean?"

Richard raised his hands. "The Black school looks like a dump, and the White school looks like a place you want to learn in."

"Well, let's go in," Jerome said. He looked back at Isaac. "Do you want to come?"

"I think I'll stay right here," said Isaac. "Someone will need to pick you two up when they throw you out on your butts."

Richard pulled Jerome by the arm. "Do you think they would throw us out?" he asked uneasily.

"Man, come on." Jerome pushed Richard in the back.

When they went into the school, they did not see anyone, so they just started walking around. They could see a big difference between the two schools. The White school building was in good condition, while the Black school was all run down and needed plenty of work.

Everything seemed bright and alive at the White school, whereas everything at the Black school seemed to be dark and dull.

"Hey!" a voice came from behind them.

"I think we're in trouble," Jerome said in a low voice.

They turned around to see a White man. "You two need to get to the classroom down the hall on the left. There was a big spill that needs to be cleaned up."

Richard looked at the man, and before he could say anything, Jerome said, "Yes, sir, right away."

"Well, go, go," he said as he gestured with his hands. "We don't pay you to stand around and do nothing."

They turned around and started walking. "What did you say that for?" Richard asked.

"This will give us a chance to walk around and look at the place."

They found the mop and bucket and headed toward the classroom.

All the students were sitting at their desks, and one boy was at the chalkboard working on a math problem. He seemed to be having difficulty with the problem, so he just stood there looking at the board.

The teacher standing there was starting to lose her patience. "If you would pay attention in class instead of joking around so much, you would be able to answer this problem. Maybe we should move you to the little children's classroom. You might be able to do their work." Everyone in the class started laughing, which made him feel even worse.

Richard saw everyone laughing, so he started laughing. The boy looked at Richard and became furious. "What you laughing at, nigger mop boy?" His tone and look brought the whole classroom to silence.

Richard walked over to the chalkboard and picked up the chalk and started solving the problem. When he completed the answer, he put the chalk down and walked out of the classroom.

The teacher looked at the problem and Richard's solution. "That's correct," she said in a low voice, surprised that the answer was correct.

Jerome walked to the chalkboard, grabbed the chalk, and wrote a big A plus next to the problem, then circled it.

He handed the boy the mop. "If you can't answer a simple problem like that, you better get used to that mop in your hand." Jerome turned around and walked away. When he came to the bucket of water, he kicked it over, then looked at the boy, who still had the mop in his hand. "Now *you* clean it up, mop boy." He walked out the door.

When Jerome was outside the door, he took off running. "Run, Richard!" Richard looked back, not knowing what was going on, but he started running. When they made it outside the school, they saw Isaac lying in the back of the wagon asleep. "Isaac, let's go, let's go!" Jerome yelled as they got closer to the wagon.

Isaac looked up, not fully awake, and saw Jerome and Richard running toward him. "Oh no, what did they do now?" he asked himself as he quickly climbed into the front of the wagon.

"Go, go," Jerome said. They climbed into the back of the wagon.

"Haaaw, haaaw." Isaac snapped the reins and did not slow down until they were out of sight of the school. "Now what did you two do this time?"

Richard replied, "I only showed some dumb White boy that I am smarter than him, and then I left." He pointed at Jerome. "Now I don't know what Jerome did, because he came out of the classroom hollering run! So I started running."

Richard and Isaac both looked at Jerome. "What?" Jerome said, holding his hands out.

"What did you do?" Richard asked.

"All I did was tell the White boy that if he can't answer that easy problem, he needed to get used to having a mop in his hand."

"That's it, you had me running for that?"

"Well I did kick over the bucket of water and said 'Clean it up, mop boy.'" Jerome and Richard started laughing and gave each other a high-five. Isaac just shook his head.

When they arrived back at the mission, Jerome and Richard talked to Mrs. Edward about the best way to transition the children into the school, especially the children whose families were transitioning out of the mission. Since the students would no longer be at the mission, they wanted to make sure they were ready. After they finished going over everything with Mrs. Edward, they went down to visit June and her mother.

When they got close to the house, they could see June and Sarah on the porch studying. Richard looked at Jerome, "I'm going to call that girl, Professor. All she do is study. If she's not working, she is studying. I bet she study in her sleep."

Jerome looked at Richard. "If we ever get home, you can bet that I am going to follow her example and take school much more seriously. She has a hunger to learn, and she has opened my eyes to the importance of education."

"I think that's one of the things I love about her."

Richard stopped walking and with raised eyebrows grabbed Jerome by the arm. "Did you use the love word? The player of players, the mac daddy of them all, cannot be using the love word. The one who says he is too much for one woman. Pinch me, it can't be true."

"I see you got jokes. You know what I mean. I mean I love her dedication to learning."

"You can tell that to somebody who don't know you. I never thought I'd see the day a girl hook the great JT," Richard said.

Jerome stood there straight-faced, not knowing what to say because he knew it was true.

They continued walking, when suddenly, Jerome grabbed Richard by the arm. "What about you? Sarah got you hooked."

"At least I can admit it, but you can't."

"That's because nobody hooks JT."

"You can tell that to somebody who don't know any better," Richard said as he walked up to the porch.

Sarah looked up. "Tell what to somebody?"

Richard gave her a big smile. "That I am hooked on you."

"You are so crazy," she said with a blushing smile.

"Who *you* hooked on?" Richard asked Jerome. The three of them waited for an answer. Jerome stood in silence, giving Richard a hard look.

He then turned to June. "You know I am hooked on you," he said sheepishly.

June smiled, "I is hooked on you too." Then they all started laughing.

The four sat on the porch talking and enjoying each other's company. "So what were you all doing at the school today?" Sarah asked.

"We believe the children are ready to go to the school, so we were just looking it over," Jerome said.

"Do you think they are?" she asked.

"We believe they can fit right in," Jerome said with confidence.

"That's great," Sarah said. "I believe with a little more work, June will be ready to go to school and fit right in my class."

June looked up, surprised at what she had just heard. "You really think I is almost ready?"

"Yes, I do," Sarah said as she gave June a hug.

Richard looked over at June. "As much as you study, you going to be teaching the class real soon."

June sat up real proud, "I is gon' be teaching. Mrs. Edward said if I keep working with my learning, someday I could teach at the mission. That's why I work so hard."

Jerome said, "I knew the first time I saw you with that book in your hand that you were special, and I see that teaching is your calling."

Sarah became very serious when she turned to Richard. "You need to be careful around Christopher. When he saw you wave at me, he became very angry and was mad for the rest of the day."

"I'm not worried about him," Richard said, blowing it off like it was no big deal.

"Nevertheless, promise me you'll be real careful around him."

"Don't worry."

"Promise me," Sarah said in a more persuasive voice.

"I promise." Richard said to Jerome in a low voice, "She cares."

It was getting late, so Jerome and Richard headed back to the mission. "I think Sarah has a good point," said Jerome.

"About what?" Richard asked.

"About Christopher…that fool is crazy. We need to make sure we are together at all times when we leave this mission."

"If you say so, but I ain't worried about that chump."

"Remember, we ain't home, and the rules are different," Jerome warned.

Richard had a bewildered look on his face as he thought about what Jerome said.

The next day, Jerome and Richard let the children know they believed they were ready to go to regular school. Some were excited, and a few were hesitant. Jerome assured them that they were ready, that in fact they were ahead of some of the students their age at the school. That gave the students relief, since they trusted and believed Jerome and Richard.

Lunchtime arrived, and the children had settled down and were eating. Jerome and Richard were talking to June while their lunch was being prepared. While their attention was away from the children, a man came up to one of the tables and asked them to point out Richard. They pointed him out, and the man disappeared.

The man was in the corner of the dining area, keeping an eye on where Jerome and Richard were sitting. Jerome got up and said something to Richard, then walked out the door.

When Jerome was out of sight, the man in the corner came over to the table. "Are you Richard?" he asked, with panic in his voice.

"Yeah."

"It's Sarah, she got hurt at the school, and she is asking for you," said the man.

Richard jumped up from the table. "What happened?"

"I'm not sure. I was just told to come and get you because she wanted you by her side."

"Well, let's go. Take me to her!"

They headed for the door, and Richard stopped at one of the tables. "Tell Jerome that Sarah is hurt and I went to the school to see about her."

"Come on, let's go," the man said, waving at Richard, hoping to get out of there before Jerome came back. They both jumped in the wagon and headed to town.

Several minutes later, Jerome walked back into the dining area. Looking around, he did not see Richard, which gave him concern because one of them was always with the children. He walked over to where June was working. "Have you seen Rich?"

"He was sitting over there and then he and some man rushed out," she said.

"What man?" Jerome asked with concern.

"I is never seen him before. Is everything okay?"

"I don't know, but this don't look good," Jerome said.

Jerome rushed over to where the children were eating. "Did anyone see Richard?" he asked frantically.

"We saw him leave with a man."

"What man?"

"A man came over here and asked us to point out Richard. When you left, he went and talked to Richard. Then Richard said to tell you that Sarah was hurt and he went to see about her."

Jerome clapped his hands to get the children's attention. "All right, listen up, after you finish lunch, school will be out for the day." The children started clapping and celebrating. "I will see everyone tomorrow." Jerome quickly headed out of the dining area. "I got to find Isaac," he said under his breath.

Jerome was running all over, looking for Isaac when he found him working in the barn. "We got to go to town now. Richard went off with someone who said Sarah is hurt."

"What happened?" Isaac asked nervously.

"I don't know, but I think he has been set up by that damn Christopher. Ain't no telling what's going to happen if we don't get there quick."

Isaac quickly hitched up the wagon and they headed to town.

When they arrived, Jerome saw Christopher coming out between two buildings looking very nervous. "Stop the wagon," Jerome said as he jumped out of the wagon before it came to a complete stop. He ran over to Christopher and grabbed him by the collar. "What did you do to Rich? I know you lured him down here. What did you do?"

Christopher looked shocked. "I didn't know they were going to do what they did. All I wanted them to do is rough him up, but he fought back, which made them angrier. I told them to stop, but they kept kicking and hitting him with boards. I kept hollering at them to stop, but they would not listen. They just kept kicking and hitting. They went crazy and I could not stop them. I did not know what to do, so I ran. I didn't mean for all that to happen. I really didn't."

"Where is he, where is he?" Jerome asked desperately, vigorously shaking him.

"He's behind the building," Christopher said meekly.

Jerome and Isaac took off and headed to the back of the building. "I didn't mean for it to go that far!" Christopher hollered. He then took off running in the opposite direction.

Jerome and Isaac arrived at the back of the building. Richard was lying there motionless with bruises and blood all over his face, to the point he was nearly unrecognizable.

"Oh my God!" Jerome put his hands on his head, not knowing what to do. "Go get help!" he hollered at Isaac.

Isaac took off running to the front of the building. "Help, help!" he hollered, trying to get the attention of anyone who would help.

Jerome got on the ground and put Richard's head in his lap. Richard looked up at Jerome with his eyes half closed, barely able to talk. "He got me. I can't believe I fell for that." His eyes then completely closed as his head fell to the side on Jerome's lap.

"No, no," Jerome said in a panic, and he looked up to see if anyone was coming. He then pulled Richard's head up to cradle it in between his hands and tenderly rested his forehead on Richard's as the tears ran down his cheeks.

CHAPTER 29

Richard looked up. "He's coming around!" Everyone standing over him showed a sign of relief.

"Oh, man," Jerome said as he rose up, rubbing the back of his head. He looked up at Richard.

"You all right? I thought you were dead," Jerome said still rubbing the back of his head.

Everyone who had gathered around looked at each other in confusion.

"As hard as his head is, I think he knocked what little sense he had out when he hit that floor," said Richard. Everyone started laughing, which eased the tension. Jerome looked at everyone, incredibly confused about what was going on.

"Back up everyone, back up," a teacher said as he made his way to Jerome. "Are you all right?" He examined his eyes, evaluating him for signs of a concussion.

Still a little dazed, Jerome replied, "I think I'm okay, just a little dizzy and confused about what's going on. I'm just glad Rich is okay."

Richard, shaking his head, said, "He done lost it."

"Get him to the nurse's office." The teacher helped Jerome to his feet. Jerome stood there, still a little dizzy.

"I'll take him," Richard said.

Jerome, leaning on Richard, asked, "We did win, didn't we?"

Richard glanced back at everyone and reassured them, "He's all right." They then headed to the nurse's office.

"Why would you think I was dead? You busted your head, not me," Richard said as they walked.

"It's a long story. I'll tell you about it later. How long was I out?"

"You were out at least two minutes."

"That's it?" Jerome asked, incredulous.

"What you mean? That's it? Ain't that long enough?"

"You ain't going to believe what I have to tell you," said Jerome seriously.

They walked into the nurse's office. She looked over Jerome and wanted to observe him to make sure he did not have a serious injury or a concussion.

"I'll catch up with you later, gotta get to my next class," said Richard. Jerome gave him a head gesture as he sat in his chair, stunned that he was only out a couple of minutes when everything he experienced seemed to be months.

Jerome sat in the nurse's office for about an hour. After the hour, the nurse felt that he was okay. He told the nurse that he would like to be excused for the rest of the day. She agreed and signed him out.

Jerome was walking home with a dozen thoughts running through his head. He thought he must be crazy when he found himself missing the life he had when he was unconscious. He especially found himself missing June. He missed how important he felt when everyone looked up to him and how it made him feel when he helped someone.

He looked at his life and the way it was before he was unconscious. For the first time, he saw himself as arrogant and egotistic in the present, and he did not like it. At that moment, he decided that he was going to change and be the person he had been when he was unconscious. He was excited because he knew he could become that person. The only thing he knew he could not change was seeing June, and that made him sad. He knew he had the memories and he would hold on to them. He swore to himself that he would never forget her and the influence she'd had on him.

It was later that evening when Richard came over to see Jerome. "How you doing?"

"I'm all right."

"We ran a couple of games after school, and on my way home I thought I would stop by," Richard said, obviously still concerned about Jerome.

"You got your butt kicked, didn't you?" Jerome smirked.

"What makes you think we lost?"

"Because I wasn't there," Jerome said with a smile.

"Well, we came close in both games," Richard said defensively. "I'm ready to hear this long story you have to tell me because you were acting pretty weird."

"Not now. I am working on my paper for Mrs. Wilkins' class."

Richard sat up, shocked at what he was hearing. "You doing your homework?"

"Yeah, so you got to go so I can finish it. You need to get home and do yours, and if you're not here in the morning early enough to get to class on time, I'll be gone," Jerome said.

Richard got up, looking at Jerome like he done lost his mind. "I'll see you in the morning then," he said as he walked slowly to the door, not recognizing his best friend.

"And you better be on time," Jerome insisted.

Richard stood outside, dazed and confused. Then he smiled because he saw a different Jerome and he liked it.

The next day, Richard was at Jerome's house early enough to get to school on time. "Let's go, I don't want to be late," Jerome said with a sense of urgency. They started walking at a quick pace, and at every block Jerome checked the time.

"Slow down, we're going to get there in time," Richard said, struggling to keep up with Jerome's pace.

Jerome slowed down and looked at Richard. "Did you get your paper done?"

"Look at you, sounding like Mrs. Wilkins. Of course I got my paper done," Richard replied. "Did you?"

"Yeah."

It was early when they arrived to the classroom. Richard headed to the back where they sat every day. Jerome stopped and sat in the front row. Richard looked back and saw Jerome sitting in the front row, so he headed back to the front and sat down. As it got closer to the start of the class, students started to enter the room. Everyone was shocked to see Jerome and Richard already in class and sitting up front. Everyone came up to shake Jerome's hand and ask how he was doing after the incident the day before.

Mrs. Wilkins could hear the noise coming from her classroom before she made it to the door. "Settle down," she said as she walked in. She put her books and folders on her desk, then saw Jerome and Richard sitting quietly up front. Shocked, she gave them a smile. Then she gave her attention to the rest of the class. "Settle down and take your seats. Does everyone have your assignments?" Everyone got quiet, and a disappointed look flashed across her face.

After roll call was taken, Mrs. Wilkins looked up and asked brightly, "Who wants to go first?"

Jerome quickly raised his hand. "I'll go first, Mrs. Wilkins."

Everyone was shocked, and even Mrs. Wilkins was speechless for a moment. "Come on up, Jerome," she said. There was reluctance in her voice, hoping that he was not going to get up there and start clowning around in his usual way.

Jerome got up and walked slowly to the front and faced the class. Everyone sat quietly in anticipation of what they were about to hear. Jerome looked out at the class and he could tell that everyone was on edge of their seats as they waited for him to start. At that moment, Jerome could tell that his fellow students looked up to him and the things he did set an example that they would follow. He knew then he had a responsibility to do the right thing.

Just when he was about to start, the door opened and a young lady walked in.

"June!" Jerome gasped, with a bewildered look. He could have sworn he felt his heart skip a beat.

Richard looked up, then turned around and said to the person behind him, "I think that fall on his head is still affecting him. He thinks it's June, when everybody knows it's September."

"Come in," Mrs. Wilkins said with a smile. The young lady handed her a paper. Mrs. Wilkins read the paper, then said, "This is Charlotte Pleasant, who is related to me, so you better be nice to her. She just moved here from Chicago and will be joining our class. Charlotte, take a seat anywhere."

As she walked to her seat, Jerome was looking at her like he had seen a ghost. She was the spitting image of June, and he could not stop staring at her. Mrs. Wilkins clapped her hands. "All right, Jerome, you can put your eyes back on your paper; we're ready to hear from you." Everyone started laughing.

Slightly embarrassed, but still amazed, Jerome glanced at Charlotte, who smiled at him.

"Okay, Jerome, you can start." Everything became serious again as everyone anticipated what Jerome was going to do.

Jerome looked down at his paper for a moment, cleared his throat and took a deep breath, then looked up.

"The question put before us is how learning about our past can help us in the present. It has been said that if you don't learn from the past, you are bound to repeat it. I say that part of our past needs to be repeated. The part where our forefathers would die to learn to read and write. If we had half the dedication our forefathers had for learning, there would be fewer Blacks so far behind when it comes to education." He paused for a moment. "Respect. Respect for our elders is another part of our past that needs to be repeated. In the past, our elders were respected for the things they endured, their wisdom, and the sacrifices they made for their future generations. If it wasn't for our forefathers enduring their challenges, sacrificing, and dying for their beliefs, we would not be here to enjoy the freedoms we have today. The question we need to ask ourselves is if they could look down on us today, would they be proud of what they see, or would they be hurt and disappointed? Would they think the sacrifices they made and the thing they fought and died for worth it, or would they think it was all for nothing? The least we can do is show respect to our forefathers by doing the best we can in school, respecting our elders, and making the future better for our people. These are the things they believed in, fought for, and died for."

Everyone was quiet, staring in disbelief that this was coming from Jerome, the person who never took his classes seriously. Mrs. Wilkins stood there in disbelief as tears swelled up in her eyes.

She removed her glasses and took a tissue and wiped her eyes. "Well done, well done, Jerome, you may take a seat."

Jerome walked to his seat, sat down, and looked straight forward, not saying a word. Richard's mouth was wide open. It was hard to believe what he had just heard had come from his best friend.

After Jerome sat down there was a different atmosphere in the classroom. Jerome being serious seemed to make everyone else serious. There were several other students who got up to speak, and there were the ones who were happy that the class was ending before their turn, knowing they were not ready. Mrs. Wilkins made it clear that the rest of the students would do their speech tomorrow.

Everyone was leaving the classroom when Charlotte walked up to Jerome. "The speech you gave was really deep," she said, smiling. "I never really thought about the things you said would be disrespectful to our forefathers, but the way you put it really makes you think. You must really enjoy this class."

"Well, before yesterday I thought it was a waste," Jerome said honestly.

"Really? The way you gave that speech sounded like you put a lot of thought into it."

"It's amazing when you get a taste of the past and how it puts things into perspective."

"A taste of the past? I don't understand," she said, interested but uncertain.

Jerome smiled, "I'll explain it to you someday."

Richard ran up to Jerome, "Let's go, it's game time, we need to get back at those chumps for yesterday. With you back, they won't be talking all that smack."

"I think I need at least another day before I get back out there," Jerome said.

"Oh yeah, you did take a hard fall yesterday, which I think has gone and made you a little crazy. I guess I'll have to go and represent then," Richard said, patting Jerome on the shoulder before he took off running to the gym.

"Let me walk you to your next class," Jerome offered.

"I don't have a class until third period," Charlotte replied.

"I don't either. I can show you around if you'd like," Jerome said, suddenly feeling a little self-conscious and excited at the same time.

"What happened yesterday?" Charlotte asked as they started walking.

"While playing ball, I took a hard fall and I lost consciousness for a few minutes."

"Are you okay?"

"Yeah, I'll be fine," Jerome said with a smile. "Enough about me. Tell me about you. Big-time city like Chicago, so what brought you to our little town in Louisiana?"

"Chicago is really getting rough, and my mother thought it wasn't a good environment for me, so here I am." She shrugged.

"Why Louisiana?"

"Hey, my roots are from here. This is going to sound crazy, but it has been said that my great, great, well, one of those greats, escaped from a plantation here in Louisiana, with the help of two strange young men, and made her way to Illinois. It's been said that the two young men were from the future."

"No, that can't be." Jerome thought about how much it sounded like his experience when he was unconscious.

"I know, I know, it sounds strange," Charlotte said, feeling a little embarrassed for telling him.

"You never know, strange things happen to make the world go round," Jerome said with a smile. "So, you and old lady Wilkins are cousins?" He saw the look on her face and clarified. "Old Lady Wilkins is what everyone calls her. My fault, Mrs. Wilkins," Jerome said quickly, hoping he did not offend her.

"Both of our ancestries started here in Louisiana—two sisters with different mothers fathered by the same slave owner. One sister escaped to Illinois and the other one lived here in Louisiana. So that is how my side ended up in Illinois," she said.

They continued to walk and talk until their next class. After school, Jerome walked her home. He could see how she, in many ways, reminded him of June.

Charlotte looked up at Jerome. "You know, I feel a strange connection with you...like I've known you for a long time," she said shyly.

Jerome smiled. He felt he got his June back and was going to make sure he didn't lose her again.

www.ingramcontent.com/pod-product-compliance
Lightning Source LLC
Chambersburg PA
CBHW021153310726
48971CB00002B/610